The Beauty Queen

ALSO BY SALLY-ANNE MARTYN

The Clinic
The Home
The Beauty Queen

THE BEAUTY QUEEN

SALLY ANNE-MARTYN

JOFFE BOOKS

Joffe Books, London
www.joffebooks.com

First published in Great Britain in 2024

© Sally-Anne Martyn 2024

This book is a work of fiction. Names, characters, businesses, organizations, places and events are either the product of the author's imagination or are used fictitiously. Any resemblance to actual persons, living or dead, events or locales is entirely coincidental. The spelling used is British English except where fidelity to the author's rendering of accent or dialect supersedes this. The right of Sally-Anne Martyn to be identified as author of this work has been asserted in accordance with the Copyright, Designs and Patents Act 1988.

No part of this book may be used or reproduced in any manner for the purpose of training artificial intelligence technologies or systems. In accordance with Article 4(3) of the Digital Single Market Directive 2019/790, Joffe Books expressly reserves this work from the text and data mining exception.

Cover art by Nick Castle

ISBN: 978-1-83526-920-6

For Mum — Thank you for everything, I love you.

The Sunshine Sands Echo — Monday 6 September 1982

BLONDE BEAUTY MISSING IN SEASIDE MYSTERY
By lead writer, Jeremy Lowden

Speculation surrounds the usually happy resort this morning as police continue to search for the newly crowned Miss Sunshine Sands. Seventeen-year-old Jane Delway was last seen celebrating her win with friends and family at a restaurant on Saturday night. Wowing the judges with her sparkling personality and enviable figure, Delway was the runaway winner of the coveted gold crown and £1,000 cash prize.

Jane's mother, Ms Marion Delway, sobbed as she spoke outside the Forget-Me-Not boarding house, where they had been staying during the competition.

'Jane is such a kind girl, she wouldn't hurt a fly. A beautiful soul inside and out. It's not like her to go off without telling me where she's going. If anyone has any information at all, I beg you to let the police know. Winning Miss Sunshine Sands was a dream for her, it should have been the happiest night of her life.'

The town's mayor and head judge of the competition, Len Erwitt, also spoke about the disappearance.

'The whole town is of course in terrible shock and our thoughts go out to Ms Delway at this worrying time. Sunshine Sands is proud to be a safe place for all the family and we've provided many happy memories for thousands of holidaymakers over the years. I don't believe there's anything untoward here, Jane has most likely taken herself off for a bit of space. Winning something as prestigious as this can be a bit

overwhelming, but I expect she'll be back home soon. In the meantime, we'll continue to provide five-star holidays for our visitors and our venues will be open as usual.'

Local police are paying particular interest to the beach following the discovery of a pink satin sash that washed up on the shore just hours after the competition. It was the twenty-fifth anniversary of the contest, which sees the winner going on to compete in Miss Seaside UK for a £10,000 prize. The contest has long been a bone of contention with local women's groups, who see the pageant as demeaning and sexist, something the town council strongly disputes. Television personality and local comedian Charlie Bailey has stated previously:

'Miss Sunshine Sands celebrates women. There's nothing wrong with showing off your body if it's something you're proud of. If you ask me, it's just jealousy from women more used to burning their bras than paying attention to their looks.'

It is not known at this time whether the competition will continue on to its twenty-sixth year in 1983.

The police have urged anyone that might have information as to Jane's whereabouts to call the station on 0433 50733.

CHAPTER 1

2022
Zoe

Zoe opened the car boot and grabbed her suitcase handle, yanking it towards her. She let out a small '*aaah*' as the muscles in her lower back spasmed, and froze, waiting for it to pass, her fingers still gripping the luggage. It felt, on a daily basis, as if her body was berating her for never completing that yoga course, or opening the plastic seal on the Pilates DVD that now gathered dust on her shelf.

A seagull landed on the pay-and-display machine alongside her car, cocking its head and watching her with its avaricious eyes.

'I've nothing for you,' she said, slowly rising vertebra by vertebra until she was upright, the suitcase by her side.

A gaggle of women and a man passed by, a stray handbag hitting Zoe on the back. The girl turned, eyes wide, pink lipstick smudged.

'I'm so sorry!' she slurred, her eyes trying to focus on Zoe's face.

The others turned to see what was keeping their friend.

'Come on, Katy, we'll miss Happy Hour,' a jet-haired man said, wearing a sash with *Gay Best Friend* emblazoned across it.

'When are you getting married?' Zoe asked.

Katy turned to the man for an answer.

'Jesus Christ, you're a right state,' he said to her, then looked at Zoe. 'Next Saturday, if she's sobered up by then.' He took the bride-to-be's arm and led her away. 'Come on, Lady Jane, let's get you a lemonade, sans alcohol.'

Zoe watched them skip off down the road, fuelled by hope, love and vodka.

The salt air carried gentle murmurs of laughter from the end of the pier across the road. She watched the Ferris wheel turning, multi-coloured lights sparkling against the grey September afternoon sky. Her gaze pulled back to the outline of Dunes and the customers sat outside on the benches. She watched for a while, taking in the vaguely familiar view, waiting for a sensation, anything to take over her body. She felt nothing, and that brought relief.

The gull flapped its giant wings and let out a loud *ha-ha-ha* as it flew into the air, joining a flock circling a nearby chip shop. Zoe inhaled the scent of hot oil and vinegar, her stomach rumbling. *Later*, she promised herself. First, she would check in and then wander back down for a takeaway dinner. The thought of salty chips motivated her to lift the heavy suitcase onto the pavement as she took out her purse to pay for the parking.

As she held her card to the machine, she looked up to the Forget-Me-Not boarding house, an Edwardian mid-terrace with plastic baskets of pansies lining the windowsills. The sign had seen better days, the *g* slightly off-kilter and blue lettering faded at the edges. A fluffy white dog appeared at the window, its black nose smudging the glass. It yapped in her direction, needle teeth bared for her welcome. An elderly couple sat seemingly unaware, dead-eyed and sipping tea from dainty cups. Zoe flung her laptop bag and handbag over her shoulder and lifted the case, dragging it through a low metal gate and up to the chipped, scarlet-painted steps.

'Let me help you, miss.'

Zoe turned to see a man in work overalls marching towards her up the short path. A roll-up hung from his dry bottom lip, flapping up and down as he spoke. He carried a spade which he stabbed into the ground, the blade slicing into a small patch of grass, narrowly missing a ruddy-cheeked garden gnome with its weathered, gurning face staring bleakly ahead.

'I can manage,' Zoe insisted, heaving the case up the first step.

The man wrestled the handle from her fingers and took it from her, the smell of freshly dug soil, creosote and tobacco wafting past her nostrils.

'Thanks,' Zoe muttered, as he lifted it up to the front door.

She followed him into the reception area, and her first impression was the odour of damp with top notes of furniture polish. The yapping dog ran out of the dining room and scuttled down the tiled hall towards them, its tiny claws clattering along the floor.

'Geed away, Princess!' the man commanded, shooing the dog away with his hand as he dropped her case with a thud by the reception desk. 'What have you got in here, bricks?'

Zoe resisted reminding him that she hadn't wanted him to carry it for her in the first place.

A sign on the desk read, *Ring for reception*. As she reached over to press it, the man beat her to it, slamming his palm down on the brass bell. Princess barked from the other end of the hall, all the time eyeing the gruff man but not daring to pounce forward. On the desk sat an array of small ornaments, tiny porcelain ladies in Victorian dress fanning themselves, and a tall vase of faux flowers, their once-bright petals now faded and frayed.

'Are you the owner here?' Zoe asked, trying to make polite conversation.

He laughed huffily. 'General dogsbody. Bits and bobs, here and there.'

A woman appeared from a room at the back, Princess's yaps turning to high-pitched whines as she followed her to reception.

'Thank you, Trevor, I'll take it from here.'

The landlady of the Forget-Me-Not boarding house was in her late sixties, with yellowish-blonde hair back-combed into a chignon and a smudge of cerise lipstick that didn't reach the corners of her mouth. Her thin eyebrows were drawn on in such a way to give her the look of someone permanently suspicious. She wore a purple Lurex wraparound top that strained over her large bust and a pencil skirt that revealed a map of varicose veins on ample calves.

'Mrs Kincade?' she asked.

'Ms.'

The woman gave her a hint of a disapproving look, before smiling tightly. 'Of course, my apologies.'

'But you can call me Zoe.'

The woman thought for a moment, then continued, 'Of course, and you must call me Dolly.' Dolly opened a large leather-bound guestbook, her pen pausing above Zoe's name. She looked up, studying Zoe's face. 'Is this your first time in Sunshine Sands?'

'Yes, first time at an English seaside resort — well, apart from day trips to Blackpool.'

Dolly's shoulders relaxed. 'Well, we give Blackpool a run for its money here, don't we, Trevor?'

'Oh aye,' Trevor said. 'We might not have the illuminations, but we make up for it in old-fashioned hospitality, and a certain class you won't find anywhere else this side of the Pennines.'

The three of them turned as a couple walked out of the dining room. The beer-bellied husband wore a stained white vest, ginger back and shoulder hairs sprouting from reddened skin. He belched loudly, putting a hand to his mouth as he apologised to Dolly. His red-faced wife hit him on the arm.

'It's the kippers, they play havoc with his insides,' she said as they passed, making their way up a flight of stairs.

Zoe glanced around the hallway at the framed photographs of entertainers gone by, the odd scrawled dedication showing appreciation for the hospitality. Freddie Starr, Bob Monkhouse and Cilla Black among others. Zoe's eyes rested on a photograph of what looked like the young Dolly. She was standing in front of the boarding house, next to an older man wearing heavy spectacles and a beige cardigan. The man held aloft a plaque, and a small brass plate below pronounced Bernard Simpson the winner of Sunshine Sands Boarding House of the Year 1982. His smile was proud as punch, in contrast to Dolly, who scowled through a curtain of lank mousy hair. Other men stood by their side, a man wearing mayoral chains and a moustached man wearing a tuxedo and dickie bow, thick curly hair atop a grinning face.

'Is that you?' asked Zoe, pointing to the girl.

'Aye, she was a sullen beggar back then,' Trevor said, chuckling, his laughter fading as Dolly glared at him.

'You might be able to help with my article,' Zoe said.

'Article?' Dolly said, her eyes narrowing, shoulders slowly moving back.

Trevor edged away, his eyes blinking to the floor.

'I'm a journalist, for the *National Mail*. I'm here to cover the talent show — well, that and the British seaside boom post-Covid in general.'

Dolly regarded her, then smiled thinly. 'Boom? It's barely been more than a whimper, ducky. Not that we mind here, we like to keep Sunshine Sands a little lower key. We don't care for the brashness of Blackpool — quality over quantity.'

A fly buzzed past Zoe's head, landing on the reception desk. In the blink of an eye, Dolly pulled out a plastic fly swatter from beneath the counter and brought it down on the unsuspecting insect. She returned the plastic tool of death to its place as Trevor scooped the unfortunate fly into his palm and dropped it in a bin. In the pause that followed, a grandfather clock at the end of the hall ticked away, making the seconds of silence feel like minutes.

'Will either of you be attending the Grand Talent Show?' Zoe said, putting on her brightest *I haven't just witnessed you dispatch a fly with the skill of a cowboy shooting beer bottles from a log* smile.

'I've nothing to do with any of that, we just keep our heads down, beds made and tea flowing here,' Dolly said. 'We don't like a fuss at the Forget-Me-Not.'

Zoe took a leaflet from a box on the desk, a map of the seafront and pier. She opened it out as she spoke, as if it was an afterthought. 'And of course, Sunshine Sands has the added mystery of that beauty queen going missing all those years ago. That must cast a shadow?' Zoe looked up from the leaflet to Dolly and Trevor.

Both stared at her blankly.

'That was here, right? What was her name? *Jane* something?'

Dolly took a key from a hook on the wall, jangling it rapidly in the air. 'Now then, we had you in the Crowther Suite but given that you're a journalist I think we'll upgrade you to the Grayson.' She looked over to a framed photograph of a gurning Larry Grayson standing beside the beige-cardiganed man. 'Not that Mr Grayson ever stayed here, it seemed only the Grand was good enough for him. Still, as you can see, my dad was a little starstruck.'

Zoe studied Dolly's dad, his thin smile and dead eyes feeling suddenly familiar.

Dolly handed her the key, which was attached to an oversized wooden keyring with her room name scorched into it.

'Thank y—'

Zoe was cut off by Princess, who began yapping manically. She felt a rush of air behind her as the door opened and four windswept figures bundled through with an assortment of suitcases and beach paraphernalia.

'I told you we'd be able to buy a windbreaker here,' a red-cheeked woman scorned.

'I'm not wasting money on a new one while we've got a perfectly good one already.' The man — her husband, Zoe presumed — hit a framed picture with the wooden leg of the windbreaker, sending it crashing to the floor.

'Derek!' the woman cried out as a framed photo of Cannon and Ball crashed to the floor. It landed face up, their comedic images obscured behind shattered glass.

Trevor rushed over, urging their two children to step away from the detritus that had spread across the hallway.

'If you hadn't been on at me,' the man retorted.

Dolly stepped from behind the desk. 'Mr and Mrs Collins! Welcome back to the Forget-Me-Not. I trust you had a good journey?'

As the red-faced Mrs Collins uttered grovelling apologies, Mr Collins continued to wrestle with the windbreaker as he cursed the roadworks on the M6. Dolly crouched down to the floor, gathering up the larger pieces of glass and cradling the frame.

'Trevor will have this reframed in no time,' Dolly said. Then she tapped the picture gently and winked at Mrs Collins. 'They weren't my favourites anyway.'

Trevor ambled over to join them, ushering the excitable children past the tiny shards of glass that only a hoover could hope to catch.

'Now then,' he said, 'I bet you two would enjoy a nice glass of lemonade?'

The mother continued to apologise profusely to Dolly as she followed her and the broken photo to the desk. Zoe lugged her case to the top of the stairs, pausing when Dolly called up after her.

'Dinner's at seven on the dot.'

'Oh, I'm fine. I was just going to go to the chip shop,' Zoe said.

'No,' Dolly said sharply, the female guest behind cowering back.

Zoe wasn't sure she'd heard correctly. 'Pardon?'

'I've made a welcome dinner especially for you and my guests.'

'Honestly, I'd—'

Dolly held her stare, her tangerine-painted nails tapping rapidly against the banister.

'Seven o'clock. I'll see you then,' Zoe said.

* * *

The landing of the Forget-Me-Not was far less 'showbiz' than the reception and hallway downstairs. A plug-in air-freshener was fighting a losing battle against the fug of bacon fat that rose from the kitchen below, and the fusty carpet was so old, the ghosts of previous residents' feet were worn into the thread. Instead of autographed photos of celebrities gone by, there were cheaply framed prints of white horses running across blue sand, and doe-eyed street urchins that looked down at her with sadness. On a mahogany cabinet, stuffed bodies of various deceased animals peered out from glass bell jars, age and time reducing them to scrawny caricatures of their former selves.

Zoe passed the Crowther Suite, peeking in to see what she could have had before the room upgrade. A hoover started up, driven across the dark carpet by a cleaner, her face drawn and pale. She didn't acknowledge Zoe's presence as she continued to push and pull the vacuum cleaner with such ferocity that when she hit the base of a set of drawers, the TV on top shook.

Zoe turned the key in the door of the Grayson Suite. As she entered the room she could only assume that Larry Grayson's snubbing of the boarding house had offended Dolly more than she had let on. Though a small sign on the dresser proclaimed *No smoking*, there was a distinct whiff of stale cigarette smoke in the stuffy air, and the once magnolia walls now bore a faint tint of yellow. If this was the upgrade, she dreaded to think what the rest of the Crowther Suite was like. Zoe wasn't a hotel snob — if it was clean and the bed was comfortable, she could sleep anywhere. Before she'd had children, she had been a reporter in war-torn areas across the world.

Back then she had been lucky to have more than a sleeping bag and ground sheet.

On a set of drawers opposite the bed, a glass-eyed owl stared at her from within a bell jar, its wings slightly raised as if it were about to fly away. Zoe grimaced, taking an embroidered tray cloth and placing it over the dome to hide the bird's glare.

She lifted the strap of the laptop bag over her head and put the bag on the floor, rubbing her shoulder, which now had a red welt mark on it. She walked across the room and attempted to unlatch the sash window and let some air in, but the brass fitting was stuck tight.

She kicked her shoes off and took her phone from her bag, shuffling back onto the double bed and leaning against the pink padded satin headboard and two limp floral pillows. She dialled her daughter's number.

'Belle?'

'Yes, Mummy.'

'All OK there?'

'When are you coming home?'

'I only just got here.'

'Why are you there?'

'I told you, I have to work. I'll be back in a couple of days. Are you having a nice time with Daddy?'

'Yes, we had Chinese for tea.'

Zoe's stomach rumbled.

'That sounds nice. Are Dylan and Alice OK?'

'Dylan's in his room and Alice is playing cards with Heidi. Shall I get her?'

Zoe imagined Heidi, their dad's new girlfriend, bonding over Uno with her daughter, and a twinge of jealousy spiked her insides.

'No, leave her to have fun. I'm going to have a quick sleep now. Give my love to Alice and Dylan and I'll message you all before bed, OK?'

'OK, Mummy, love you.'

'Love you too, Belle, speak later. I miss—'

Belle cut the call off. Zoe took a small bottle from her handbag and uncrewed the lid. She tipped a pill into her palm and threw it to the back of her throat, swallowing it with a gulp of tepid water from a bottle on her bedside table. She set her phone alarm for two hours' time so she wouldn't miss dinner, and lay back on the bed, trying to fluff life back into the flat pillows, tossing and turning to avoid the mattress springs that dug in her body. She closed her eyes and thought about her children and her ex with his young and beautiful girlfriend. Heidi was lovely; she had met her briefly when she dropped the kids off. The new girlfriend had been understandably nervous, stuttering as she offered Zoe a cup of tea she likely hoped would be refused. It wasn't Heidi's fault the marriage had failed: Zoe alone took responsibility for that.

Somewhere outside an ice cream van played its plinky tune and hungry seagulls cawed. As she drifted off to sleep, she heard a door opening and closing nearby, muffled arguing between adults as their lemonade-fuelled children ran wild.

CHAPTER 2

'Zoe,' Dolly called across the small dining room. 'You're over here.'

Zoe put back the dining chair she was preparing to sit down on and headed over to where Dolly stood, the landlady clutching the back of another chair at a small table set for one. The butter-yellow lampshade above created a sickly glow in the room, barely illuminating assorted tables dotted about and set ready for the other guests.

'I've reserved a special table for you — we can't have you writing negative reviews of the Forget-Me-Not, can we now?'

'Thank you,' said Zoe, sitting down and pulling herself to the distinctly *un*-special table flush to the wall, her chair barely able to move back for the drinks trolley directly behind her. She felt woozy from her sleep and the tablet she had taken, unable to shake the persistent haze of dreams and memories.

'I'm early,' she said, looking around the empty dining room.

'Punctual,' said Dolly, looking up to a white clock on the wall, each tick-tock echoing around the room.

There were clocks everywhere in the boarding house, no space where you weren't aware of the passing of time, which

Zoe found ironic given the place seemed to be stuck in the last century.

Zoe counted seven other tables, all set up with an assortment of condiments and claret-coloured napkins fanning out from each wine glass. The placemats featured a pen-and-ink image of Sunshine Sands seafront, which Zoe traced with her finger, running it over the Grand hotel, the arcades and down to the pier. 'I see that the talent contest is going to be held in the same place as the beauty contest — Dunes Bar, isn't it?'

Dolly regarded her for a moment. 'I believe so, yes. Like I said, I'm not involved in that side of things anymore. But if it brings more visitors to me, I suppose I can't complain.' She whispered down to Zoe, her tone begrudging, 'We've even got *Londoners* here.'

Zoe nodded. She knew when an interview, official or not, had run dry. A young couple entered the dining room.

'Mr and Mrs Ashcroft,' Dolly called out, 'you're by the window, the *honeymoon* table.' She leaned down to Zoe. 'Young Sophie has been coming to Sunshine Sands for years, with her family. Now she chooses to spend her honeymoon with me.' Pride washed over her otherwise surly demeanour.

The young lovers giggled, holding hands all the way to their table, never letting go, even when trying to pull the chairs out. Their cheeks were flushed with love and no doubt endless sex. Zoe tried to remember those days and that feeling. There had been passion for a few years, but like many marriages, it had dwindled with time, children, and familiarity that had bred contempt like bacteria in a Petri dish.

She took her phone from her handbag and scrolled her social media apps, twenty alerts waiting to be read.

'Ah-ah.' Dolly wagged her index finger back and forth. When she had Zoe's attention, Dolly pointed to a sign by the door. It was a picture of a mobile phone set in a red circle, a red line struck through it.

Zoe let out a small laugh, then realised by the look on Dolly's face she wasn't joking. She put her phone back in her bag, vowing never to chastise her children again for technology at the dinner table.

'What can I get you to drink? We have wine, lager and soft drinks.'

'Do you have any Malbec?'

Dolly frowned, before stepping back to the drinks trolley. She screwed up her eyes as she peered at the labels, lifting one bottle at a time and holding them at a distance from her face.

'Anything red will do,' Zoe said, looking uneasily at the stuffed mole framed in a box above her head.

Dolly picked up a half-empty bottle and unscrewed the metal cap. She took the paper napkin from Zoe's wine glass and filled it almost to the brim. Zoe took a sip, trying not to flinch at the oxidised beverage.

'Thank you, that's lovely,' she lied.

The faint sound of chatter and a door closing was followed by creaking stairs, and two more residents entered the dining room.

'You're over there.' Dolly gestured to a table behind the lovers, then leaned down to Zoe again, her hand shielding her mouth and speaking with a hint of disdain. 'The *Londoners*.'

Zoe smiled and mouthed a silent *hello* to them as they took their seats.

'Is there a menu?' Zoe asked.

'Chef has cooked a special meal for everyone tonight, I'm sure you won't be disappointed. Beef and onion pie!' she exclaimed with pride.

'Oh, that's great. Is there a vegan option?'

Dolly's mouth contorted into a tight smile. 'I'll see what I can do.'

'Sorry, I wasn't expecting dinner, I would have said—'

Dolly waved her hand in the air. 'No, no. No, we're nothing if not flexible at the Forget-Me-Not.'

She marched out of the dining room, leaving Zoe wishing she'd stuck up for herself earlier and just got chips. The two women from London were in their thirties, both immaculately dressed in designer clothes, a chain-strapped Stella McCartney handbag hanging over the back of one of their chairs. They spoke in low voices, each eyeing their surroundings with derision and barely disguised disgust.

The choice of accommodation in Sunshine Sands was limited to boarding houses like this one or cheap chain hotels located on the outskirts of the town. The Grand, which stood on the south end of the seafront and had once been the jewel in Sunshine Sands' hospitality crown, had been derelict since the early nineties, a permanent reminder of the halcyon days of the English seaside.

Dolly came back into the dining room holding a plate aloft, followed by two elderly holidaymakers and their middle-aged son. Dolly showed them to a table set for three, and Zoe watched in fascination as the older woman shook open the serviette and tucked it into the younger man's jumper as her husband rolled his eyes.

Dolly put a plate in front of Zoe.

'I'm sorry, dear, if only we'd have had a bit more notice.'

Zoe looked down to the plate of boiled potatoes and carrots, flakes of pastry in the space where the beef pie had been unceremoniously removed.

'This will be fine, honestly.' Zoe smiled, vinegary chips still on her mind.

Dolly put a hand on Zoe's arm, the cold touch of her fingertips causing Zoe to flinch.

'I'll make sure you have something better tomorrow evening.'

Zoe wanted to protest, not wanting to be beholden to the boarding house each night. She didn't remember dinner being included and if she had realised, she'd have let the woman know in advance it wasn't needed or wanted. In her time, Zoe had interviewed many powerful and difficult subjects; it really shouldn't have been as hard as it was to voice her opinion now.

'Thank you, that's very kind.'

The young groom called from the window table and Dolly left to see to him. Dolly and the couple exchanged pleasantries, the landlady's hand resting on the young man's shoulder. Dolly pointed to their glasses and then left the room, the two of them giggling nervously like misbehaving schoolchildren.

Zoe dug her fork into a potato, which crumbled into a small, dry pile. She took the bottle of ketchup from the table and shook it over the food, a glob of sauce landing in a dollop on the carrots. A raised voice on another table caught her attention, the other guests surreptitiously craning their necks to see.

A giant of a man, ruddy-cheeked and wearing a short-sleeved Hawaiian shirt was trying to wrestle his pint back from his wife, who sat opposite.

'That's enough,' she scolded, her voice stark in the sudden silence.

'I'll say when I've had enough,' he boomed.

'You're drunk.'

'Not drunk enough, because I can still hear you yabbering on,' he replied, taking the pint glass back from her and draining the remains in several loud gulps.

The designer couple exchanged raised eyebrows, before turning back to their food.

His wife threw her chair back and stormed out, bumping into Dolly as the landlady entered the dining room, clutching a bottle of cheap fizz.

'Is everything alright?' Dolly asked, looking over the woman's shoulder to the Hawaiian-shirted man.

'Another pint of lager please,' he demanded, his fingers clicking in the air.

All eyes watched as Dolly put the bottle down on an empty table and strode towards him.

'I think you've had quite enough for tonight, Mr Morton,' she said, each consonant landing like a slap.

Mr Morton blinked at her, soundlessly opening and closing his mouth like a goldfish.

'I think your wife—' she turned her head to the room — 'and my other guests, would prefer you to go back to your room now.'

He sat back in his chair, folding his arms defiantly across his chest.

'I'd like another pint, please.'

Dolly smiled gently, as if she were about to ease off. His triumphant grin vanished as she walked around him, yanking his chair back. The giant of a man gripped the sides of his seat so as not to slip off. She hooked her elbow under his arm and manhandled him to his feet.

'Oi, what you doing?' he said, before crying out in pain as her hand gripped the back of his neck, pushing him past the other tables.

'I won't have you disturbing my dining room, Mr Morton. Let's get you to your room and you can sleep it off.'

He waved his thick arms and biceps in the air, but his resistance was futile. As she manhandled him out of the door, he relented, mumbling pathetic apologies.

'Blimey, you wouldn't want to go home to Dolly a pound short in your pay packet would you?' the young groom joked.

His bride tapped his knee playfully. 'Ssshhh, she might hear you, then you'll be in trouble too.'

The Londoners shook their heads and stood to leave, the food on their plates barely touched. Zoe wondered where they would be going to eat now — she hadn't been able to find much beyond fish and chips and burger bars when she had researched restaurants pre-visit. Of the eight tables in the dining room, only three were now occupied. If other hotels and boarding houses were doing, or rather not doing, similar business, the outlook for the English seaside was bleak indeed.

At eight o'clock, exactly one hour after the strict mealtime had started, a young man burst through the door. Freshly showered, his exotic aftershave was a welcome relief from the odour of school dinners and cheap wine that permeated the dining room. He mouthed polite hellos to the remaining guests and sat at a table set for two. When Dolly entered, Zoe expected the second argument of the night with this latecomer to the table. Instead, the landlady placed a full plate in front of him and patted his back. The food he had been given was different to the stock meal the rest of the residents had had to endure. Roast potatoes, glazed carrots and slices of chicken breast, swimming in rich gravy.

He dug into his food, shovelling it down as if he hadn't eaten for days. So fast that when he stopped, he had to catch his breath, his hand resting on his chest. No sooner had he mopped up the last of his gravy with a slice of bread than Dolly reappeared with a bowl of ice cream topped with spray cream and ruby-red cocktail cherries.

The newlyweds said their farewells, their hands clasped together like lobster claws. They were followed by the couple and their adult son, who arranged to meet in the bigger of their two bedrooms for a game of rummy. Zoe approached the young man's table.

'I hope you don't mind me saying, but you smell amazing. What is that?'

He smiled, picking up a paper napkin and dabbing his mouth. 'Tom Ford.'

Expensive aftershave that she had once bought her ex for Christmas, begrudging the money spent when he had handed her an envelope containing a £50 voucher for a clothes shop she rarely frequented.

'How long are you on holiday for?'

'I'm not, I'm a seasonal performer.' He slumped back, a hand resting on his belly as he let out a sigh. 'Though I think they'll have to carry me on the stage tomorrow.'

'What do you do? Sing, dance?'

'All of the above when called for.'

'What show?'

'I do general stuff throughout the summer, tomorrow the talent show.'

'At Dunes?' Zoe said.

He smiled. 'Yes. Have you got a ticket?'

'Press pass,' she said, patting her pocket.

He laughed. 'That makes it sound very grand. I hope it lives up to your expectations. If your expectations are good, that is.' He winked.

'I'm sure it will,' she said, looking to the empty place opposite him. 'Expecting a date?'

'No,' he said, a mock look of resignation on his face, 'my boyfriend and I are no more — he left me for a juggler in a travelling circus. He's apparently cavorting with an aerial acrobat in Rhyl now.'

'Brutal,' Zoe said.

The door opened and Dolly appeared, carrying a plate of food. She eyed Zoe long enough to make it clear that her time in the dining room had come to an end. Zoe said her goodbyes as Dolly sat down opposite the young man, inaudible low whispers passing between them as she left the room.

***

On the landing she heard deep snores coming from the Cilla Black Suite, with an accompanying pleading of 'For God's sake, Mike, turn on your side,' followed by another deep, throaty snore. The door to the Monkhouse Suite opened and out came the older son of the couple, clutching a pack of playing cards.

'Goodnight,' Zoe said.

He gave a tight, self-conscious smile, shuffling past her and disappearing into the room next door.

Zoe stood by her bedroom window, watching as the jewel-coloured lights of the pier fairground twinkled in the dusk. On the road below, a small group of young women exited a minibus and hung around the back waiting for their cases. They were dressed in sweatshirts and pyjama bottoms, a couple with their hair wound in giant curlers. Once they had their luggage, the driver scanned a piece of paper and pointed them in the right direction, each wheeling large suitcases to their respective seafront boarding houses and hotels.

Zoe fell back onto the bed, resting her laptop on her stomach. She clicked on a folder on the home screen, opening various documents: thumbnail images of colour photographs and old newspaper articles.

Whatever Happened to Baby Jane?

The Mystery of the Missing Beauty Queen

Dazzled by the Bright Lights of Sunshine Sands

The photographs that accompanied the stories showed a line of girls in swimwear. Some looked no older than sixteen, a couple in their twenties, lined up like dolls in a toy shop. In another photograph the mayor, wearing his mayoral chain, placed a crown on the head of Jane, her eyes watery with shock, a hand raised in a wave.

Zoe searched the internet, finding nothing new since yesterday's search. She opened a new tab and brought up the Friendbook page *What Happened to Jane Delway?*

The pinned post had new comments, which had begun to appear with the news of the talent show a couple of months ago:

@ElliThompson
I think it's so disrespectful to have this dumb talent show, without any mention of poor Jane or the other women who went missing back then. How would the mayor like it if it were his daughter???

@ClareJones
100%, they just cover that sexist shit up and brush it under the carpet.

@OwenWebb
Snowflakes ahoy...

@ClareJones
Oh fuck off @OwenWebb.

@OwenWebb
I say bring back the tits and ass competitions, even I'd go to that dump by the sea if they did that.

@ClareJones
@OwenWebb thanks for proving my point, f*ckwit. @Admin can you block the troll??

Zoe clicked on Owen's profile, an avatar of a cartoon character she didn't recognise and endless posts about a local pizza delivery company and bitcoin opportunities. His contribution to her page was a litany of dumb and antagonising comments. She clicked on the 'block' button and watched his profile disappear.

Over the years there had been hundreds of theories about Jane, from jumping onto a boat and sailing off into the night with a Russian warship, to being kidnapped by a women's rights organisation and spending the rest of her days atoning for her sins. The supposed return of British holidaymakers to the English coast and the announcement of the talent show had created a new flurry of interest, though nothing useful to Zoe.

Other women had vanished in Sunshine Sands in the years before Jane's disappearance, but none had garnered the attention that she had. A young, blonde beauty queen with her life ahead of her was deemed far more newsworthy than the middle-aged teacher who had disappeared while walking her spaniel along the coastline, or the drugged-up teen whose lifeless body was found outside the Lucky Jim arcade. The girl had had no history of drug use, and the woman that found her as she arrived for work that morning reported that her clothing looked torn. Her death was recorded as 'misadventure' by the local coroner and filed away, an attempt to keep Sunshine Sands' slate clean.

Zoe had only found out about the other deaths thanks to a Channel 5 unsolved cases documentary, one in which, of course, Jane took centre stage. The blot on the history of this seaside town might never have resurfaced at all, if it wasn't for the rising appetite for true crime and endless media content.

An email alert slid onto the screen and Zoe opened it.

Amelia Langford (a.langford@bzmedia.com)
Subject: Sunshine Sands
Dear Zoe,

I hope you arrived safely and all's going well?

I spoke to Mike, but was unable to get an advance, I'm afraid. It seems that all belts are being tightened at the moment. If you could get the article to me within the week then payment will be made asap. Just so you know, he's keen to get a bit of controversy in the piece re sexism (past & current). He's not looking for anything flowery, just something to get the reader comments flying! If there's anyone I can put you in contact with, just shout!

Let's catch up when you're back, champers on me!
Best,
Amelia
Features editor — National Mail Publications

Zoe closed her laptop and fell back against the thin pillows. It was bad enough having to ask for an advance, let alone be refused. At least she wasn't home to hear the bill reminders hit the doormat.

She checked her phone to see if her kids had left her any messages — there was nothing. She posted in their family WhatsApp group: *Goodnight. Love you Xxx*, followed by four pink hearts. The door to a room on the other side of the landing slammed shut and low giggles turned to aroused moans. Zoe turned off the small lamp next to her bed and pulled the duvet over her head.

It felt like she had barely slept when she awoke hours later. She tapped her phone: 2.15 a.m. The last time Jane Delway's mother had reported seeing her daughter.

CHAPTER 3

Zoe froze on the landing when a floorboard creaked beneath her foot, her body tensing when a muffled snore and sleepy groan came from a room to her right. She continued past the other guestrooms, with only the dull glow of an orange table lamp lighting her way. One careful step at a time, she descended the stairs, feeling like an errant teenager escaping the house to meet up with a boy.

As she closed the front door behind her, a whip of cold air swept over her body. She took a woollen beanie from her pocket and pulled it over her head. She was almost at the gate when Princess began to yap from within the boarding house, and light snapped on at the top floor. Zoe ran to a purple wheelie bin, hiding behind it as she watched Dolly sweep the curtain to the side and yank up the sash window. The landlady peered up and down the street as Princess continued to bark, setting off a relay of barks and howls along the road. Zoe's heart pounded in her chest as she crouched further down, inexplicably terrified about what might happen if she was caught sneaking out.

Eventually, after shouting at Princess to 'pipe down', Dolly drew the window back down and turned the light off.

Zoe crossed over the wide road that separated the hotels, boarding houses and shops from the beach and pier. She jumped over the tramlines and onto the promenade near the entrance to the pier. The funfair was now in darkness, the silhouette of the motionless Ferris wheel blurring into the dark sea beyond. Polystyrene chip trays bounced along the tarmac, the dull beat of music reverberating from behind blackened windows along the road. Zoe stopped short when she saw something glittering on the edge of the beach wall. She bent down and picked it up.

She spun the silver plastic tiara in her hand, *Bride* spelled out in tiny pink gems. Zoe balanced it on top of an overflowing bin attached to a lamppost, and read the poster attached to the metal pole above.

SUNSHINE SANDS GRAND TALENT SHOW
Hosted by the Queen of the North — Miss B. Havin'
Featuring ex–Passion Island contestants
Ann-Marie Hook & Bella Dee
Dunes Bar, North Pier,
Sunshine Sands
Saturday 3 September

Tomorrow the resort would come alive with excitement — at least, she expected that's what the council were hoping for. She knew they would have paid good money for the reality stars, desperate to stretch their fifteen minutes of fame beyond their eight weeks appearing on *Passion Island*. Crouching down, she scrambled through the railings and jumped down onto the sandy beach. She took off her trainers and socks, stepping onto the cold, dark sand, which sunk beneath her feet. Passing crumbling sandcastles and discarded ice lolly wrappers, she made her way under the pier and stood in the shallows of the sea as waves crashed against the giant timber supports. Names were crudely carved into the wood, true love promised *4eva* and temporary grudges marked for the passer-by to note for evermore. Zoe moved forward, the icy waves lapping at her ankles. Oblivious to the freezing water, she walked further still until the waves skimmed her thighs, her jeans now soaked through to her skin. She stared out to sea, picturing that pink sash, soaked and dirty with sand.

A burning end of a cigarette fell from the pier and blew down in front of her eyes. She followed its embers, glowing and fading until they were extinguished in the dark waters. Voices from above faded as their footsteps rattled away back down the pier and suddenly Zoe felt the cold spiking her skin. She had two days to gather all she needed to write the article for the paper.

It was somewhere she had avoided for so long, but when the opportunity had arisen for her to come back, it felt like fate intervening. Forty years of trying to block out the pain and to hold on to what memories she did have had taken their toll on her health, her marriage and her ability to live in any kind of peace. It was time to revisit all those places, to see if she could get some closure and maybe finally find out what had happened to Jane Delway. The winner of Miss Sunshine Sands 1982, a young woman whose life had promised so much. A beautiful teenager, an adored daughter. Her sister.

CHAPTER 4

1982
Jane

A small boy ran up the aisle of the packed coach, batting the day trippers and holidaymakers with a plastic lightsabre that glowed neon blue in the darkness. The trail of tiny spotlights on the coach roof illuminated as the sun rose, and the passengers began to stir. Jane peered outside the rain-sodden window as the coach left the motorway, chugging up a slip road. Her little sister yawned and stretched her limbs as far as they would go, the palm of her hand pushing against the side of Jane's head, squashing her face against the damp coach window. Jane gently moved her small hand away and propped her up in her seat.

'Wake up, Zoe.'

'Where are we?' said Zoe, crawling over her big sister, peering out to the dimly lit car park.

'The services,' Jane replied, yawning.

Jane felt a sharp scratch in her head and cried out, 'Ow!'

She turned to see her mum looming over her from the seat behind, a comb held like a weapon in her hand.

'You can't get off the coach with your hair like that, your perm's all flattened at the back.'

'I'll do it,' Jane protested, grabbing the comb, strands of her golden hair twisted in its teeth. 'It's not like anyone's going to care what I look like at six o'clock in the morning.'

'Of course they will. All eyes will be on you, Jane. Miss Sunshine Sands is never off duty, remember that.'

'I'm not Miss Sunshine Sands!'

'*Yet*,' her mum said, sitting back down and taking a lipstick out of her handbag. She applied a coat to her lips and smacked them together. 'I've a feeling in my bones.'

Jane handed the comb back through the seats and turned to her sister. 'Do you need the toilet, Zoe?'

Zoe nodded and Jane shuffled across the seat, forcing her sleepy sister into the aisle. Jane felt her mum's hands tucking in the label on the back of her T-shirt and wriggled away.

'Come on, I'll buy you some sweets while we're there,' Jane said.

'None for you, Jane, not until after the competition,' her mum warned.

Jane ignored her, navigating her sister past feet and handbags strewn in the aisle. A hand swept over her backside and she snapped her head round to see a middle-aged man and his friend chuckling, signalling to her with a slow wink. Jane blinked rapidly, her cheeks flushed with embarrassment as she hurried off the coach.

* * *

The hand dryers in the toilets whirred and water splattered from grimy sinks. Jane looked in the mirror, teasing her hair with her fingers.

'You OK, Zoe?' she called out.

A lock slid open and Zoe appeared, brushing down the ruffles of her rah-rah skirt.

'Wash your hands and we'll go and get something from the shop,' Jane said.

In the shop Zoe picked out penny sweets from a display and the assistant dropped them into a paper bag. Jane was distracted by the smell of fried breakfast; she hadn't eaten properly the day before and her hunger was starting to make her feel sick. She left Zoe deciding between a penny shrimp and a jelly snake and went to the café across the way. A jolly-faced woman with ruddy cheeks, wearing a white tabard and cap, looked up from a griddle where she was turning sausages and bacon.

'What can I get you, love?'

Jane hesitated, looking back to where the coach stood. The man behind her exhaled impatiently as she turned back to the server.

'Fried egg sandwich, please.'

In one swift move, the woman slid an egg from the griddle between two pieces of bread, handing it to Jane wrapped in a serviette. Before she had chance to say thank you, she had been moved along by the man behind, who barked his order of four bacon sandwiches. Jane looked over to Zoe, who was paying for her sweets, balancing the paper bag under her arm as she sorted through a handful of coins. Jane took greedy bites of the egg sandwich, cursing as a drop of yolk dripped onto her jumper. She threw the remains in the bin and wiped at the stain with a dry serviette. Zoe wandered out of the sweet shop, scanning the service station.

'Hey.' Jane caught her eye. 'Over here.'

Zoe skipped over, showing her the sweets.

'Come on,' Jane urged, her hand on Zoe's back, 'we don't want to miss the coach.'

They walked outside, a group of passengers having a last-minute smoke by the coach doors.

'Do you think you'll win?' Zoe asked as they rushed along.

Jane smiled down at her sister. 'Who knows, there are lots of pretty girls in every town in the country.'

'But you're the prettiest,' said Zoe, a chewy sweet tangled in her teeth.

Jane laughed. 'I've just bought you sweets, your opinion is biased.'

'If you do win . . .' Zoe paused, looking down into the bag of sweets.

'What?'

'You . . . you won't leave home?'

Jane stopped and turned to Zoe, a hand on her shoulder. 'Well, I'll have to leave home eventually. That happens when you grow up, but not for a few years yet.'

Zoe exhaled and dug her hand into the paper bag of sweets, fishing out a jelly fish and stuffing it in her mouth. Jane put her hand in the bag and took out a deceptively sugary cola bottle, wincing as the sour taste hit her tongue.

'Don't tell Mum.'

* * *

'I can't wait to have a bath and an early night,' Jane said, plonking back down onto the coach seat, Zoe sliding in beside her.

'You've got to go to some kind of welcome event today,' her mum said, her face peering between the seats.

Jane groaned as her mum passed a sheet of paper through the gap.

'Here's your schedule for the next two days.'

Jane looked at it in dismay, a page full of commitments for all entrants of Miss Sunshine Sands.

'It's a big deal,' her mum said. 'You can't not show up or they'll notice. It'll affect your chances.'

Jane passed the paper back and slumped in her seat as the coach began to chug away from the services. She noticed a woman running across the car park, carrying a baby and dragging a small child behind her.

'Stop!' Jane called down to the driver.

He jammed the brakes on, and the coach groaned to a sudden halt, causing hot tea to spill from polystyrene cups and unbuckled kids to lurch forward in their seats. The coach doors hissed open, and the red-faced woman stepped on gasping for breath. She made her way to her seat and admonished her sleeping husband, who had failed to notice her absence. Other passengers sniggered under their breath, wives and girlfriends holding onto their partners' arms in the sure knowledge they would never leave them behind at a motorway service station.

Jane thought about her own future and marriage — not that there was even a boyfriend yet. She'd only ever been on one date, at the Ritzy cinema. It had fizzled to a disappointing end before the credits rolled. As if the universe was listening, a young man of about eighteen leaned across the seats in front of them.

'You work on the deli in town, yeah?'

Jane looked up at him. He grinned, and his eyes sparkled with 'Jack the Lad' charm.

'Yes, that's right.' She smiled, feeling the eyes of her mother burning into the back of her head. 'I've seen you there. You never buy much.'

His cheeks flushed. 'I—'

Zoe piped up, 'She won't be there long anyway, she's going to win Miss Sunshine Sands.'

'Zoe!' Jane tapped her little sister's arm.

The teenager's eyes widened. 'A beauty queen? That beats slicing ham and cheese for a living.'

'Well, I most likely won't win.'

'She will,' Zoe said.

'Of course you'll win!' he agreed. He paused for a moment, seemed to gather confidence. 'Hey, do you fancy grabbing a drink tonight? There's a good club there and—'

'No, she wouldn't,' Jane's mum called out from the seat behind. 'She's got things to do.'

Jane shrugged at the young man. He waited a moment, as if expecting her to say something else, but she couldn't, paralysed by her mother's presence. He smiled awkwardly, then ambled back to his seat, his ego in tatters. Jane held her stomach, a sudden rush of bile rising in her throat. She tried to burp away the eggy taste in her throat, but it was no good.

'Oh God.' Jane scrambled from her seat, knocking Zoe sideways.

'You OK, Jane?' her mum said.

Jane ran to the back of the coach, pushing the toilet door open and locking it behind her, dropping to her knees and clutching the toilet seat. When she opened the door again, she was met with grimaces from the other passengers.

***

By the time the coach pulled into the car park at Sunshine Sands it was 10 a.m. The weary passengers peered at the distant tide as they trudged off the bus. The kids, free from the confines of the coach and high on sugary snacks, ran in circles around the car park. The pot-bellied coach driver opened the side door and pulled out suitcases and various bundles of folded chairs and umbrellas. The holidaymakers swarmed over the bags like locusts, grabbing their things and corralling children to follow them.

'Here's ours,' Jane said, pulling two cases from the middle of the pile.

'I can see mine too,' Zoe said, grabbing a small pink backpack.

The three of them took their bags and walked along the promenade with its row of boarding houses. *No Vacancies* signs hung in the front windows, apart from one with an overgrown garden and wilting geraniums in window boxes. Jane's mum shook her head.

'Thank goodness that's not our accommodation,' she said, marching onwards.

'Found it!' called out Zoe, pointing at the Forget-Me-Not boarding house.

Their mum smiled with relief. It was clean and bright, foil windmills spinning in the light summer breeze, a rainbow of colour hitting the white walls.

They trudged up the red stone steps and through the front door, a bell ringing as it opened. A slight and balding middle-aged man stood behind the reception desk. He blew his nose into a large cotton handkerchief, wiping it left and right before scrunching it up and putting it in his cardigan pocket.

'Welcome to the Forget-Me-Not.' He suddenly turned to the wall, urgently pulling his handkerchief from his pocket and sneezing loudly into it.

'Bless you,' Jane said, as the man blew his nose again.

He sniffed into his hankie and returned it to his pocket, holding out his hand.

'Bernard Simpson.'

Jane's mum hesitated, grimacing slightly as she tentatively shook the hand he had held the handkerchief in.

'Marion Delway, and these are my daughters, Jane and Zoe.'

He looked beyond Marion to the two girls, his inspecting eyes magnified through thick lenses. Zoe sidled closer to Jane, who took her young sister's hand.

He ran a finger down a list of names in a spiral-bound book. 'Delway, Delway . . . ah yes, here we are. Just the two nights?'

'That's right, Jane is here for the beauty contest.'

He opened a drawer beneath the desk and took out a key ring with a silver key hanging from it; 'Your room key.'

He turned towards a door in the back and called out, 'Dolly!' before facing Marion again. 'Breakfast is between seven and nine thirty. We ask all residents to be back by 11 p.m. and that noise is kept to a minimum at all times.'

Jane frowned. 'What happens if we need to be out later than eleven?'

Bernard looked at her as if he didn't understand why she'd ask such a thing.

'Well, you wait until 7 a.m. and the door will be unlocked again.'

Dolly appeared from the back, her mousy hair, parted in the middle, held back from her face with two kirby grips. She wore a baggy cardigan over a floral tabard, her head down.

'Can you show our guests to their room please, Dolly?'

Dolly muttered under her breath and took the keys from Bernard. Marion looked to Jane, raising an eyebrow as Dolly padded past them and up the stairs without saying a word. Zoe skipped after her, followed by Marion and Jane. Bernard raised his head from the reception desk and watched as Jane walked away, his eyes fixed on her legs. When Marion urged Jane to hurry, Bernard snapped his gaze away and began idly leafing through the guestbook on the desk.

* * *

Dolly turned the lock with the smaller of the two keys and pushed the handle down, opening the door to a sizeable room with a bay window. The walls were papered with purple-and-pink floral wallpaper, the patterns disorientating Jane for a moment. Heavy curtains framed the window, in front of which a camp-bed had been made up. A double bed was positioned opposite, looking out to the view.

'Thank you,' said Marion, taking the keys from Dolly.

Dolly eyed Jane's white court shoes, then lowered her head and left, closing the door behind her.

'She's a chatty one, isn't she?' Marion sneered. 'Jealous of you, most likely.'

'Don't say that, Mum,' Jane snapped.

Marion tutted and took her suitcase over to the wardrobe, opening the wooden door and pulling out a handful of metal coat hangers. Jane walked over to the put-up bed by the window where Zoe sat, playing with a Sindy doll she had taken from her backpack.

She looked out of the window, watching as families walked along the seafront, faces beaming despite the strong gusts of westerly wind. Across the road, on the promenade she saw a woman her mum's age in a sparkly leotard and tutu, tap-dancing on top of a small wooden box. An older man accompanied her on an accordion, holidaymakers throwing coins into a hat as they passed. Lovers walked hand in hand among children who skipped along, their faces buried in clouds of candyfloss.

'Shall we go for a walk to the beach soon?' Jane asked Zoe.

Zoe opened her mouth to speak as Marion chipped in. 'You'll need to be getting ready for this afternoon.'

Jane pulled a face at Zoe, unseen by Marion. She giggled and went back to combing her doll's hair.

There was a knock at the door.

'Get that will you, Jane?' Marion said, running her hand down a satin dress she held in the air.

Jane opened the door to find Bernard standing there, balancing a pile of neatly folded towels in his arms.

'I've brought you these. Dolly forgot to put them in the bathroom for you.'

'Oh, thank you.' Jane reached forward and tried to take them from him, but he drew them further into his body for a second, forcing her closer, before releasing them. The skin around his nostrils was red and stubble was breaking through his pale skin. He looked like he was about to whisper something to her, when Marion pulled the door wide open and he took a step back.

'About the timings . . .'

'Timings?' he said, pushing back stray strands of hair over his bald patch.

'The contest is Saturday, and as much as we'd all like to be back in bed by 11 p.m., I'm sure it will be a lot later, and you said—'

'Of course. It's not normal rules, but I'll let you have this.' He put his hand in his pocket and took out a small bunch of keys, freeing one from the metal ring. 'It's a spare front door key, mind you don't lose it and make sure it's back with me on Sunday.'

Marion smiled. 'Thank you.'

Bernard kept his eyes fixed on Jane as Marion closed the door on him.

'What a strange man,' she said, taking the towels from Jane and carrying them to the tiny en-suite bathroom.

'Sssh,' Jane urged, 'he'll hear you.'

'I'll run you a bath and Zoe can have your water afterwards,' Marion said, already turning the taps.

'Do I have to have a bath?' Zoe groaned, dropping her Sindy doll back in her backpack and taking out a teddy bear.

Marion marched to the dressing table and took out a cigarette from her bag, lighting it with a Swan Vesta match.

'You don't want potatoes growing behind your ears, do you?' Marion said, exhaling smoke into the room.

Jane leaned over Zoe and opened a window, shooting a look of disapproval at her mum.

'I'm glad I still fit into my dress,' Marion said, turning to the dressing-table mirror and sucking her stomach in as she swung from side to side. 'You never know, there might be some eligible men there.'

'Mum!' Jane cried.

'I'm not over the hill yet, you know. There's life in the old dog yet.' Marion stubbed out her cigarette in a small brass ashtray and picked up a tube of lipstick. She removed the lid and drew it across her lips, smacking them together as she plumped up her hair.

Jane went to the bathroom to check on the water, swishing her hand around the barely warm flow from the taps.

'I've got the perfect outfit for you, Jane,' Marion called from the bedroom.

'I can pick my own clothes,' Jane protested.

Her mum ignored her, and began to sing an old song that she sung whenever her mind was on something else.

* * *

Jane stood in front of the wardrobe, looking into the oval mirror fixed to its door. She wore an emerald-green satin wrap dress, a thin gold belt cinching in her waist. Her mum had

had her on a diet for the past four weeks, ever since she'd won the regional heat. The egg sandwich had been her only treat since then and now it was down a toilet somewhere on the M6. She could only hope there was food at the reception they were heading to.

'What a picture!' Her mum clasped her hands together as Jane turned around. She retrieved a small camera from her bag and took a photo, the flash hurting Jane's eyes.

'Mum!'

'Can't a mother be proud?'

Her mum pouted, the guilt-inspiring look which always had Jane apologising, even though she rarely knew what she was apologising for. Marion joined her at the mirror and put an arm around her, looking at their reflections.

'Lucky for you, you got your looks from me and didn't end up with your good-for-nothing father's nose.'

Jane gritted her teeth. The berating of her long-departed dad was so ingrained in her mum's psyche, it was useless protesting. Her mum had burned most of his and Zoe's dad's photos on a gin-fuelled night in 1974, not long after Zoe's dad, her second attempt at a happy marriage, had fled to Spain with a young barmaid from the local pub. As much as she loved her mum, and felt loyal to her, there were times when she understood why both men had found the need to escape. What began as wild romance and excitement invariably ended with Marion's disappointment in the dull reality of domestic life and their inability to provide her with the trappings she felt she deserved.

Jane looked down at Zoe, who was struggling to tie the laces on her pumps. 'Do you need help?'

'I can do it,' Zoe said proudly, as she managed to make them into a bow.

Marion placed a ragged fox stole across her shoulders, handed down to her by her own mother. Its eyes, two black beads slightly off-kilter, gave it a slightly crazed appearance. Her mum claimed to friends that it was a gift from a suitor she had holidayed with in the south of France. Jane knew that though her mind wandered around the world, her mum's physical being had never travelled further south than Birmingham.

'Come on, you two, we've got to find the place first.'

Jane pulled Zoe up from the bed and led her out of the room. 'Let's get a bit of sea air.'

As they reached the bottom stair in the boarding house, the sound of clipping heels travelled down the hallway and two young women appeared. One wore tight satin trousers with a batwing top that exposed a pale shoulder, the other wore a clingy black dress. Their arms were linked and they pressed their heads together in conspiratory giggles.

'Don't forget to be back by eleven,' Bernard commanded.

The young women sneered, one of them taking a cigarette out of her handbag.

Bernard pointed to a sign. 'No smoking in communal areas.'

The girls cackled as they went through the front door, their laughter disappearing into the street.

'No respect, not like back in our day,' Marion said.

'Absolutely. Luckily, I don't have these problems with Dolly. She knows better.' He locked a drawer beneath the reception desk and walked back to the kitchen.

As they passed the dining room, Jane saw Dolly wiping the tables down, a Walkman heavy in her cardigan pocket as she hummed to herself. She looked up to meet Jane's gaze. Dolly frowned, putting her attention back to the table and rearranging the salt and pepper pots.

Marion, Jane and Zoe walked along the seafront, the sisters arm in arm as their mother followed behind. Jane's feet were already hurting in the new heels Marion had insisted she wear. Zoe giddily pointed to the boats that bobbed up and down in the sea, small dots on the horizon. On the beach, people sat in deck chairs, cardigans pulled around them as they ate ice creams and drank tea from silver flasks, determined to make the most of the last week of summer. The lights sparkled on the pier, a Ferris wheel turning and cars descending on a rollercoaster as faint screams carried through the air.

Zoe let go of Jane's arm and grabbed her mum's. 'Can we go to the fair, Mum? Please?'

Marion shook her away. 'Not now, and it will be too late by the time Jane's done. We'll all be ready for bed.'

Zoe let go of her arm, the disappointment clear on her face. As she walked closer to Jane, her elder sister put her arm out and drew her in, whispering in her ear, '*Definitely* tomorrow, little one.'

Zoe beamed up at her then skipped ahead, humming her favourite pop song.

A sandwich board outside the Lucky Jim arcade directed them to a flight of stairs behind a red rope. A burly security guard stepped forward as they headed towards it, his arms crossed tightly over his chest as he eyed them up and down.

'We're here for the reception,' Marion said, pushing forward and meeting his stern gaze with her own. 'Miss Sunshine Sands?' She motioned to Jane as if she were *Exhibit A*.

He unclipped the rope, holding his hand out in the direction of the stairs. Marion smiled curtly and ushered Jane and Zoe through. Jane was halfway up the stairs when she stopped abruptly, clutching her churning stomach.

'I can't.'

'Oh, yes you can,' Marion snapped, 'and you will.'

Jane felt her breath shorten, her chest feeling like it was held in an ever-tightening vice.

'She's not well, Mum,' Zoe said, wrapping her arms around Jane.

Marion softened. 'It's just a bit of nerves, love. That's normal.'

'I feel sick,' Jane groaned.

Zoe's brow crumpled as she watched her sister trying to take deep breaths. 'Should we get a doctor, Mum?'

Marion sighed and took Jane's hand, pulling her upwards. 'Now, come along, Jane, this is no time to act like a child. I've not come all this way only for you to back out now.'

Jane didn't argue, and let her mum lead her up the stairs. Zoe followed behind, her small hand on her sister's back. There was no more time for second thoughts. Marion pushed open the door, bringing Jane through with her. The heavy door swung back, hitting Zoe in the head before Jane could catch it. She cried out, but her voice was lost in the sea of chatter and low jazz music that filled the room.

'Are you OK?' Jane said.

Zoe nodded, rubbing the skin.

The men wore suits with ties and the women an array of short taffeta dresses and cocktail attire. They clutched glasses of champagne and balanced tiny canapés in their palms, giving the new arrivals the once-over. Marion poked Jane in the ribs.

'Smile.'

Jane looked around the room, the faces peering back at her. Soon they averted their gaze and continued chatting, and Jane managed to take a full breath. Through the gathered group, a man in his late forties emerged, a heavy gold chain laid over his suit.

'Welcome!' he said, his hand outstretched. 'I'm Mayor Erwitt, but you can call me Len.'

Marion took his hand and did a slight curtsey, placing her foot a little too far back and almost toppling over.

'Pleased to meet you, Mayor. I'm Marion and this is Jane.'

Len turned to Jane. 'Clearly one of our contestants,' he said, offering his hand to her. His handshake was limp, barely holding Jane's hand in his. He looked to Zoe, who was lingering behind and eyeing a plate of cheese and grapes set out on a table. 'And who is this lovely young lady? A future Miss Sunshine Sands?'

Zoe smiled, revealing a gap in her teeth where the adult tooth had yet to appear. Marion looked incredulous at the suggestion, leaning forward and saying, 'That one's more into climbing trees and reading books, Mayor. I don't hold out much hope.'

She spoke as if she wouldn't be heard, but Zoe's smile quickly faded, and she returned her attention to the food on display. Jane hated it when her mum spoke about Zoe in that way, almost as much as she resented the almost constant flattery she received. There was no middle ground between the treatment of the two sisters. Although both dads had left Marion, it was Zoe's who had committed the ultimate crime of being unfaithful. Zoe was the image of her dad, a constant reminder of Marion's humiliation, and now it seemed she was doomed to receive the punishment for his actions.

'Well, feel free to mingle and enjoy the night. Now, Jane, you can pick up your uniform for the beach photographs tomorrow morning over there.' Len pointed to a woman standing by a table stacked high with clothing. 'There'll be lots of photographs taken and a reporter present, so plenty of chance to get seen.'

Marion let out an excited 'Ooooh', nudging Jane. 'How exciting!'

A woman dressed in a twinset and pearls waved at Len from across the room.

'I'd better go, the wife is calling.' He gave a dramatic eyeroll and strode off, giving cursory hellos as he weaved through the guests.

'Come on then, let's mingle,' Marion said excitedly, heading towards a small group standing around a tall table of drinks.

Jane begrudgingly followed, trying her best to appear happy and enthusiastic as the other contestants glanced furtively as she passed, studying the competition. Jane turned to make sure her little sister was following and noticed a bump appearing on her forehead.

'I didn't realise it had hit you so hard,' Jane said, crouching down to take a closer look.

Zoe rubbed at the lump, flinching as she ran her fingers across it.

'It's OK,' Zoe said, tears pooling in her eyes.

'Do you feel dizzy?'

Zoe shook her head.

'If you start to then you'll tell me? Promise?'

'Pinky promise,' said Zoe.

They linked their little fingers together, Zoe eyeing the reddening bump with concern. Zoe skipped after their mum, who was talking to a couple from Birmingham.

'This is Mr and Mrs Jenkins, Jane. Their daughter Claire models for catalogues,' Marion explained.

'Have you done much modelling?' Mrs Jenkins asked, a crystal brooch sparkling against her black velvet dress.

'Not yet,' Marion interrupted, 'she hasn't got an agent. We're hoping she might find one after the contest.'

'I could always pass your details on to our Claire's, you never know.'

Marion's face lit up like a Christmas tree. 'That would be wonderful, thank you.'

Marion opened up her handbag and took out a headshot Jane had had done in the town shopping centre. Beneath her bright-eyed image was her name and their home telephone number. Marion grimaced as the woman folded it neatly down the middle and slid it into her bag.

'I'll do what I can, no promises,' Mrs Jenkins said, snapping her handbag clasp back together.

'Fancy folding up a photograph!' Marion gasped as they walked over to the table to collect Jane's uniform for the beach shoot. 'Nobody's going to take you on with a great crease across your face.'

Jane looked down to Zoe, crossing her eyes and sticking her tongue out. Zoe giggled, stopping abruptly when their mum glared down at her. The woman at the uniform table looked Jane up and down and sorted through various T-shirts and shorts. She handed them over to Jane, who checked the labels.

'I'm a ten and these are an eight?'

'They come up big, love. You don't want to be wearing a baggy T-shirt when you're trying to show off that figure, do you?'

Marion took the clothes from Jane and put them in her bag.

'I'm sure they'll fit just fine,' she smiled, thanking the woman, who was busy straightening what was left of the clothes.

As they walked across the room a young photographer tapped Jane on the shoulder.

'May I?'

Before Jane could reply, Marion had already given her consent and was suggesting the best ways to pose in order to get the best shot.

'One leg forward, Jane. No! Not that far. Chin up, that's right.'

The photographer moved around her, the shutter snapping like a tiny machine gun. He made Jane feel comfortable, a kind face in a room full of sneering strangers.

'Beautiful,' he said as he snapped away. 'Perfect.'

When he had finished, he winked and smiled at her. 'Thank you.' Then left to catch more images of the girls and dignitaries in the room.

'I think he had a soft spot for you,' Marion cooed.

Jane shrugged off her words and her knack of invading any private thoughts she had.

* * *

The party began to thin out once faces had been shown and the majority of the complimentary food had been eaten. The mayor had given a protracted speech about the town and what being Miss Sunshine Sands would mean for the winner. More local engagements, and then of course moving on to the next level and the chance of a £10,000 prize.

'We'd never have to do without again,' her mum said, a dreamy look in her eye.

Jane felt a hand brush her shoulder, a man she recognised from the TV.

'I don't think I've had the pleasure,' the moustached man said.

He wore a frilly shirt and dickie bow and took Jane's hand, placing a wet kiss on it.

'*Charlie Bailey?*' Marion exclaimed, her eyes wide and hand on her chest.

The man grinned, before taking Marion's hand and delivering another kiss.

'Are we all having fun so far?' he said.

Most people in England knew Charlie Bailey, a stalwart of the working men's clubs and a quiz show on Yorkshire TV. Saturday nights were always the same: steak, chips and peas in front of the television watching *How's Your Father?*, a show thick with innuendo and jokes that kept just the right side of 'blue' so that children could watch with their parents. Summers he spent at various seaside resorts, selling out the theatre for the season.

'Oh, yes! Could I have your autograph? We love your show. We're all big fans!' Marion gushed, already taking a notepad and pen out of her handbag and handing it to him.

Charlie grinned. 'Of course, always happy to oblige.' He winked at Marion and she blushed like a lovesick teenager.

He put the notepad down on a table. 'Who shall I sign it to?'

'Marion. Well, Marion and Jane, she's a contestant tomorrow night.'

Charlie scribbled his signature and handed it to Marion.

'That's very kind. Isn't it kind, Jane?'

Zoe pushed in between Marion and Jane. 'Can I have one too?'

'Don't be so rude,' Marion said. 'I do apologise, Mr Bailey.'

Charlie gave Zoe a toothy grin. 'No matter at all, of course you can.'

Marion scowled at Zoe as Charlie signed another piece of paper and handed it to the young girl, who pushed it into her pocket before skipping off to the buffet table.

Charlie scribbled on a third page, tore it out and slid it into Jane's hand. 'I'll see you tomorrow, no doubt,' he said.

Then, directing his attention to Marion, 'There'll be no missing a looker like you in the crowds.'

'Oh, you charmer, you,' Marion giggled.

Charlie said his goodbyes and walked away, other party-goers and contestants trying to get his attention as he joined Len Erwitt and his wife, who were putting their coats on.

Marion read out the autograph: 'To Marion, by far my best-looking fan. Best wishes, Charlie B.' She smiled broadly. 'He put a kiss too. I should get this framed.' She carefully closed the notepad and put it away. 'Right, best get an early night, you've a busy day ahead, Jane.' She swanned ahead, high on his compliment and the brush with fame.

Jane walked behind as they headed back to the boarding house, glancing down at the scrap of signed paper Charlie had given her.

To Jane, I'm staying at the Grand, room 139. Come and see me, I can give you some winning pointers. Charlie X

CHAPTER 5

2022
Zoe

'You missed breakfast, Zoe,' Dolly accused.

Zoe tried to stifle a yawn as she reached the bottom stair.

'Sorry, I turned my alarm off and fell back to sleep.'

Dolly pursed her lips. 'If you could just let me know the night before if you're not joining us.'

'Like I said, it wasn't intended,' Zoe said crisply. Then, softening her tone, 'I don't suppose there's any chance of a coffee?'

Dolly regarded her and gave a put-upon sigh. 'There might be some left in the urn if you look sharp.'

'Thanks,' Zoe said, as Dolly brushed past her and disappeared into the kitchen.

Zoe sat down in the dining room at her previously allotted table. The honeymooners were by the window, both leaning into a brochure.

'Exciting plans for today?' Zoe called out.

They turned to her, their faces bright.

'Nothing special, we're just going to take a walk along the front,' the young woman said.

'Sophie wants to go to the fortune teller,' her husband said, rolling his eyes.

Sophie tapped him playfully. 'I've heard she's really good. I looked her up online. Dan's not keen, as you can tell.'

Zoe smiled. 'Well, there's lots to keep him entertained while you find out about the future.'

'You've been here before?' Dan said.

Zoe glanced at the doorway, making sure Dolly wasn't within earshot.

'A long time ago. It's changed a lot since then.'

'With your mum and dad?'

Zoe felt her heart begin to race at the mention of her mum and that time. Marion screaming out Jane's name as she dragged Zoe along the seafront searching for her sister. Holidaymakers looking at her mum as if she were mad. And she was really — at least, driven that way.

'My mum and sister.'

'They didn't fancy coming back with you?' Sophie said, her eyes bright.

Zoe took a long intake of breath, not prepared to be the one being interrogated.

'My mum died quite a few years ago, and my sister.'

Sophie's smile faded. 'I'm so sorry.' Her cheeks reddened and she looked to Dan for support.

The moment of silence was broken by Dan, who quickly changed the subject.

'Sophie wants to keep busy this morning, keep her mind off later.'

'Later?' Zoe said, relaxing again.

Sophie beamed. 'I'm in the talent contest, the one on the pier. I'll be dancing. They're filming it apparently, so it might lead somewhere. I'm nervous as hell!'

'No need for nerves,' Dan said, taking his wife's hand. 'She's very talented, could have gone to stage school.'

Zoe reached for the small notebook in her handbag, a biro clipped onto the cover, aware that she had spent little time on the job she was being paid to do.

'Do you mind if I ask you some questions about the show for my article?' she asked, already up from her chair and making her way to their table.

Dan jumped up and pulled an extra chair over so she could join them, gesturing for Zoe to sit between them. While she was grateful for the enthusiasm, she was slightly perturbed by being the thorn between two roses.

'Thank you,' she said. 'Can I ask your full names?'

'Daniel Ashcroft.'

She wrote it down then looked to Sophie, who hesitated for a moment.

'Ashcroft, Sophie Ashcroft.' She grinned widely. 'I'm still not used to it.'

'How long have you been married?'

'Five days,' they said in unison.

'Congratulations. So, the talent show is interrupting your honeymoon?'

Zoe was already finding an angle to the story she could write: *Even love couldn't get in the way of the show!*

'Not really, we planned the honeymoon around it,' Sophie explained. 'We couldn't afford two holidays, so we decided this would be it. We came a few days ago so we had a break beforehand.'

Zoe nodded, jotting notes down. 'And do you feel a talent show like this helps bring more people to resorts like Sunshine Sands?'

'Definitely. People should support our holiday towns, otherwise we'll lose them for good,' said Sophie.

'Not everyone can afford a holiday abroad,' Dan piped up. 'Besides, when the weather's good, there's nowhere better, is there?'

The three of them glanced out of the window as a woman walked by, clutching her hat to her head to prevent it being blown away.

'Have you other family coming to watch?'

Sophie shook her head. 'My dad couldn't get time off work — he works nights in a hospital.'

'But your mum will be watching over you, won't she?'

Zoe looked at Sophie, waiting for an explanation.

'We lost her earlier this year.'

'Oh, I'm so sorry.' Zoe put her pen down on the table.

'She would have been so proud,' Dan continued. 'She was a bit of a star herself, wasn't she, Sophie? She was a runner-up in a beauty contest they held here, the last one they ever did.'

Zoe felt her stomach knot and her pulse quicken. She took the pen in her fingers again, trying to keep her shaking fingers still.

'You know, when the winner went missing. Your mum reckoned she got drunk and fell in the sea, didn't she, Soph?'

'Well, that's what they thought at first, but then there was talk she'd run off with someone, an older man. Someone famous.'

'Do you know who the man was?' Zoe asked, leaning towards Sophie, willing her to have a name.

Sophie shook her head. 'A comedian or something, I don't think they knew really.'

Dolly approached the table, a wave of agitation rippling across her face. She placed a mug of coffee in front of Zoe, somewhat roughly. 'I'm afraid I'm going to have to clear the dining room now, the cleaner needs to get in to hoover and wipe down.'

'Dolly might know,' Sophie said, draining her teacup.

'Might know what?' Dolly asked.

'Sophie was just telling me that her mum was a contestant in Miss Sunshine Sands 1982, the same year as that girl went missing.'

Zoe watched Dolly's reaction, a slight flicker in her eyes as she sucked in a breath.

'Yes, Sophie mentioned that. Like I said, Zoe, Sophie and her family have been coming to Sunshine Sands for years,' Dolly bristled, before turning her attention to the newlyweds. 'Well, come on, you two, I thought you had plans for a morning on the pier. You'd best get out while that rain holds off.'

'Did you need to ask us anything else?' Dan said.

Zoe felt the glare of Dolly from above. 'No, that's great, thank you. Go and enjoy your day together.'

As the Ashcrofts gathered their things, Dolly began clearing around them, plates crashing into each other. Zoe took a sip of the lukewarm coffee, flinching at its bitterness. She'd just put the barely drunk mug down when Dolly held out her hand to take it from her. Zoe took another sip, then handed it over. As she got up to leave, Dolly put her hand out and grabbed Zoe's arm, pinching the skin.

'If you don't mind, I'd rather you didn't interrogate my guests while they're on holiday.'

'Pardon?'

'The Forget-Me-Not is a place to relax and have fun. I'd rather it not become a boardroom for your work. I have their privacy to consider, people come here to relax—'

'But—'

'Not to be hounded by the press.'

Zoe managed to stifle a laugh. One lone reporter talking over coffee to fellow guests about a beauty pageant was hardly the stuff of Fleet Street.

'I'm sorry, Dolly, I won't do it again.'

Rain began to patter against the window as Dan and Sophie ran by outside. He held his jacket over her head to protect her from the downpour.

Dolly placed the empty mug on a tray. 'Dinner at seven?'

***

The traffic was at a standstill, tail-to-tail coaches packed with passengers who looked out to the arcades and sea with excitement, unperturbed by the wind and rain. The circus was in town, if only for a day and a night. A marquee was being set up on the promenade next to the beach, workers shouting to each other as metal poles clanked and tarpaulins whooshed in the air. Cars filled the public car park next to the Harbour

Lights fish and chip shop. A young teen slapped a leaflet into her palm: 'Wash and Wave, £10 all day.'

Zoe looked down at the leaflet, then at the young girl who had already roller-skated away to the next bystander. She stuffed the leaflet in her handbag, not wanting the girl to see her throw it in the bin. She had also once been a leaflet girl, posting flyers through letterboxes in their village to advertise her mum's foray into selling Avon products. Marion's business venture had ended when she tried to sell the stock at higher prices and pocket the money to pay for a holiday to the Algarve.

A multi-coloured truck drove past, metallic rainbow streamers flying out from the wing mirrors and handles, an arch of balloons swaying precariously over the open-topped trailer. Gloria Gaynor played out from a loudspeaker secured to the cab with a bungee as three drag queens lip-synced into microphones, ignoring the downpour as they threw handfuls of glitter and confetti onto unsuspecting tourists. Zoe laughed as the queens paraded around the tiny space as best they could without falling over the low sides.

Some passers-by clapped in time to the music and children waved, as others sneered and shook their heads in disapproval. For a moment Zoe remembered that at one time there had been joy at Sunshine Sands, she *had* laughed and played, before that night when everything had been stolen away from her.

* * *

The sweet smell of candyfloss and hot greasy donuts paved her way as she walked down the pier towards Dunes. Despite the northerly wind blowing a gale, hardy holidaymakers sat on the benches that ran the length of the pier, supping hot tea from takeaway cups and wrestling slippery seafood out of shallow containers with cocktail sticks. A child chased a clown-shaped helium balloon as its ribbon freed itself from her chubby fingers and began to float away, her sobs muffled in the embrace of a concerned dad who watched helplessly as it snapped back and forth out to sea.

She was surprised the manager of Dunes had agreed to talk — there had been much resistance to journalists getting involved in the weekend's celebration, apart from one who wrote for the local paper and was likely to be nothing but glowing about an event in their own town. The last thing the town council needed was any kind of negativity about a place already steeped in controversy and decline.

Her phone began to ring, and she shuffled around in her handbag to retrieve it.

'Hi, Dylan, how's things?'

'Where are you? What's that noise?'

Zoe attempted to shield her phone beneath her jacket. 'It's the wind, I'm on the pier in Sunshine Sa—'

'Can I go to Carla's party next weekend?'

'I'm great, thanks. How are you?'

'Eh?'

'Never mind.' Zoe stepped to the side to avoid a mobility scooter that was heading straight for her. 'You're with me next weekend.'

'Yeah, I know, but it's an eighteenth and it's at her house.'

'Do her parents know?'

'I don't know, I suppose so.'

'Let's chat when I'm home.'

'I need to let her know now.'

Zoe noticed the time: she was late.

'OK, fine, but midnight curfew?'

'Muuum.'

'Got to go, I'll call later. Love you.'

She ended the call and dropped her phone into her bag, walking quickly past the funfair and towards the entrance to the bar.

Dunes sat on the very end of the pier with just a narrow walkway around the rear. It was hexagonal in shape and clad with white wooden slats. The large window frames were freshly painted in turquoise blue. Posters for the talent show were stuck inside each window and a larger one on a sandwich board outside. The two reality stars' faces were prominent, neither of which Zoe recognised. She stood for a moment outside the entrance. It looked so different now and in the light of day. Her only memories from then were the blaring music, bodies rushing in and out, the dancing, cheering and then frantic searching. Zoe pushed through the doors before her head told her to turn and run.

There was a small lobby before entering the venue. Zoe took out her phone and unlocked it, pointing it at the walls and taking snapshots. A potted history of one of the oldest piers in England. Victorian mill workers lifting long skirts so they could paddle in the sea, lovers reunited after the war embracing their newfound freedom. Later images included photos of local dignitaries alongside famous comedians of the day. All of the Forget-Me-Not luminaries were there — Larry Grayson, Leslie Crowther and Bobby Ball pulling on bright braces to the amusement of those gathered. Her eyes focused in on one taken the year her sister disappeared, a formal gathering of men standing before a red velvet curtain. Zoe studied their faces. On the mount below the photograph were their names: Dolly's dad and the former owner of the Forget-Me-Not, Bernard Simpson; Mayor Len Erwitt; DCI Bob Previtt and Charlie Bailey. Zoe took a picture and zoomed in on Charlie Bailey's grin in all its toothy glory.

She thought about what Sophie had said: a comedian. Her head suddenly felt light, her knees like jelly. Zoe crouched down and sat on the floor, waiting for the dizziness to pass.

'You alright, love?' A cleaner carrying a mop and bucket stood over her, the disinfectant in the water making Zoe want to gag.

'I'm fine, I just came over a bit funny. Hot and dizzy.'

'The menopause is a bugger, isn't it?'

Zoe didn't know whether to be thankful for the understanding or insulted that she looked clearly of an age where the menopause was the first thing this woman thought of.

'Yes, that must be it,' Zoe said, rising to her feet again and putting her phone in her back pocket.

'Our Ginny swears by ashwagandha tea, says she's never felt better. Mind you, I think it was getting rid of her feckless husband that really did the trick.'

The cleaner didn't wait for Zoe to respond as she pushed open the double doors to the bar, the mop handle whacking the woodwork. Zoe caught the doors before they swung shut and entered the bar as the cleaner joined her colleague by a stack of chairs in the corner.

Zoe approached a man standing behind the bar polishing glasses with a tea towel.

'Colin?'

The man looked up and when she realised he had his AirPods in, she spoke louder. 'I'm here to see Colin Myers?'

The barman nodded and disappeared through a door at the back of the bar. Zoe wandered around the venue. It was coming to the end of the season and the tell-tale signs of summer wear and tear were beginning to show. A few scrapes on the wall, chipped window ledges and giant rubber plants that looked ready to hibernate for the winter.

The cleaners began brushing and mopping the dance floor. Boxes full of Hawaiian flowers on string sat about the place and at the other end of the room where the stage was, a silver foil curtain was being hung. A rain-drenched family of four appeared through the doors and made their way to the bar. When the barmaid told the dad they weren't open due to the upcoming show, he swore loudly and ushered his family away, leaving the unperturbed barmaid to carry on filling baskets with packets of crisps.

'Ah, Miss Kincade,' a man called as he walked theatrically from a door behind the bar. 'Apologies for the tardiness, so many plates spinning at the moment.' He held out his hand for her to shake. 'Colin Myers.'

Zoe shook it. 'Not a problem at all, I haven't been here long.'

He gestured for Zoe to sit down at a table and clicked his fingers at the barmaid, who dropped a packet of crisps on the bar and scuttled over.

'Can I get you a drink?' Colin asked.

'Yes, please. Tea would be lovely,' Zoe said, taking her notepad and pen from her bag.

'Tea for two, please, Janet.'

Zoe noted Colin's outfit: faded jeans, a striped shirt and a colourful cravat wrapped around his neck. His hair was silver and thinning, swept over his head and held tight with hairspray to hide a bald patch.

'It's all very exciting, I'm so glad you're here to cover it all,' he said.

Zoe nodded. 'There certainly seems to be a lot of buzz,' she said. 'Have you sold all the tickets for the show tonight?'

'Oh, yes,' Colin said, sitting up straight as Janet appeared with a tray holding two cups and saucers, a teapot, milk, sugar and a plate of biscuits.

'Thank you, darling,' Colin cooed.

He turned back to Zoe. 'We could have sold twice the amount, and if it weren't for health and safety I'm sure we would have.'

'Who's in charge of managing everything to do with the talent show?'

'Gary, an ambitious wannabe Simon Cowell brought in from down south. If it's a success he gets to take a share of the profits.'

The cleaners began to move the tables and chairs back, unceremoniously dragging them across the laminate floor. Colin flinched at the screeching as he poured the tea.

'Are any of the old guard still around? Len Erwitt, the old mayor?'

'Len? Blimey, he's long since gone. Must be thirty-odd years now, got some kind of illness. Very sad really, had to go into care as I remember.'

'Are any of the other judges around from that time?'

Colin threw his head back, his fingers on his chin.

'Now you're asking. I'm not sure about the plod, and Charlie Bailey? I suppose it's like all the entertainers of that time, just quietly retired off to some leafy house in Buckinghamshire. He must have made a fair amount of money in his time.'

'What about Bernard Simpson?' she asked, opening the picture she'd just taken on her phone and turning it to him.

Colin took out a pair of glasses from his pocket and held them over his nose.

'Ah, Bernard Simpson wasn't a judge, but he was part of the same private men's club in town. Now, what was it called?' He looked thoughtfully up to the ceiling of Dunes, then around the room to the bar and the beer taps. 'The Boddington Club!' he said, snapping his fingers. 'That was it. A poor man's Masons, if you ask me.'

'Were there a lot of members?'

He shook his head. 'I don't know. But it was like a secret society of men patting each other on the back and giving each other a foot up for building projects and beer licences, that sort of thing. Small-town corruption dressed up in dickie bows and secret handshakes. Bernard let them use the boarding house for meetings, after-house drinks and all that. He's long gone now though, and the club frittered away after the beauty queen incident.'

'Why do you think that was?'

'I couldn't say for sure, but probably for the best they're all out of the picture now, as far as the town goes. No disrespect to them, but it helps us move on.'

Zoe felt her stomach turn. 'Move on?'

'Well, they never managed to shake the scandal of the missing beauty queen and neither did Sunshine Sands. Len clung onto his mayoral chains for dear life after that, bless him.'

'What do you think happened to her?'

Colin shrugged. 'Took the money and ran. By all accounts she had an overbearing mother that wouldn't leave her be, so as soon as she had the £1,000, which was a lot of money back then, she got the next coach out of town. London, probably. Bright lights and promises of fame, usually ending up in strip clubs and substance abuse, of course.'

It was a theory Zoe had considered many times. In some ways it would have been easier to accept: the shame and inability to come home, rather than simply not wanting to.

Their meeting was interrupted by loud singing and laughter as the drag queens from the truck burst through the doors. Their presence took Zoe's breath away, all cheekbones, platform shoes and glitter.

'You look like drowned rats!' Colin teased.

One of the drag queens held her arms out and shook them, water sprinkling to the floor.

'How did you get on? Anyone fall off the truck?' Colin said.

'No, but the coastal winds have given me frostbite in very delicate parts of my body,' one replied, their hand over their privates.

'Miss Kincade, meet our wonderful cabaret performers and our host, Miss B. Havin'.'

Miss B. Havin' doffed an imaginary cap to Zoe, glitter falling to the floor like confetti. They smiled at Zoe as if waiting for her to say something.

'Nice to meet you,' Zoe said, holding her hand out. 'You must be excited to be hosting.'

Miss B. Havin' smiled at her curiously and nodded, squeezing her hand.

'Miss Kincade is writing a piece for the *National Mail*, so be careful what secrets you reveal,' Colin warned, playfully.

'Oh, let's talk,' one of them said, flicking their long red acrylic mane over their shoulder. 'I'm sure I can get the readers' comments blazing.'

Zoe smiled. 'That's what we aim for.'

'I can give you the lowdown,' said Miss B. Havin'. 'I have time over dinner.'

'That'd be great, thank you. I'm at the Forget-Me-Not, do you know it?'

Colin opened his mouth to speak but Miss B. Havin' cut in.

'Yes I know it.' They smiled. 'Meet you at seven?'

The queens said their goodbyes before marching across the floor and disappearing behind the silver curtains. At the side of the room, the two cleaners looked at the now glitter-strewn floor in disgust.

CHAPTER 6

In the ear-splitting din of the amusement arcade, Zoe watched the two-pence coins move forwards and back, the heavy pile teetering tantalisingly on the edge but not budging. She took another coin from the plastic pot and paused, letting it drop at a long-learned precise moment, a familiar buzz inside her as it landed perfectly, pushing multiple coins down to the next level. A little boy stood watching; he was the same height as the coin drop, his eyes wide as the heavy pile slid forward and the coins cascaded and clattered down into the metal tray beneath.

Zoe scooped them into the tub realising, once the winning rush was over, she was now beholden to either carry them back to the boarding house or get rid of them all again. She turned to the boy and held out the tub.

'Here you go, have fun.'

The little boy didn't say anything, just took the money tentatively as if she might grab it back at any moment. She made her way through the blinging and flashing arcade, children weaving around her, parents frantically trying to keep up. She spotted Dan and Sophie hunched over a claw machine. Daniel was laser-focused on a plush toy kitten that repeatedly fell back down on the other toys, no matter how many times the claw appeared to secure it. Sophie laughed, her hand gently patting his back.

'You know you can buy those for a fiver in the souvenir shop, don't you?' Zoe said, smiling at the couple.

Daniel kept his eyes forward. 'It's not the same, I have to *win* one.'

They all followed the mechanical claw as it grasped a plush kitten and drew it up above the pile of furry bodies below. Sophie's fingers gripped the cotton of Dan's T-shirt as he held his breath, then let out a short sharp gasp as it jerked and the toy slipped slightly, before it moved forward towards the shoot. It was only inches away from freedom when the claw loosened its grip slightly, and the pastel-pink kitten fell headfirst back into the pile. Dan slammed his palm down on the control panel.

'Better luck next time,' Zoe said, as Sophie consoled her arcade-weary husband.

Zoe left as Dan rummaged around in his pockets to find more fifty-pence pieces, ignoring Sophie's assurances she would survive without a plush pastel kitten.

The seagulls were in full screech, fighting to be heard above the dance tunes that blasted from the waltzers and dodgems. She watched as a fairground worker rode on the back of a dodgem, the cartoonish car weaving around the shiny floor, two young women steering it sharply to avoid oncoming traffic. It was a blue — no, green car that Jane had taken her in. She had made a fuss about the seat belt not being secure, and then proceeded to drive so slowly around the oval platform that the ride's alternate name, 'bumper cars', was redundant.

Madame Eloise's fortune-telling booth was a small gypsy caravan placed next to the Ghost House. Zoe walked up the wooden steps to see a handwritten postcard had been pinned to heavy purple curtains, which were drawn across the small doorway.

Madame Eloise will be back soon.

Zoe looked up and down the pier, before edging the curtain apart a little and peering into the caravan. Illuminated by an orange lava lamp, the caravan was a treasure trove of all things clairvoyant. Shelves of crystals and eastern idols, a variety of small crystal balls and boxes of tarot cards.

Two metal chairs were placed either side of a small round table in the centre of the room. The table was covered in a purple-and-silver velvet cloth, in the centre of which sat a large crystal ball and a stack of tarot cards. Zoe didn't remember the fortune teller from all those years ago, she had been more interested in sticks of rocks and donkeys than knowing what the future held. Maybe they should have consulted Eloise that day — maybe then they would have left before the contest and their lives wouldn't have been shattered in the space of a night.

Zoe reached out to the tarot cards, her fingertips tracing the nine of cups.

'Don't touch those!'

Zoe shot back, hitting her head against the low ceiling. 'Sorry, I was just—'

'You *never* touch someone else's tarot cards,' the woman scorned, as she marched forward and grabbed them, cradling them as if holding a baby bird. 'Not that you should even be in here — didn't you read the sign?'

She wore a black turtleneck and a long flowing skirt, fringed with gold sequins that tinkled and swished as she moved. Her hair was jet-black, the whitish grey roots just beginning to emerge.

'I'm sorry,' Zoe said again, 'I—'

'It's twenty pounds to read your palm, forty for the tarot and the crystal ball reading sixty pounds.'

Zoe didn't realise that a glimpse into the future could be so pricey, but she had put herself in a position of no return, at least not without looking like an intruding lunatic.

'Tarot, please.'

Eloise relaxed her body and gestured for Zoe to sit in one of the metal chairs. The clairvoyant began to shuffle the cards, her hands wrinkled and fingers bony as she slid and rearranged with the skill of a magician. Her accent was indeterminable, somewhere between Spanish and the north of England.

'Have you lived in Sunshine Sands long?' Zoe asked, trying to fill the silence.

Eloise didn't look up, her focus solely on the cards, which she cut and piled up several times before spreading them across the table in one swift move.

'Think of a question in your mind — don't tell me. Focus on what you want the cards to reveal.'

If she had known it would be so easy to solve the mystery of Jane's disappearance, she would have come to Eloise much sooner, Zoe thought. She attempted to push all thoughts of being grifted by a seaside entertainer out of her mind and focused on her question.

'Do you have one?' Eloise asked.

'Yes, I'd like to know—'

'Don't!' Eloise held her hand up, a halting palm in front of Zoe's face. 'Keep it in your mind, but don't tell me.'

Zoe held her lips tightly together, trying to suppress her amusement at the seriousness of Eloise. Six years ago she had gone to a 'psychic night' at the local pub, and had been told that a new baby was on the horizon within the year. Vodka and red wine had caused her to inform the crestfallen man that she had had a hysterectomy the previous year, to which he valiantly counter-argued that it may be from a surrogate.

'Choose six cards, don't think about it too much. Pick the ones you are drawn to.'

Zoe looked down to the spread of cards, already anxious about which to pick, her fingers lingering over them.

'I have lived here fifty years,' Eloise said, watching Zoe's hands. 'Don't think, just go where you are guided.'

Zoe pulled out a card, then another. Her hand travelled down the spread, and she took out four more. 'So, you were here when the girl went missing? And the other women?'

Eloise gathered up the unpicked cards and put them to the side, before taking the six chosen ones and turning them over. She looked up, her focus shifting from the cards to Zoe. 'Yes, I was there then. A long time ago now.' She drew her attention back to the table. 'Terribly sad.'

She had the same nonchalant expression as Dolly at the mention of Jane. As if women dying and disappearing was as interesting as last week's television schedule. Zoe understood it: the world moves on after death and tragedy — it must. Only those directly affected live with the aftershock. Zoe looked up as the rain began to increase in its intensity, battering against the roof of the caravan, punctuated by the squeals of those outside on the pier, caught in the downpour as they ran for cover.

Zoe looked down at the cards, relieved to see the Death card absent.

'You have been through a lot of change in the past couple of years, a relationship ending?'

Zoe nodded and went to explain, but Eloise put her finger to her lips, then continued.

'Four children, one of them is in spirit?'

Zoe felt her stomach tense. Eloise closed her eyes and took a deep breath.

'She's safe with the angels, my dear.'

Zoe didn't believe in anything after this life, not a heaven and not a hell. In her teens she had dabbled in Christianity, searching for peace and answers. She had found neither.

'You aren't married.'

Zoe shook her head. 'No. Well, technically yes, separated.'

Eloise prodded at a card. 'This one tells me there is another man on the horizon. You are wary and this is wise, but try and be open to new experiences, let go of the hurt. You're searching for something . . . or *someone*?'

Zoe shifted in her chair.

'Be careful,' Eloise said abruptly.

'Why?' Zoe asked, Eloise's sombre tone disturbing her.

'Some things are best left in the past,' said the fortune teller, smiling wryly. 'Like ex-husbands.' She returned her attention to the cards and showered Zoe with promises of financial stability and a long life. There would be a house move, somewhere by the sea. A career opportunity away from her current job that she should seriously consider.

'Is there anything else you'd like to know? Have I answered your question?'

'Not really, but it's OK.' Zoe reached into her bag for her purse.

'Maybe the crystal ball would help,' Eloise said, her hands already resting on the spherical glass.

Zoe was about to protest, but as if she really could read her mind, Eloise added, 'No charge. I like my customers to have the answers they require.'

Eloise closed her eyes, her brow furrowed in concentration. When she opened them again, she peered intently into the crystal ball, her eyes searching within it. Zoe began to get restless, not wanting to waste any more time here when she could be getting on with her article in the relative warmth of the boarding house.

'You asked about the missing girl when you first sat down,' Eloise stated.

Zoe shifted forward, trying to peer into the ball to see what Eloise was looking at, but all she saw were reflections of their surroundings and her own distorted image.

'I can see her,' she said, her chest rising and falling with each rapidly increasing breath.

'Who? Who can you see? Jane?'

Eloise kept her gaze on the crystal ball, her expression increasingly troubled.

'Tell me what you see,' Zoe demanded.

Eloise looked up at her and then back down into the glass. 'Why are you looking for this girl?'

'She's my sister.'

Eloise pulled her hands away from the crystal ball, staring at Zoe.

'What did you see? Tell me.'

'Nothing, I see nothing. The images I see can disappear just as soon as they arrive,' she said, taking a silk square of cloth and placing it over the crystal ball. 'You should go.'

'Was it her?'

Eloise gathered the cards up and put them into a small blue velvet pouch, avoiding Zoe's gaze as she spoke. 'No need to pay for the reading, dear.'

'Try again,' Zoe pleaded, snatching the cloth from the crystal ball.

'It doesn't work like that.' Eloise pushed her chair back and stood up, taking the pouch of cards and placing them on a shelf as Zoe looked forlornly into the translucent glass. She didn't know what to believe, but the shock and distress on Eloise's face was real enough. She took her purse out of her bag and threw two twenty-pound notes on the table, and without saying goodbye, yanked the curtains to the booth aside and ran down the steps. She shielded her eyes from the rain which was slowing to a drizzle, the sun now making a valiant attempt to break through charcoal-grey clouds.

'Fancy a scare?' a young woman said, complete with plastic fanged teeth and bite marks painted on her slim white neck. Zoe spun away from the Ghost House and marched down the pier, weaving in and out of the crowds, faces blurring into a haze and voices indistinguishable below the noise of fairground music that played out of speakers along the seafront.

When Zoe entered the boarding house, the London women were at the reception desk, their designer cases by their sides. They spoke in low, measured voices. Dolly was the other side of the desk, lips pursed, eyes fixed in a stony gaze.

'I did have Trevor look at the boiler, but I suppose I'll have to get someone out. If you'd mentioned it before I could have swapped your room,' Dolly said.

One of the London women glanced nervously at her friend before speaking. 'I think we'd still like to leave, if that's OK.'

Dolly snatched the keys from one of the women's hands and threw them in a drawer. 'Well, I'm afraid I can't refund you any money. This is very short notice, you know.'

'That's fine,' the woman said, her voice weak.

They didn't notice Zoe pass them and walk up the stairs. She heard the front door to the boarding house close as she entered her bedroom and ran to peek out of the window. The two women wheeled their cases down the path, a taxi already waiting on the road. Footsteps stomped up the stairs and across the landing and up to the attic rooms where Dolly's living space was. Zoe listened as the feet padded back and forth. She could hear Dolly chastising somebody — muffled, inaudible words. She looked back out the road as the taxi sped away, envying the two women who were likely winding their way to another place. One with rolltop baths and room service, she presumed.

CHAPTER 7

1982
Jane

Jane stepped out of the shower and onto a thin bathmat which slipped slightly on the damp tiled floor. Her mum was singing to herself in the bedroom, her mood considerably lighter since her brush with Charlie Bailey the previous evening. Jane hadn't told her mum about Charlie's invitation, partly because she wasn't 100% sure of his intent, but also, she knew that it would take the shine off her mum's buoyant mood.

'Don't forget to shave your bikini line!' Marion called.

Jane dried her face on a towel and wiped the mirror with her palm, her troubled reflection staring back at her. Maybe she should go to Charlie's hotel and not tell her mum, maybe it was just an opportunity to learn more about the competition. Her mum was right about one thing, she needed to make more effort now she was here. Growing up, there had been a hundred warnings about not taking sweets from strangers or accepting offers to view puppies from strange men in beat-up old cars. But Charlie was famous, and famous people didn't do bad things because they had too much to lose. Her thoughts were broken by a sharp knock on the door.

'Are you nearly done in there? I need to powder my nose.'

Jane opened the bathroom door and her mum rushed past her, muttering about time and outfits as she shut the door and bolted it.

Marion had laid out Jane's uniform for today's beach event. A white T-shirt with *Sunshine Sands* emblazoned across the chest and a pair of tiny red satin shorts. Jane fell onto the bed next to them, picking up the T-shirt and holding it out above her. She hoped it was warm outside; it had hardly been T-shirt weather so far and the organisers were unlikely to let contestants wear cardigans for the photo shoot. The chain flushed in the bathroom, followed by taps turning off and on, before her mum appeared back in the room.

'Our Doreen is going to be green with envy when I tell her about meeting Charlie,' Marion gushed. 'She's never let me forget her brush with Lionel Blair. I mean, he only sat opposite her at a dinner party, it wasn't as if they even spoke.'

Jane was used to Marion's rants about her older sister. Born ten years before her and the apple of their parents' eye, Doreen had married a wealthy businessman from Birmingham and lived in a large, detached house complete with an ornamental pond and a hostess trolley. As far as Jane was aware, her aunt had never said a bad word about Marion. She had always been generous at birthdays and Christmas, showering them with expensive gifts, something that had only served to agitate Marion further.

Jane put down the T-shirt and buried her head in the pillow, closing her eyes and drifting off to sleep, until she felt the tap of a hand on her shoulder. Zoe beamed as she held out a small box.

'What is it?' Jane asked, sitting back up in the bed.

'Open it,' Zoe urged.

Jane took the lid off and removed a tiny piece of tissue paper, to reveal a silver dolphin pendant.

'It's lovely! Is it for me?'

Zoe nodded. 'It's for luck. I bought it with my pocket money.'

Jane took it out of the box and unhooked it. 'That's so kind of you. Can you fasten it for me?'

She lifted her hair as Zoe fumbled with the clasp.

'There!' Zoe exclaimed. 'Do you like it?'

Jane got up from the bed and walked over to the dressing table, holding the pendant between her fingers.

'I love it.' She hugged her sister tight. 'And I love *you*, Zoe. I always will, *always*.'

* * *

It was only 9 a.m., but the gathering on the beach of contestants, judges and dignitaries had drawn a large crowd of onlookers. The sun had yet to appear from behind grey clouds, causing the exposed flesh of the contestants to prickle with goosebumps.

'Take it off,' Marion demanded, pulling Jane's cardigan from her shoulders.

The T-shirt was tight across her bust, the lettering transfer stretched to the point that there were tiny cracks in the decal. Jane pulled at the shorts, which only just covered her buttocks. Marion slapped her hand away.

'Now stand tall, chest out. This is your chance to make an impression before tonight.'

Jane shuddered as the wind whipped across her skin, pulling a strand of hair away that had stuck to her freshly glossed lips. The photographer from the previous night approached them.

'Hello again. Over here, darlin', come have your picture taken with the others. I'm Dave, by the way, the official photographer for the contest.'

Marion held out her hand, which he shook with his free hand. 'Make sure you get her best side.'

Dave smiled and put his arm around Jane, leading her over to a gaggle of other girls that were giggling and hopping around from one foot to the other to keep warm.

'Right now, ladies, if you could all face me and give me a winning smile.' He motioned for them to huddle closer. 'That's it, now let's see those chests out.'

The young women and girls did as they were told, pushing out their chests to reveal the *Sunshine Sands* logo. There were nervous ripples of laughter between them as they stood body to body, arms wrapped around each other.

'Beautiful,' Dave shouted, clicking away as he crouched down on the damp sand. He took the camera away from his face and called over to another group. 'Mr Bailey, Len, would you do us the honour?'

The girls shifted around in the sand to make room for Charlie Bailey and Mayor Erwitt. There had been strict instructions for them to wear heels and keep them on throughout the morning; as a result, the contestants found themselves sinking and stumbling with each movement. Jane bent down and stuck a finger in her shoe, removing gritty sand that rubbed on her skin. When she stood up again, a voice whispered in her ear.

'You never came to see me,' Charlie said, wrapping his arm around her waist.

Jane glanced from side to side, relieved to see that the other girls were focused on Dave and hadn't heard this interaction.

'This way, everybody — after three, a big *Cheese!* One, two, three . . .'

As the flash bulb popped it wasn't joy on Jane's face, but shock, as Charlie's chubby hand slid down her body and pinched her backside.

CHAPTER 8

2022
Zoe

Zoe sat at the small table in the dining room of the boarding house, attempting to write her article. Free afternoon tea and biscuits were on offer daily in the dining room, slightly stale custard creams and bourbons piled high on chipped china plates. She stared at the blank screen, waiting for inspiration to strike. She typed the opening sentence and deleted it three times. A sudden barrage of shouting began outside, and she stood up, knocking a cup of tea over her laptop.

'Shit, shit.'

Zoe wiped the keypad with her sleeve and looked out to see the young man she had met in the dining room the previous night. He was walking towards the boarding house with a group of men behind him shouting. He had his head down as the jeers followed. She opened the small window at the top as the voices cut through the air.

'Gay boy freak!'

'Fuck off out of our town.'

She scrambled for her phone and unlocked it, turning on the video and recording the men as they continued to shout as the man opened the gate.

'That's right, run back home to your mum, queer lad.'

Zoe shouted through the window, 'Why don't you all fuck off, you dickheads.'

She felt her heart racing as their attention turned to her. Zoe rarely lost her temper and avoided confrontation, but when she did it was increasingly explosive.

The men laughed at her, patting each other's backs and continuing to chant a song about fairies. The door to the Forget-Me-Not slammed shut.

Zoe stopped filming and ran out to the hall to meet the man head on.

'Are you OK? We should call the police.'

He looked at her, his hands shaking. He wore a plain black T-shirt and Levi's, his hair a short, dark buzz cut.

'No, it's fine, they'll get bored eventually. Did your interview with Colin go well this morning?'

Zoe wondered how her morning meeting had reached him, musing that it was impossible to do anything in a small town without everyone knowing.

'Yes . . . sorry, how did you hear about that? I mean, not that it matters.'

'We met this morning.'

'Oh God, I really am losing my mind. Remind me?'

'"I Will Survive"?'

Zoe narrowed her eyes, then it clicked.

'Miss B. Havin'?'

'That's right! But you can call me Clark.'

Footsteps beat down the stairs and Dolly appeared. Princess bounded behind her, yapping in excitement.

'What's all the commotion? What's all that shouting?'

'It's fine, Dolly, just some drunken idiots being lairy.'

Dolly grabbed a baseball bat from behind reception and brushed past them, yanking the door open and peering outside. Zoe looked to Clark, eyes wide, and went to move forward to retrieve the bat. Clark put his hand out to halt her as one of the drunks called out, 'Ooh look, it's Mrs Doubtfire!'

Zoe froze as Dolly lifted the bat and descended the steps. The garden gate clinked open, and the jeers turned to cries of pleading as wood met skin with a dull thud.

'I'll report you to the police, you mad old bitch. You could have broken my arm.'

The shouting was replaced with rapid footsteps as the men beat a hasty retreat. Dolly returned to the doorway in silence, the bat still swinging loosely in her hand, her expression distant. She ran the back of her hand across her forehead to clear strands of hair that had fallen from her bun.

Trevor burst through the front door, breathless and clutching his chest. He glanced up to Zoe and Clark, before easing the bat from Dolly's hand.

'Come on, Dolls, let's get you a cuppa.'

Dolly said nothing, her face still vacant. She let Trevor take her arm and lead her past them and into the kitchen, the door closing behind them.

Zoe looked back to Clark. 'What the hell?'

'You won't miss breakfast again in a hurry, will you?' he warned, a playful smile on his lips as he went through to the dining room.

* * *

'Tea or coffee?'

'Vodka?'

Zoe shrugged apologetically.

'Coffee will have to do then.'

Zoe drained the last of the bitter coffee from the silver urn and joined Clark at the table.

'You can report them, you know, I recorded some of it.' She went to reach for her phone.

He put his palm out, stopping her from showing him. 'It's fine, I'm a big boy, I can take it. Besides, I think Dolly did more than the police ever would.'

'It might be Dolly getting a visit from the police; it sounded like quite a whack.'

Clark shook his head. 'They leave Dolly alone in Sunshine Sands, she's an institution. Besides, what Neanderthal like him would admit to being scared off by a sixty-something landlady?'

Zoe moved her notes into a pile and closed her laptop.

'I didn't realise there'd be so much research involved in covering a talent show.' He peered closer at one of the pages. 'Jane Delway, wasn't that the—'

'Missing girl, yes.'

'I don't think they'll thank you for including that. Sunshine Sands likes to brush problems under its sand-strewn carpet.'

'So I gather.'

'This town isn't one for facing its dark past. It might affect business, after all.'

A slim, silver-haired man walked by the window and waved at Clark. He wore jeans and a short-sleeved Ralph Lauren shirt. He had tanned skin that hinted at a life spent somewhere other than Sunshine Sands.

'Who's that?' Zoe asked.

'Dave, he's taking the photos for the contest. Used to be the local paper's photographer back in the day. Moved to London but comes back occasionally, when there's an event on.'

Zoe glanced down at her research. 'Dave Cooper?'

'Blimey, you're good at this journalist lark, aren't you?' Clark quipped, his eyebrows raised. 'Dolly can't stand him.'

'Why?'

'Part of the history of Sunshine Sands. He was one of the clique who ruled the town back in the day. Dolly's tirade against the patriarchy.' He shook a clenched fist in the air.

Dave opened the gate to the boarding house and made his way up the short path.

'He's come to chat logistics with me for tonight,' Clark explained. 'He's going to do some filming too, make a little video of the night which hopefully I can use for my showreel.'

Zoe looked to the dining room door as Dave appeared.

'Sorry I'm late, got held up with some clients.' He shook Clark's hand then turned to Zoe.

'This is Zoe, she's here to cover the talent show for . . .' Clark looked to Zoe for the answer.

Zoe shook Dave's hand. 'The *National Mail*.'

Dave nodded slowly, a glint in his eye. 'Writing for the big boys, eh?'

She let go of his hand. 'My boss is a woman.'

'Fair enough,' he smiled. 'Well, you're welcome to use some of my photos if they're of use?'

'I'll bear that in mind, thank you.' Zoe gathered up her laptop and notes. 'I'll leave you guys to it.'

Dave smiled. 'Sure. Nice to meet you, Zoe.'

'You too. Actually, could I take your details, just in case?'

Dave patted his jacket pocket and took out a thin stack of cards, taking one from the top and handing it to her. She was more used to being given Instagram handles than business cards. As she took it from him, he caught her gaze, holding it a second longer than usual. Clark raised an eyebrow and smiled at Zoe.

'See you here at seven?' Clark said, before miming the swing of a baseball bat. 'Sharp.'

* * *

Zoe took out the photographs she had collected over the years and spread them across the floor. She looked at the group photo on the beach, full of wide-eyed, smiling girls. A mix of huge perms, back-combed to within an inch of their lives and Princess Diana cuts. Everyone looked so happy — apart from

Jane, who looked as if she had seen a ghost. Charlie Bailey stood by her side, a wide TV-friendly grin pasted from ear to ear. She remembered her mum's obsession with him, talking as if he might sweep Marion off her feet and take her off to his mansion in Surrey.

Zoe had written to Charlie twenty years ago, just after her mum died, getting his agent's number from a contact at the newspaper. She had wanted to know what he remembered about that time, but all she received in return was a signed photograph. As a little girl she thought he had seemed nice, giving her sweets, and making her mum so happy that she was nice to Zoe. Part of her remembered wishing that he *would* marry their mum and whisk them all away to a happier life, though she wondered whether she would be taken along for the ride or left behind with her Aunty Doreen.

As it was, after Jane went missing, all that had been left for Marion was to return to their two-up two-down with just one child, her least favourite. Once her mother had drunk herself into an early grave, Zoe felt free to go back to the time that her mum had refused to ever talk about again. She had begun collecting everything she could, no matter how irrelevant. Something that might help her make sense of it all. It wasn't until recently she had found all the names of the judges; the internet had been more or less devoid of the details of the contest. Then as the resort had fallen to wrack and ruin due to falling visitor numbers, the place itself only turned up on YouTube videos of wannabe filmmakers discovering abandoned buildings. Zoe picked up a large scrapbook which contained most of her findings.

As she opened it up, a programme from Charlie's summer show *How's Your Father?* fell to the floor. She picked it up as someone knocked on the door.

'Hello?' Zoe said.

'I've come to clean your room.'

Zoe opened the door to find the cleaner staring back at her.

'It's OK, I don't need room service today.'

The woman's eyes narrowed, her bucket filled with cleaning materials, swinging by her side.

'Dolly likes all rooms cleaned daily and I won't get my money if they're not.'

'Just tell her you've cleaned it. It's fine, I won't say anything. I promise.'

The cleaner looked at Zoe's hands, her eyes fixed on the programme. Zoe held it out.

'It's from the 1980s—'

'I know,' the woman said, her voice uneven. 'I wouldn't be showing that around here if I were you.'

'Why?' Zoe said, a derisive laugh escaping her mouth.

'She'll go mad, that's why, you'll set her off.'

'Who? Dolly?'

The woman withdrew physically, stepping away from the door and scuttling towards the next room.

'Do you remember Charlie Bailey? Do you know about him?' Zoe asked.

The cleaner knocked on the next door and when there was no answer she took out a key and unlocked it before turning to Zoe and whispering, '*Everybody* knows about Charlie Bailey.'

CHAPTER 9

The dining room was full. Joining all the residents from the previous night were a family from Manchester, and an elderly couple who spoke only to niggle at each other.

Dolly had shot Zoe a disapproving look when she moved her cutlery to Clark's table, but had been nothing but sunshine and light when Clark spoke to her, him apologising for any inconvenience it might cause.

'Not at all, Clark,' she had smiled, 'you can sit with whomever you like.'

As Dolly moved through the dining room, filling water jugs and chatting to the residents, Zoe turned on her recording app.

'You don't mind, do you?' she said, motioning to her phone.

Clark shook his head and took a sip of water.

'How did you get the gig presenting the talent show?' Zoe asked.

'They wanted to update the event, move away from the past, and what better way than to have a drag queen in charge of proceedings? I've been doing the *Laughing Girls!* show on South Pier for a few years now, so I suppose I was an easy option.'

'I think you're being modest.'

'You saw me dancing on the truck, right? Did I strike you as modest?'

Zoe laughed. 'No, but it's a different kind of talent to host something, good looks alone won't cut it.'

'Flattery will get you everywhere.' He thought for a moment and continued, 'I went to stage school, earned my stripes as a campsite entertainer. I guess I'm qualified one way or another.'

Zoe scribbled in her notepad then looked up at him.

'Are you subjected to a lot of abuse like you were this morning?'

'Only since my role in the show was announced. Let's just say some people in town have very traditional ideas; they don't want folk like us getting ideas, or positions above our stations.'

'Homophobic?'

'Every kind of phobic.'

Dolly entered the dining room, carrying two plates of chips and nuggets which she placed in front of two snotty-nosed toddlers.

'Dolly likes you though?'

'Oh, yes,' Clark said. 'She took me in after my mum died. I was only four.'

'Oh, I'm sorry. She must have been very young?'

'Yeah. It was a drug overdose. She used to work here in the kitchen. Dolly tried to help her, but it was no use. She was very troubled about things that had happened to her here and there was nothing anyone could do to change that. Then after it happened, after she died, Dolly stepped in to look after me.'

'Does she have kids of her own?'

'No. Never married, except to this place.' He stuck his fork into his shepherd's pie, and it remained upright.

Dolly appeared like a spectre over his shoulder. 'How's your dinner?'

Clark rescued his fork from the mashed potato. 'Amazing as always, Dolly.'

'Excellent. I'll make you a packed lunch for tomorrow, I know you're going to be busy.'

The grateful smile on his face disappeared as Dolly hurried off to answer a bell at the reception desk.

'She means well,' said Clark, spooning a mouthful of food into his mouth and grimacing, 'and she's not had it easy.'

'Oh?' Zoe picked up her pen.

'After that girl went missing—' Clark took a swig of wine and swallowed the food down — 'they almost lost this place. Barely anyone came the next year, or the year after that.'

'To Sunshine Sands?'

'Well, the resort has suffered for years, but I mean *here*.' He tapped the table. 'Her dad was suspected at the time as he went AWOL the same night. It came to nothing, but mud sticks, doesn't it?'

Zoe had vague memories of the bespectacled man in the hallway all those years ago, quietly lurking about. Her mum had warned her and Jane to keep clear of him, as he gave her the jitters.

'Was he anything to do with the competition?'

Clark shook his head. 'No, I don't think so, but Jane stayed here with her family, so I suppose he was an obvious suspect. I think that's why Dolly doesn't want to think about it all, too painful losing her dad. I would steer clear of talking to her about it if I were you.'

Zoe nodded, feeling a newfound understanding for the brisk responses she'd had from Dolly. The landlady was worried that she might dig up old dirt and cause more issues. It wasn't personal.

Zoe pushed the food around her plate, picking out the mushrooms and wincing at the oily texture. The newlyweds fawned by the window, Daniel seeming to reassure Sophie.

'Do you want to come with me tonight to the rehearsal?' Clark asked.

'Really? That would be great.'

'I'm sure they'll love the coverage you're giving them.'

Zoe and Clark got up from the table as Dolly appeared.

'Not staying for dessert?' she asked, pouting slightly at Clark.

'Got to get to Dunes to prepare for the rehearsal.'

Zoe noticed a flicker of Dolly's eyelid.

'The sooner this madness is over, the sooner we can get back to normality,' she huffed.

Sophie rushed past them, followed by Daniel, apologising for brushing Zoe's arm.

'Don't be too late,' Dolly said, patting Clark's arm, 'you'll need your beauty sleep for tomorrow.'

'I won't, *Mum*,' he joked.

Dolly shook her head, smiling, and marched back to the tables to see to the remaining guests.

CHAPTER 10

Zoe phoned the kids but there was no answer. No sooner had she cut the call off than a text message appeared from Dylan.

Out for dinner with Dad and Heidi, will call in morning. All fine here.

She tried to count the number of times they had gone out for dinner as a family in the past five years, and didn't need all her fingers to do so. She heard Daniel and Sophie rushing out of their room, Daniel trying to calm Sophie's fractured nerves with soothing words.

'You'll be fine, honestly, Soph.'

Zoe yanked up her jeans, her fingers hooked in the belt loops, pulling the stretchy denim over the flesh of her hips and willing the button to meet its hole. She remembered menopausal friends of hers clutching their stomachs in disbelief: '*And . . . you get this band of fat around your middle just like that, and you'll never get rid of it!*'

At the time she had secretly smiled, *as if*. Now here she stood in front of the mirror, wearing loose tops to try and hide the roll around her middle that seemed to have appeared overnight.

She grabbed her phone and the room keys and threw them in her handbag along with her notepad and pen. As she closed the bedroom door she heard raised voices at the bottom of the stairs. Rounding the corner, she caught a glimpse of the top of Trevor's and Dolly's heads.

'I didn't know she was a journalist,' Dolly hissed. 'And now she's trying to interrogate the cleaner as well as the guests.'

'Can't you tell her you need the room back?'

'For what?'

'I don't know. But she'll be gone soon, won't she?'

'And in the meantime, she'll have interviewed half the town about it. I won't have it, Trevor.'

Trevor put an arm around Dolly. 'Now then, stop worrying. Nothing will come up about your dad, it's old news.'

Zoe felt her heart racing. She was considering tiptoeing back to her bedroom when Princess spotted her from behind Dolly's slippered feet. The dog bounded up the stairs, barking.

'Princess!' Dolly called, turning round, her eyes wide when she saw Zoe.

Zoe casually made her way down the stairs, a fixed smile on her face. 'I'm just going out.'

'Anywhere nice?' Dolly asked with a tight smile that didn't reach her eyes.

Trevor took a bag of loose tobacco out of his pocket and began rolling a thin cigarette, tiny threads of tobacco escaping from his trembling hands.

'Dunes Bar.'

Trevor looked up at her, his forehead crinkled. He placed the cigarette in his mouth and went to light it.

'Not in here,' Dolly said sharply.

Trevor put the lighter back in his pocket and picked up his tool bag. 'Right, Dolly, I'm off home. I'll see you in the morning.' He put a hand on the landlady's forearm and glanced between her and Zoe. 'Just call if you want me to come round, you know, any odd jobs and that.'

Dolly brushed it away. 'I'll be fine.' She watched him leave then turned her attention back to Zoe.

'It's only a rehearsal tonight, I doubt there'll be anything there for you to write about.'

'Oh, we'll see,' Zoe said. 'Clark is going to get me in, friend of the star and all that.'

Her attempt at lightening the mood fell flat. Princess was sniffing and inhaling the bottom of the cellar door in the hall. Dolly pushed the dog away with her foot.

'Is that where you store the dog food?' Zoe joked.

'No. Old furniture and tools,' Dolly said dryly.

Clark ran down the stairs, taking two at a time. When he reached Zoe, he placed his hands on her shoulders.

'Mothers' meeting?'

'I've got something for you, Clark,' Dolly said, going back into the kitchen and returning with a thin plastic carrier bag. 'There's snacks for later and a carton of juice.'

'Thanks, Dolly,' Clark said, giving her a kiss on her cheek. 'Right, we'd better be off, otherwise I'll be facing the wrath of Gary.' He crouched down to put the bag of food into a large holdall, Princess trying to nose her way into it. Clark scooped her up in his arms and let the dog lick his face. 'Who's a good girl?'

Dolly hastily took the dog back from him. 'You'd best get on, they'll be waiting for you.' She cradled Princess, ruffling her fur as she fixed Zoe with an unnerving gaze.

CHAPTER 11

1982
Jane

The auburn-haired presenter waited for the director to count her down into her segment. Her smile was camera-ready, microphone poised beneath her chin.

'You join me, Joy Benson, in Sunshine Sands, where excitement is growing for the annual beauty contest, due to be held over there on the North Pier.'

The camera swung to the right to take in the pier, then returned its focus to Joy.

'The skies may be grey now, but by 8 p.m. tonight, the resort will be alight with winning smiles and dazzling gowns.'

Two young kids entered the shot, pulling faces and pushing each other back and forth.

'The contestants have travelled from all over the UK to take part, where the lucky winner will receive a whopping one thousand pounds, but perhaps, more importantly, that coveted jewel-encrusted crown. Let's speak to some of the people gathered here, see what they think to tonight's event.'

Joy moved two steps to her left, to where a small group had been held back.

'What's your name and how far have you travelled?' Joy held the microphone out to a young girl.

'Helen, and I'm from Doncaster.'

'Will you be going to the contest tonight?'

'Oh yes, I can't wait! I wish I was old enough to enter.'

Joy moved along to a middle-aged couple, the woman stuttering and blushing as the camera turned to her.

'I'm Sheila and this is Tony. We've come all the way from Newcastle.'

'For the contest?' Joy asked.

The husband leaned forward to speak into the microphone. 'No, this is our holiday, but I'll tell you what, I'm not complaining. Look at these girls!' He gestured to the contestants, who waved on cue.

A loud cheer rippled from the other men gathered, as his wife shook her head and rolled her eyes. Joy laughed and moved along the row to where Dolly stood, a fish out of water staring straight into the camera.

'And what's your name?' Joy asked.

When Dolly didn't answer, Joy moved the microphone closer to her mouth, leaning further towards her. Dolly turned to Joy.

'Pardon?'

'What's your name?'

'Dolly.'

'And are you looking forward to the beauty contest, Dolly?'

Dolly stared into the camera, her eyebrows stitched in a frown. The camera panned away swiftly as Joy moved on.

'Now, over here we have a very well-known face, not only in Sunshine Sands but the whole of the UK. He's here with two of the hopefuls, Jane Delway and Donna Baines. How are you enjoying the build-up to the contest, Charlie?'

Charlie pulled Jane and Donna in tightly. 'I've had worse mornings!'

Joy cackled. 'Yes, I can see you have your hands full here keeping the contestants entertained.'

'We just want to make sure all the girls here have a great time. Winning is important, of course, but so is having a time to remember.'

'And you will be judging the contest, along with the mayor and a local DCI. Any favourites so far?'

The camera turned to the rest of the girls, who giggled nervously.

'Not at all,' said Charlie, a more serious tone to his voice. 'As you can see, they're all stunners. The real test will be how they hold themselves and express their talent on the night.'

Joy turned back to the camera, which zoomed in, framing her face.

'So, that's it from me at Sunshine Sands, we'll be back tomorrow to speak to the winner. Over to you in the studio.'

Joy's TV smile dropped as soon as the camera was lowered, asking the director if it was a good piece. Jane wriggled away from Charlie and made her way back towards her mum and Zoe, who were watching from the edge of the beach. As she walked, her heels sank into the sand, causing her to wobble. She reached out to stop herself from falling, catching hold of somebody's arm.

Dolly looked down at her, letting Jane use her to pull herself upright.

'I'm so sorry, I thought I was going to go head down in the sand,' Jane said, taking off her heels and knocking them together to get rid of the sand. 'Has your dad given you time off?'

Dolly shook her head. 'No,' she said sharply, 'I came out to get some milk for the afternoon teas and coffees.' She held a carrier bag by her side, the handles stretching from the weight of its contents.

'And ended up on the beach?'

'I like to see the donkeys,' she explained, her head down. 'I always do, each morning. I bring the leftover carrots and feed them.'

'That's nice,' Jane said. 'And you got to be on TV.'

Dolly raised her head and looked across at the director. 'He asked me to come and stand with the group of people, I didn't know why. I didn't know I'd be on some stupid television show.'

As much as she wanted to be nice to Dolly, Jane was finding it increasingly difficult to warm to her. Perhaps there was a good reason nobody spoke to her. Dolly was the type of person her mum would describe as *not the full shilling*. She didn't seem to know what was happening around her and if she did, there was no response to it, happy or sad. There was a girl who worked in the supermarket with Jane who was just the same. She didn't join the others at break, and if it weren't for her name badge, nobody would know what to call her.

'Do you want to walk with us? We're going back to the boarding house in a minute.'

Dolly shook her head, her hair covering half of her face as she lowered it. 'No, I should be back by now.'

Dolly trudged quickly across the sand, not making eye contact with any of the crowds. Zoe watched Len Erwitt reach out a hand to her, but Dolly arced around him, avoiding his touch.

'How did you do?' Marion said. 'Do you think you'll be on the telly?'

Jane shrugged. 'They were more interested in Charlie.'

'Well,' Marion said, 'it'll soon be you that's centre stage. Then it'll be a different story.'

The three of them waited on the pavement, looking for a gap in the traffic to cross over the busy road. Jane held on to Zoe's hand, squeezing tightly as a tram passed, a huge blown-up image of Charlie Bailey pasted to the side. For a split-second she envied Dolly: no expectations of her other than to do her job and keep a low profile, and no attention from creeps like Charlie Bailey.

As they were about to step out onto the road, a voice called out, 'Hey, Jane!'

She turned to see Dave running across the sand, her cardigan in his hand.

'You forgot this,' he said, handing it to her.

'How did you know it was mine?' Jane asked, tucking it under her arm.

'There's a name tag sewn in it.' He grinned.

Jane glared at her mum, the embarrassment rising within her.

'Listen, a few of the contestants are going to grab some food, nothing fancy, probably just donuts and a terrible coffee on the pier?'

'Thank you, but I need to get back to—'

'You should go, Jane,' Marion interrupted.

Jane looked to her mum, surprised she was encouraging her to wander off from her ever-controlling gaze.

'You might get to know some of the other girls better,' her mum said, her eyes wide and teeth gritted.

Dave waited patiently for Jane's response. Feeling trapped with no way out, she turned to Dave and smiled. 'Great, OK then.'

Marion beamed triumphantly as Zoe stepped forward.

'Can I—'

'No, Zoe. You can come back with me, these young folk don't need a hanger-on.'

Jane gave Zoe a sympathetic glance, then turned and followed Dave down the windswept promenade.

* * *

'We wondered where you'd got to!' A girl in a Sunshine Sands T-shirt and shorts ran up to Dave and grabbed his hand.

She pulled him into a gaggle of contestants where another young man stood. He wore smart jeans and a thin lemon pullover, a canvas bag thrown over his shoulder. Jane caught up with the group and felt instantly out of place with their breezy familiarity and ease with each other.

'Jane, this is Jeremy, our local hack,' Dave said.

Jane shook her head.

'A journalist,' one of the girls explained, then speaking further as if Jane was a five-year-old child, 'he's doing the write up for the contest.'

Jane felt her cheeks flush. 'Oh, right, of course.'

The attention was quickly off Jane as the other girls dragged Dave and Jeremy down the pier. Holidaymakers watched and pointed as the gaggle of glamorous young women giggled and called out as they marched towards the funfair. If she turned and went back now, they wouldn't miss her. Jane was about to do just that when Dave noticed her hesitating.

'Donuts?'

He was standing by the small wooden booth at the front of the queue. Jane joined him, inhaling the heady scent of frying batter and sugar. Her rumbling stomach quelled her desire to leave.

'Yes, please.'

As Dave ordered, Jane watched the rings of uncooked dough move along the tiny conveyor belt, dropping into the hot fat and sizzling on the surface. After a generous dunking in a tray of sugar, the server handed over the paper bag of steaming-hot donuts.

'Here you go,' he said, carefully taking one out and handing it to Jane.

She passed it from hand to hand until it had cooled just enough to eat, the coating of sugar covering her lips and sprinkling down onto her T-shirt.

Dave handed her a paper napkin.

'Shall we go on the Ghost Train, Dave?' a young woman with red curls and matching ruby lipstick called.

'Blimey, let me finish my donuts first!' He grinned.

The tribe wandered slowly down the pier, licking their sugared fingers and screwing up the paper bags and flinging them into a bin. A young girl ran up to them, asking for a photo and the girls gathered excitedly, ushering the child into the centre.

'Come on, Jane,' Dave said, waving at her to join the others.

Jane looked from the young child's family to the group, all watching her impatiently. She pulled her cardigan around herself and edged into the back of the shot as the child's dad snapped away on his camera.

'Smile, it might never happen!' the child's dad said, raising the camera to his eye.

Jane did as she was told, putting on her best beauty pageant face as the flash popped. The young girl bobbed up and down with excitement, thanking the girls and running back to her parents.

'How cute!' said the red-haired contestant. 'Now, who's for a scare?'

* * *

A pair of wooden doors burst open and a small train appeared, each open-topped compartment containing wide-eyed holidaymakers, crying out in dramatic fear. A child, no more than five, had his head buried inside his dad's jumper, the father stroking his head to comfort him.

Once the previous passengers had departed, the beauty contestants jumped into the empty seats.

'I'll wait here,' Jeremy said. 'Not my kind of thing.'

'Spoilsport,' Dave chided, guiding Jane into the last compartment at the back of the train.

He pulled the safety bar down over their laps, clicking it into place. Jane smiled nervously at him as the other girls laughed and whooped in anticipation of the ride ahead. A bored-looking teen in a glass booth pressed a button and the train lurched forward, causing Jane to cry out as her spine knocked against the back of the rigid metal seat.

'You scared?' Dave asked.

'No, it was just—'

Before she could explain, he had draped his arm around the back of her, resting it on the cart.

'Nothing to be frightened of in here, just a kids' ride really.'

Jane kept her eyes forward as they moved along the rails and through the wooden doors.

Fluorescent painted ghouls and creatures surrounded them in the darkness. A ghost dropped from the ceiling, causing all to scream out and then laugh at their own skittishness.

'See, I told you — kids' stuff really,' Dave said, sliding his arm forward and draping it across Jane's shoulder.

She leaned forward a touch, enough for Dave to take his arm away. He was good-looking and he was kind, but Jane wasn't ready for this clumsy attempt at intimacy. Added to that, he was at least twenty-five and she was seventeen, a young seventeen at that. She had barely more than kissed a boy before — a fumbled, wet kiss outside the school disco. The thought of it caused her to shudder.

Cotton cobwebs brushed across their faces as the train juddered through a graveyard with polystyrene gravestones and plastic grass. A trap door opened and a skeleton clanked upwards as a sound effect echoed *mwuhahahas* around the attraction. Jane shielded her eyes as the train burst out into daylight for a few seconds, the ride turning a sharp left. When she took her hands away from her face she looked down to the pier to see Dolly running into the arms of another girl dressed in black. Jane craned her neck to watch as they disappeared into another sideshow, as the Ghost train emerged into another dark corridor.

'Fancy a drink after this?' Dave whispered as they rode through a haunted island.

A pirate laughed maniacally, a skeletal parrot cawing on his shoulder.

'I should get back to Mum,' Jane replied, embarrassed her excuse made her sound so childlike.

Dave nodded. 'Fair enough, maybe grab one another time?'

Jane smiled, relieved his response wasn't mocking or mean.

As they exited the doors into the light again, Jane felt a rush of relief that the ride had ended. The other girls rushed to Jeremy, recounting the 'horror' of the ride. Dave stood by the side of the cart and held his hand out to help Jane onto the wooden platform. She took it and pulled herself up onto terra firma.

'Thanks for the donuts,' she said, 'and the spooky ride.'

Dave smiled thinly, a faint look of annoyance on his face as if he hadn't really expected her to go. Jane guessed he was used to girls fawning over him and her refusal of his offer had hurt his male pride a little. Another contestant ran over and held her arm.

'That was great, wasn't it?' she said.

'Yes, it was fun,' Jane replied, happy that one of the other girls was being friendly to her.

'You up for a quick drink with the others?' Dave asked the girl.

'Ooh yes, might as well make the most of this holiday.'

The three of them walked down the three steps back onto the pier and Dave and the girl turned towards Dunes.

'I'll see you later,' Jane said, heading away.

Dave turned and nodded. 'Enjoy the rest of your day.' His tone was cold. The girl waved at Jane before clutching Dave's arm and heading towards the club, leaving Jane to go in search of Dolly.

The strange girl had not long been on her way back to the boarding house, a place she appeared tethered to by her dad. Jane wondered if the tears had been the result of a telling-off by Bernard, the plates not being clean enough or the beds not made straight enough. It was no surprise to Jane that Dolly was so dour — with an almost constant companion like Bernard it would be difficult not to be.

Jane walked a little further up the pier and stopped at the sideshow that Dolly and the girl had gone into. A wooden sign with gothic lettering above the entrance read 'Freak Show'. The small wooden payment booth was empty, so she pulled aside the heavy red-and-white-striped canvas and peered in. There were a small group of people wandering round the exhibits, their faces a mixture of grimaces, amusement and vague repulsion. Jane stepped in and let the curtain fall behind her, the eyes of those in the tent falling to her skimpy outfit beneath the baggy cardigan, which she pulled around her.

The lighting in the exhibit was purposefully dim, green bulbs throwing ghoulish light onto rows of glass bell jars and vivariums. She walked past the cloudy containers and through to the rear of the tent where there was another canvas curtain to a back room.

Through a gap in the curtain she watched Dolly sip a cup of tea, as the girl dressed in black leaned forward and spoke in a low voice.

'They shouldn't be here, stupid girls flaunting their bodies for dirty old men.'

Jane edged forward, straining to hear as a couple walking around the Freak Show chatted about their evening plans as they passed by a lamb's foetus in a jar.

'It's started it all over again,' Dolly hissed.

The girl in black laid her hand on Dolly's arm and patted it gently. 'We have to do something about it, you can't go on like this.'

'Do what though? We're powerless.'

The darkly dressed girl sat back in her chair and thought for a moment. 'Something big, something to bring this whole insipid charade to its knees.'

A child let out a guttural wail behind Jane, and Dolly and the girl looked up at her. Jane turned and ran through the Freak Show, passing a red-faced boy who stood crying by a formaldehyde-soaked head in a jar.

***

The boarding-house dining room was quiet apart from the sound of cutlery clinking and the occasional slurp of lager or Coca-Cola. Each table whispered their conversations, not wanting their words to echo around the room. Marion had barely said a word since Jane had returned, just enough to make sure she was ready for dinner in time.

'You should have gone for drinks,' Marion said, slicing a piece of rubbery meat with a steak knife.

'I was tired,' Jane said meekly.

Marion huffed. 'Tired? You don't know the meaning of the word! When I was your age I was working two jobs just to put food on the family table.'

Zoe shuffled in her seat, trying to swallow a mouthful of carrots. Jane's stomach began to churn, the pressure of her mum's anger only adding to the pressure of the contest itself.

'I don't think you realise just how much we need the money you could win, Jane. If I didn't think you had a chance then I wouldn't have bothered coming here, but you do.' Marion's face softened. 'You're a lovely-looking young woman, Jane, there's no reason why it can't be you wearing that crown. You've just got to play the game a little bit — you know, show willing.'

Jane looked down at her half-eaten food. She should have gone for drinks with Dave, made better friends with the other girls. She was here now, she might as well try to win. She thought about Charlie's note and his offer of advice — perhaps she should at least go and meet with him and see what he had to say.

'I know, Mum, I'll do my best.'

Marion smiled. 'There's a good girl.'

The dining room door creaked open and Dolly appeared carrying a jug of orange squash. Jane sank back in her chair as the girl's eyes glanced over at her. Now she knew that Dolly and the other girl didn't want the contestants there, she wanted to avoid her as much as possible. She wondered what their plan was: throw paint as the girls walked onto the stage? Hold placards outside Dunes?

Zoe's hand shot up into the air as Dolly passed with the drink. Dolly hesitated before stopping and filling her glass. Jane moved her glass forward to save Dolly reaching over, but as soon as she had filled Zoe's she walked away and left the room.

'Who rattled her cage?' Marion said.

Zoe yawned and stretched her arms above her head.

'Time for bed?' Jane said, desperate to escape the dining room.

Marion finished the rest of her wine and picked up her handbag from the floor.

'I think we could all do with some shut-eye. Big day tomorrow, eh?' She smiled encouragingly at Jane.

Jane pasted a smile on her face. 'Yes, I can't wait.'

As they trudged through the hallway, Jane's eye was drawn to the open kitchen door, where Dolly stood in the semi-darkness staring back at her.

CHAPTER 12

2022
Zoe

'Welcome to Sunshine Sands' Got Talent 2022, we hope you're all having a great time so far.'

The contestants leaned forward in their seats, hanging onto every word Gary spoke. He wore an expensive-looking suit, and a large gold watch that caught the lights above. Zoe sat on a chair away from the entrants but close enough to hear what was being said. A couple of rows back from the contestants were the dancers, seasoned performers who sat back in their leggings and baggy T-shirts sipping from water bottles.

The opening bars to the *E.T.* soundtrack rang out and Gary stopped talking; the whole room turned to Zoe. For a split-second she wondered why she was suddenly the focus of their attention, before cursing and scrambling in her bag to find her phone.

'*Sorry,*' she mouthed to Gary, holding a hand of surrender up as she left to answer the phone.

'Hi, Dylan, what is it? I'm in a bar . . . no, not *partying*, I'm working.'

Zoe opened the main doors to Dunes and stepped onto the wooden pier, the wind gusting around her head. She put a finger to her other ear to block the sideshow music and screams from the waltzers.

'No, I haven't checked it today, what does it say? ... OK, I'll have a look now. All OK there? Great. Love you. Bye.'

Dave Cooper passed her, a friendly hello as he made his way into Dunes carrying a large case with him. His gaze lingered that second longer again; she held it, confused. Was he flirting with her? She wasn't sure she remembered how flirting even worked anymore. Zoe hung up the call and clicked on the Friendbook group, scrolling through the posts and comments until she saw it.

@CarysTyler
My mum was a contestant in the contest when Jane Delway went missing, she reckons the place was crawling with weirdos. They couldn't move without getting their backsides pinched, had to grin and bear it though. By all accounts that Charlie Bailey was a wrong'un. She said none of the organisers cared about the missing girl, just losing business and saving face. Also said some of the other contestants were really bitchy and would steal your make-up and stuff.

Zoe began typing.

Hi @CarysTyler, can you DM me? Would be great to chat. Thanks, Zoe.

* * *

Zoe pushed the heavy doors to Dunes open. Even the warm stale air of the venue was a welcome relief to the cold night. The dancers were walking through their routine as Clark yelled directions. Gary was now in front of the stage typing on his phone between exasperated glances up at the dancers.

Clark clapped in the direction of the bar and the music stopped, as did the women on stage.

'Give each other more room. Now, heads high, smiles bright. Let's go again, but this time keep that space between you and—' he looked to his notes — 'Sophie, is it?'

Sophie nodded.

'Stop when you circle back to stage right and the rest of you stop where you are then. We should have a nice semi-circle around me.' He looked back to the bar. 'Colin?'

The music began again, and the dancers moved, this time more in uniform. Dave appeared from the shadows holding a camera and began to snap away.

'Ignore Dave,' Clark instructed, 'we're taking some behind-the-scenes photos for social media, no need to pose.'

Dave turned and snapped in Zoe's direction, a flash temporarily blinding her. Zoe put her hands to her face, shooing him away while smiling. She hated having her photograph taken at the best of times, even less so when she was tired and without make-up.

The dancers were ushered off the stage and gathered in the stalls, where Colin appeared with refreshments. Clark took a glass of lemonade and swigged from it before continuing practising his own intros and stage directions. Zoe jumped as a hand rested firmly on her shoulder, the smell of musk aftershave burning her nostrils. She wriggled away from beneath the hand, looking up into Gary's eyes.

'How's it going?' he said.

'Sorry?'

'The article? I hope it's going to be a positive piece for us, I'm hoping all this will bring new life to Sunshine Sands. Your editor assured me you wouldn't be critical.'

Zoe was sure whatever her editor had said, if there were such promises, it was just to secure her access behind the scenes.

'Oh, it's going fine,' she said, non-committally.

Gary's shoulders relaxed. 'Good stuff, wouldn't want to feel duped. I know you journalists can be a sneaky lot.'

He smiled, but Zoe sensed there was an underlying warning implied. His brow furrowed as he noticed a contestant at the bar drinking a glass of wine.

'Excuse me,' he called out, marching towards her and taking the glass away, chastising her with his pointed finger.

A singer had taken her place on stage, tapping the mic and saying odd words to test it. Beside her, perched on a high stool, a young guitarist plucked at the strings as Clark spoke to him.

Zoe gathered her bag and coat and headed to the bar. There was little to report on and nobody here that could help her with what she really wanted to know. Gary was new to the town and most of the dancers and contestants weren't even born in 1982.

'Can I get you a drink?' Colin offered. 'Something stronger than tea.'

She thought about the lonely bedroom, and the baggage she was lugging around, weighing her down literally and metaphorically.

'Yes please, a vodka and Diet Coke.'

'Single or double?'

Zoe shrugged, and Colin lifted the glass to the optic twice before filling the glass with the cola.

'I think I'll join you,' he said, pouring himself a whiskey. 'Oh, I meant to say, I did a little digging after our meeting this morning.'

Zoe sat up, putting the glass on the bar.

'Seems not all the people around that time have croaked — well, not yet anyway. Have you heard of Oak Lodge?'

Zoe shook her head. 'No, is that another men's club?'

Colin smiled. 'Not exactly, it's the old folks' home up on the hill. The policeman who dealt with Jane's disappearance lives there now. Not sure he'll be much help, especially as he didn't manage to solve it at the time, but might be worth a shot?'

Zoe scribbled down the name of the home. 'Thanks, I'll see if I can get up there tomorrow morning. You never know,

I could be the journalist that manages to find out what happened to her.'

His eyes relaxed as he smirked. 'Good luck to you, might finally put an end to the mystery once and for all.'

'What mystery?' Dave Cooper pulled up a bar stool next to Zoe, his leg brushing hers.

'Miss Marple here is looking to solve the case of the missing beauty queen.'

Dave regarded her for a moment, his eyes narrowing slightly.

'Well, good luck to you. About time someone found out what happened to the poor girl.'

It was the first time someone had shown any kind of sympathy towards her sister and Zoe felt pathetically grateful.

'Do you remember her?' Zoe asked.

He sighed. 'It was a long time ago, but yes. I was a young photographer hoping to make his mark, so I was keen. I saw all the girls a lot. She was a pretty girl, I wasn't surprised she won.'

'Why?' Zoe asked. 'They were all pretty.'

Colin placed an opened bottle of lager in front of Dave, who took a sip before speaking.

'It's hard to say really. It's that "X factor" thing, isn't it? From what I can remember, most were dolled up to the nines and she was just more down to earth, girl next door. Like I say though, it was a long time ago.'

'Could I have a look at some of your old photographs? You never know, I might see something others have missed.'

'Missed?'

'I don't know, people who were around her, maybe get more of a feel for that day?'

'Of course. Maybe we could grab some lunch and chat further, there's an Italian just down the road, makes a vaguely passable carbonara.'

Colin caught her eye and winked, causing Zoe to blush. Was Dave making a pass at her? He was almost twenty years older, but so what, he was still attractive, and it was a long time since anybody had taken her out.

'That would be great, thank you.' She took another sip of her drink and put her notebook and phone in her bag. 'Shall we say twelve?'

'Absolutely.'

Onstage, Clark continued to direct the talent to the music as Gary chatted to a group of the dancers. Zoe handed her empty glass to Colin.

'Can you tell Clark I'll see him later?'

Colin nodded as she turned to Dave.

'What's the restaurant called?'

'Luciano's.'

'See you there.'

CHAPTER 13

1982
Jane

Jane woke up to the sound of rattling plates and cutlery coming from downstairs. She turned in her bed to see Zoe sleeping, her thin arm curled around a fawn teddy bear. Jane put her hand to her neck, holding the small silver dolphin between her fingers. It was 8 a.m. and the seagulls outside were readying to start their day, gentle caws floating through the air.

She longed for tomorrow when all this would be over, and she could return home and back to her life.

Peeling back the covers, she reluctantly climbed out of bed and sat herself at the dressing table.

For as long as she could remember her mum had had this dream for her to be something more than she was. With each person that had commented on her child's golden hair or bright blue eyes, she could see something growing within her mother, ideas forming and swelling. Tap-dancing, ballet, elocution lessons that resulted in Jane being further isolated from her young friends who already felt she thought she was a cut above. After the contest she would tell her mum that enough was enough, she had to live her own life.

The chain flushed in the en-suite, and Marion appeared. 'I thought I heard you stirring.' Her mum scrunched her eyes and picked at Jane's curls with the tips of her fingers. 'Maybe we should have booked you in for a perm before we came, the curls are on the turn.'

On the turn, like fruit past its sell-by date. Jane pulled away, batting at her mum's hand. 'It's fine,' she snapped.

'No need to be narky with me, don't let your nerves get the better of you.'

Jane took a blob of moisturiser from a pot on the dressing table and rubbed it into her skin with her fingertips.

'Oh, to have skin like yours again,' Marion said, peering at herself in the mirror. She pulled at her features, smoothing out the fine wrinkles. 'But maybe he prefers the more mature woman.'

'What do you mean?'

'Charlie Bailey. I've seen the way he looks at me, a woman knows these things.'

Marion took a bottle of perfume and sprayed it liberally around her neck and shoulders. Jane grimaced.

'Oi, I saw that face. I'm not over the hill yet, you know. It might come as a surprise to you to know I was once pursued by the lead singer of a *very* famous band.'

It didn't come as a surprise. It was Marion's favourite tale when the sherry was running dry and the ashtray was overflowing. She had never specified exactly who the mystery rock star was, but once when Jane had been sorting through some records, her mum had nudged her and winked when she'd taken out a Rolling Stones album.

'Life could have been very different for us all if I'd have just said yes and ignored the fact he was married.'

'We're not that badly off, are we?' Jane asked, looking at her mum in the mirror.

Marion began fiddling with her bracelet.

'I didn't want to say anything.' Marion looked over to Zoe, who was sleeping soundly on the bed. 'There's talk of redundancy at the shop. We're barely getting by as it is. It's not just the prize money, Jane, it's all the jobs that might come with it. And if you win this then it's the next stage of the contest — *ten thousand pounds!*'

Jane sighed inwardly as she pulled on a pair of jeans and a baggy T-shirt. She decided she should meet Charlie. She could always leave if he tried any funny business. Despite her protestations, a job in television would be better than the supermarket and she could help her mum and Zoe out. She decided to call the hotel — she wouldn't go to his room, she'd meet him somewhere public.

'You're not wearing that, are you?' Marion said, frowning at Jane's outfit. 'You've always got to be camera-ready, Jane, you never know who you'll see.'

Jane sat on the bed and pulled on a pair of socks before sliding her feet into her pumps, ignoring her mum's continued tuts and head shakes.

Zoe stretched and yawned on the bed, her hand pushing the teddy bear to the floor.

'Morning, Zoe,' Jane said, glad for an excuse to walk away from her mum.

Jane picked up the teddy bear and placed it next to Zoe, sitting down on the edge of the bed.

'What did you dream of?'

Zoe thought for a moment, frown lines appearing on her brow. 'I dreamed you won tonight but you tripped, and your crown fell to the floor.'

'Oh, that's not good. Maybe I should wear pumps tonight instead? Less chance of falling.' She winked at Zoe.

'You'll do no such thing, those stilettos cost almost a week's wage,' her mum piped up.

Jane stroked Zoe's hair. 'Shall we go to the funfair today?'

Zoe shot up, pulling the covers down. 'Yes, yes, yes!'

'Are you sure about that, Jane, shouldn't you take it easy today? I thought we could—'

'Mum, it's Zoe's holiday too. She's been so good tagging along so far, and she'll have to do it again tonight. Let's at least do something fun this morning.'

'Please, Mum,' Zoe begged.

Marion looked from one daughter to the other and relented. 'As long as we're back for three. I've got a mobile manicurist coming to do your nails.'

'Can I get mine done?' Zoe said.

'I'm not made of money, young lady, I can barely afford all this as it is,' her mum retorted, then, looking Jane straight in the eyes, 'Winning that money would more than cover any luxuries. Perhaps then we could get your nails done too, Zoe, another time.' Marion walked over and patted Zoe on the head, all the time smiling hopefully at Jane.

'I'll do yours, Zoe,' Jane said, ignoring her mum. 'Right, you'd best get dressed then, the waltzers are calling.'

Jane smiled as her young sister ran around the room gathering her clothes, pulling on a red T-shirt and a tartan skirt that had once belonged to Jane.

'Ready!' Zoe exclaimed.

'Teeth,' her mum ordered.

Zoe skipped out of the bedroom, the bathroom door slamming shut, causing the walls to rattle.

'That child,' her mum said, picking up her nightie from the floor and neatly folding it before placing it at the end of Zoe's bed.

'Don't be so hard on her.'

Marion glanced up before continuing to make Zoe's bed, her mouth now in a thin tight line.

'I'm not hard on her, Jane, I was exactly the same with you and it's not done you any harm.'

Jane didn't remember her mum ever telling her off, not once, not even when she spilled Ribena all over the new cream rug in the lounge.

Zoe burst back into the bedroom, grinning widely to show off her freshly brushed teeth.

'Why, what bright teeth you have, little girl,' said Jane, holding her arms out and waiting for Zoe to hug her.

'All the better to bite you with!' Zoe said, pretending to gnaw at Jane's arm.

Their mum shook her head as she ran her hands over the candlewick bedspread, smoothing the ruffles.

'Come on, then. The sooner we go out, the sooner we can be back to prepare for tonight.'

***

Zoe skipped along the seafront, an ice cream held out in front of her. She licked the melted ice cream from her hand, lapping up every drop.

'Dodgems or waltzers first?' Jane said.

'Waltzers!'

'Race you,' Jane said, getting a head start and running through the crowds, weaving in and out of people until the noises became a blur and the smells of sugar and vinegar merged. The faint voice of her mother carried on the breeze, attempting to pierce her joy.

'Be careful, Jane, you don't want to break a leg!'

She turned for a brief moment and when she turned back, she ran headfirst into Dave the photographer.

'I'm so sorry,' she said.

He checked his camera before smiling broadly. 'No need. It's not every day a pretty girl throws herself at me.'

'Did you have a good time at Dunes after I left?' Zoe asked.

'Oh yeah, top time. Shame you didn't come along.'

Jane felt her cheeks redden. She scanned the pier for Zoe, but she was nowhere to be seen. He lifted his camera to snap her.

'Oh no, don't.' Jane put her hands to her face. 'I'm not ready.'

'Don't be silly, you don't need make-up, natural beauty is always best.'

He continued to take photos of her, so she attempted to smile.

'There, that's better. Loosen up a little, turn to the side, that way. Gorgeous.'

A hand grabbed hers.

'Found you!' Zoe squealed, panting as if she had been running for miles.

'And who's this, then?' Dave asked.

He lowered his camera and began to snap Zoe, who smiled a toothy grin. Jane took her hand. 'Sorry, we have to go, I promised her we'd go to the funfair.'

'Scream if you want to go faster, eh?' he laughed.

They left Dave taking photographs of the arcades along the promenade as they headed towards the funfair and sideshows.

'Look, Jane!' Zoe ran towards the entrance of the Freak Show.

Jane grimaced. 'No, Zoe, that doesn't look fun. I took a peek in yesterday, it's a bit gruesome.'

Zoe's shoulders dropped, her face forlorn. 'I like gruesome things.'

Jane smiled and warned her, 'It might be too scary for you and I'm not staying up all night with the lights on when you get too scared to sleep.'

'Pleeease,' Zoe begged.

A boy younger than Zoe skipped out of the tent, followed by his parents, who seemed unperturbed by anything either they or he had seen. Zoe looked hopefully at her sister, her hands joined together in prayer.

'OK, but don't come running to me if you have nightmares tonight,' Jane said, both knowing full well Zoe could always come to her.

Zoe clapped her hands together and skipped to the small wooden booth by the tent opening. Jane recognised the girl in black, whose head was down counting money.

'Here—' Jane handed Zoe some coins — 'you can buy the tickets for us as it's your idea.'

Jane kept her face turned away from the girl, fearing that if she recognised her from before she wouldn't let either of them in. Zoe skipped over and handed her the money and the girl pushed two paper tickets forward, barely looking up.

Zoe ran back to Jane and took her hand, squeezing it gently. 'Let's go!' she squealed.

Inside the gloomy tent lay rows of tables, on top of which sat various glass tanks and bell jars which Jane had only briefly caught a glimpse of the previous day. She shuddered. It felt like Frankenstein's parlour, and the smell of the sawdust-covered floor permeated her nostrils. Zoe peered through a glass jar at a pickled liver floating in yellowing liquid, before moving along to gaze wide-eyed at the foetus of a lamb suspended in formaldehyde.

'Poor lamb,' Zoe said.

A more genteel display featured brightly coloured birds frozen in time atop a foliage-covered branch. It wasn't until Jane looked more closely that she realised the birds all had two heads. A pair of stuffed mice propped with wire stood on their back legs as if trying to peer above something with their tiny glass eyes.

On the walls of the tent hung a gallery of sepia photographs entitled *Circus Freaks*. A bearded woman, a giant of a man who held two adult humans aloft in his huge hands, and conjoined twins who smiled brightly at the camera. Jane felt uncomfortable gawping at the images, not knowing the kinds of lives these people had had or if they had ever imagined they would become like zoo animals, there for human entertainment.

'Is this really him?' Zoe exclaimed, now standing in front of an exhibit entitled *Caterpillar Man*.

In the display case there was a wax moulding of a man's head, attached to the limbless trunk of a body. It lay face down on a moss-covered base, presumably to add to the insect mythology he had been given.

'No, it's just wax,' she said, hoping that there wasn't anything in the case that had ever belonged to a real human being.

They moved along a row of more taxidermied animals. Zoe petted a stuffed poodle, talking to it as if she might coax it into a game of fetch. The dog sat at the feet of another wax figure, a seated man dressed in a white coat who stared ahead through lens-less wire-rimmed spectacles. Zoe read aloud the card next to the man.

'Ernest Le Terre was born in Paris and moved to Sunshine Sands in 1960. He has immortalised animals for clients all over the world, including a terrier for a member of the Royal Family.' Zoe turned to Jane with wide-eyed surprise, before continuing, *'Though now retired, Ernest occasionally takes on commissions from local residents who wish to keep their much-loved pets with them, along with his apprentice taxidermist daughter.'* Zoe thought for a moment. 'Do you think he'd stuff Tibbles when he dies?'

Jane pictured their still very much alive moggy stuffed and sitting in the corner of the lounge as they watched *Coronation Street.*

'No. I think when the time comes, we'll just bury Tibbles like normal people.'

Zoe looked disappointed, but it was short-lived as she ran over to inspect a display of foxes and badgers, frozen among gathered foliage and twigs. Jane looked to the back of the tent where she had seen Dolly and the girl, and making sure Zoe was OK she made her way there. She glanced back to the entrance and watched the girl in black busy with a queue of people paying for tickets.

The curtain was down and tied shut with strips of canvas which she carefully unknotted. She slid behind the curtain to the backroom, which was lit by a small table lamp. There were rows of haberdasher cabinets, the kind she saw in shops of times gone by. Jane opened a couple of the drawers and found little but old correspondence and stationery.

Everything was orderly, like a doctor's office. There were photographs on a table by the cabinet, black-and-white images of dour-looking family members. She recognised one of the founders of the Freak Show, the girl in black sat on a chair in front of him. A larger group of circus performers and workers stood before an old wooden rollercoaster on the pier. The man and the girl were smiling this time, the whole group appearing as one disparate family. Jane was about to leave when she noticed a poster for the beauty contest in a wastepaper basket. She went to retrieve it but it came apart in pieces, not torn, but sliced with the clean lines only scissors or a scalpel could achieve. Someone had scrawled something in thick black marker, the letters written across several cut pieces. Jane took them out of the bin and matched them up, her blood running cold as the words appeared:

Death to all.

'Can I go on the carousel now?' a voice called out behind her.

Jane spun around, her heart racing as Zoe stood in the doorway.

'I'm bored.'

Jane glanced behind her to check no one else had seen her in there and then ushered Zoe away and back into the main exhibit. 'Yes, come on. I've had enough of brains and body parts in jars for one day.'

Jane kept her head down as they exited the tent and passed the ticket booth. She was intimidated by the other contestants but the locals seemed far more alienating — it was clear they resented her and the others being there, but the depth of their anger was now apparent. Jane couldn't wait for the weekend to be over, and to be on her way home.

***

Zoe whooped and laughed as the painted horse rose and fell, appearing and then disappearing on the rotating carousel. Jane waved each time Zoe appeared, glad for the moments away from the contest preparations and her mother's watchful eyes.

The plinking machines and organ music couldn't hide the excited gasps and calls as a large group entered the pier arcade which housed the carousel. Dave had appeared again, shuffling backwards as he snapped away at the group. The excitement in the room grew, the eyes of the children on the slowing carousel no longer on their waiting parents, but the ensuing commotion.

'Is that?'

'Oh my God!'

'He's off the telly, isn't he?'

Charlie smiled for the camera and the animated crowds that had gathered, a young beauty contestant either side of him, both in their regulation T-shirts and shorts. Jane noticed the comedian's hands wrapped around their middles, his thumbs splayed, skimming their breasts. Len raised his hands in the air, urging the room to be quiet, smiling and shaking his head as it took several attempts.

'Now then, campers,' he called out, 'do you all recognise this man?'

Cheers rang out around the arcade, more holidaymakers joining the throng by the second, straining their necks to see what all the fuss was about.

'If you don't you must have been living under a rock for the past twenty years, that's all I can say!'

Charlie took his hands away from the girls' bodies and raised them in the air, waving at the crowd.

'How's your father?'

The delighted crowd called back, 'Yes please!' before breaking into peals of laughter.

Charlie shook his head, basking in the response to his most famous catchphrase. Jane's mum made her way through the crowds, catching her breath when she appeared at Jane's side.

'Why didn't you come and get me?' she hissed, tidying up her hair as she smiled in Charlie's direction.

'He's only just arrived, I didn't know he'd be here.' Jane checked the halted carousel, each rider staying on their mount, unable to locate their family members in the ever-growing crowd. Jane spotted Zoe, who was watching the commotion with glee.

'Why didn't they ask you to walk with him?' Marion said, sneering in the direction of the two girls escorting him. 'You should put yourself forward a bit more.'

Jane wondered if it was that straightforward — if the competition itself was a waste of time, and the girls just needed to curry favour with Charlie to walk away with the crown.

'He's quite a looker for his age, isn't he?' Marion gushed.

Jane shuddered.

'Ladies, gentlemen, boys and girls, for those that haven't got tickets for tonight, Charlie has kindly agreed to come and sign some autographs.'

Len motioned to Dave, who took his place by a small table and chair. Len then led Charlie over and the two of them smiled for the camera.

'If any of you would like your photograph taken with our resident star, they'll be available to buy at the information hut by the hook-a-duck stall, after 3 p.m. Official photos only, I'm afraid,' he said, motioning for a woman to lower her camera.

A queue began to form before he'd finished speaking, as starstruck holidaymakers went one by one behind the table, leaning in as Dave snapped away.

'I bet he gets this kind of attention wherever he goes, don't you, Jane?'

'I suppose,' she said, checking Zoe was still on the carousel.

'Imagine the parties I'd get to go to if I was with him, I'd meet all kinds of famous people.' Marion stared, misty-eyed, over at the table.

When the last autograph had been signed and photograph taken, Charlie stood up from behind the table, waving his thanks to all and blowing kisses to the crowd. His gaze fell on Jane and Marion, his tongue darting across his lips.

'He's coming over here!' Marion exclaimed. '*Be polite.*'

Len regarded Charlie as he crossed the arcade, smiling when he saw him join Jane and Marion.

'How is the most glamorous mother in the North?' Charlie said, kissing Marion's hand.

She blushed, before taking in the scrutiny of the holiday-makers looking on. 'Very well, thank you.'

Charlie put his arm around Jane's waist, pulling her close and whispering in her ear, 'Are you not going to take me up on my invitation?'

Jane's skin froze under his touch, and she smiled nervously as he leaned in again.

'Meet me in twenty minutes in the hotel dining room.'

His eyes flickered over to Marion, who was still beaming broadly.

'Come alone.'

He immediately stood back, waving at the crowds as Len led him through the crowd.

'What did he say?' Marion asked, excitement in her voice. 'Was it about me?'

'Just good luck for tonight,' Jane replied.

Marion's face dropped, disappointment etched on her face. 'Well, I suppose it's nice he's wishing you luck. After all, he's clearly got other favourites to win.' She watched the two chosen contestants as they ran after Len and Charlie. 'I bet they never wear baggy jeans and T-shirts.'

Zoe ran up to join them, begging to go on the waltzers. Jane looked through the doors of the arcade to the queue, then up at a giant ornate clock above the carousel.

'Maybe later, I think I'd like a bit of a walk, get some fresh air.'

Zoe huffed, stomping her foot into the ground.

'Maybe you could go with Jane,' Marion said to Zoe.

'No,' Jane said, 'I'd like to go alone.'

Now it was Marion's turn to huff, and she took Zoe's hand as Jane walked slowly towards the promenade.

CHAPTER 14

2022
Zoe

An alert on her phone woke Zoe. She felt for it in the darkness, finding it underneath the pillow beside hers. It was 2 a.m. and from the notification on the front screen she could see it was a DM from the Friendbook group member called Carys.

She sat up immediately and reached for the switch on the bedside lamp. She took her glasses from a case and opened the message.

> *Hi there,*
> *My name is Carys and I put a comment on earlier and you asked me to DM. Are you the admin for the page? Did you know Jane personally? Give me a shout if you have any questions, not sure if I can answer anything but can try.*
> *Best, Carys x*

Zoe could see Carys was still online so began to message back, hoping she'd see and respond.

Hi Carys,

Many thanks for getting back to me, I was very interested to read your comment. Yes, I knew Jane very well and I'm in contact with the family, who have never given up on finding out what happened to her. You said your mum was a contestant with her, did she ever speak to Jane? Was she aware of anything odd about anyone else connected to the competition? Could you ask her about Len Erwitt? He was the mayor at the time, and also there was a TV star who judged it, Charlie Bailey? Anything at all might be of use. Thanks so much.

Zoe.

Zoe watched as the tick indicated it had been read, and waited to see her reply. When Carys went offline her heart dipped. This, she reasoned, was because Carys had to ask her mum about it and she was unlikely to be awake in the early hours. Zoe scrolled through various news apps before giving up on a reply tonight. She turned off the light and tried to sleep, tossing from side to side. Her back was sore, and the ongoing night-time battle she had of trying to remember the events of that night in 1982 remained futile. After twenty minutes, she gave up trying to sleep. She reached for her laptop and attempted to write the article on the resort, the article she was actually getting paid for.

Music began to filter down from Dolly's room above, footsteps dancing across the floor. Zoe put her laptop to the side and lay back looking up at the ceiling, trying to tune into the music. Just as she was about to identify the song, a needle screeched across the vinyl and the music ended abruptly. At first Dolly's voice was quiet. Slow, berating, barely audible sounds, like a quiet 'telling-off' in a misbehaving child's ear. Zoe sat up as Dolly's voice got louder, angrier, and manic. She pushed the covers down and got out of bed, pulling a hoodie over her head and slipping on her shoes.

She knocked as discreetly as she could to prevent waking up the other residents. The plaque on the door to Dolly's rooms read 'Private'. When her angry voice stopped, Zoe considered scuttling back to her room, not wanting to face the woman's wrath. Before she had the chance, a lock turned and Dolly peered around the door. She was wearing a fleecy nightgown, wrapped tightly over a nightdress that reached her fluffy mule slippers. She cradled Princess in her arms.

'I wanted to check you were OK, I heard voices and—'

'She who listens at doors hears no good of herself.'

Zoe was fast regretting her intrusion. 'I wasn't, I . . . I was trying to sleep, and the music woke me up. I didn't hear anything at all, you just . . . sounded upset.'

A door opened across the landing and Mr Morton shuffled out, his vest skew-whiff over his large frame, his striped pyjama bottoms perilously low. He rubbed his eyes and yawned.

'It's OK, Mr Morton, Ms Kincade just had an issue with her radiator,' Dolly called.

'At 2 a.m.?' he croaked, scratching his exposed belly.

Dolly looked at Zoe as if to say, *Now look what you've done.* Zoe gave Mr Morton an apologetic shrug.

'I get cold all the time. Bad circulation,' she said, wrapping her arms around herself and faux shivering.

Mr Morton slunk back into his room and closed the door, leaving the two women alone again.

'Who were you talking to? Before?'

Dolly took slow deep breaths, as if preparing herself to leap from a height into a distant pool of water below. Princess opened her sleepy eyes and looked up at her owner, her tail beginning to wag anxiously. Zoe backed away, one small step at a time.

'I-I think I'll just . . . goodnight,' Zoe said, turning and scuttling back to her room.

CHAPTER 15

1982
Jane

The Grand stood like a beacon at the end of the promenade, its pristine exterior all glistening glass and freshly painted fascias. Jane walked into the foyer to find the hotel buzzing, and peered into the dining room to her right. Most of the tables were taken and waiters scurried about with silver trays and bottles of wine wrapped in linen napkins.

'I'm here to meet Charlie Bailey,' Jane said.

The receptionist looked her up and down, before picking up a telephone and dialling a number. She put her hand over the mouthpiece as she asked, 'Your name?'

'Jane. Jane Delway.'

The receptionist cleared her throat before she spoke.

'There's a Jane Delway in reception, sir. She says she has a meeting with you.'

The receptionist nodded and replaced the receiver. She held her arm out towards the dining room.

'Give the waiter Charlie's name, he'll seat you.'

Jane walked slowly into the room, feeling out of place in her stonewashed jeans and striped T-shirt. The waiter walked with his nose in the air, guiding her to a table by the window and pulling the chair out for her. She went to sit down and as she did, he expertly guided both her and the chair under the table.

'What can I get you to drink, madam?'

Jane scanned the laminated menu before her, a range of teas and alcoholic beverages.

'Do you have lemonade?'

He nodded and left her to look out of the window, the pier visible in the distance. A pianist in the corner played nondescript tunes under the polite hum of chatter and the clink of dinnerware.

A young woman from the beach photo call approached her. She was as equally well dressed as the other diners, and barely recognisable without her *Sunshine Sands* T-shirt and shorts.

'Are you nervous about tonight? I am!' she said, holding out her hand, 'I'm Dawn, by the way.'

Jane shook her hand. 'Jane. A little nervous, yes!' She glanced at the dining room doorway as someone entered, relieved to see it wasn't Charlie.

'I've spent most of the day on the toilet!' she giggled, ignoring the disapproving glances of the woman on the next table. 'What are you doing for your special talent?'

'Just a poem I wrote. Silly really, but I can't sing or dance, so . . .' She shrugged. 'You?'

'A quick rendition of "Someday I'll Fly Away". I've been practising for months, I just hope these nerves don't get the better of me.' She held her hand out flat, shaking it for effect.

'I'm sure you'll be fine,' Jane said, smiling in reassurance.

The talk in the dining room silenced and both girls turned to the doorway as Charlie Bailey entered.

'Oh my God!' Dawn exclaimed. 'Can you believe they've got a TV star judging?'

Charlie spotted Jane and headed their way.

'*He's coming over*,' Dawn hissed, eyes wide and mouth taut with excitement. 'I don't know what to say.'

Jane had never wished more for the ground to swallow her up than she did right now. In a second's time she would be revealed to be the girl that tried to curry favour with the judge by having fancy tea and buttered scones with him.

'Two for the price of one?' Charlie said as a waiter rushed to pull the chair out opposite Jane.

Dawn's expression changed from nervous excitement to confusion in a flash. Then the grains of realisation fell into place, piece by piece. Jane flushed. She didn't even know what to say to Charlie, let alone how to explain this strange meeting.

'Right,' Dawn said, stony-faced. 'I'll leave you to it, then.'

'Join us,' Jane blurted out so loudly that diners turned round to look.

Dawn looked from Jane to Charlie and let out a snort of indignation.

'I'd better go and practise a little more, if it's even worth it.'

She stomped off, joining her parents, who were waiting by the door. The three of them looked over at Jane in disgust.

'Never mind them,' said Charlie. 'Jealousy is a terrible thing.'

The waiter appeared with Jane's drink and placed it before her.

'Lemonade on a special day like this?' Charlie mocked. 'A bottle of your finest red, please.'

The waiter nodded and left.

'One glass won't hurt, you can always have a lie-down this afternoon.' He winked at her.

A small child approached the table, a pen and paper in hand. Without being asked, Charlie signed the paper and the child went on their way.

'I'm glad you came.'

'I thought it would be rude to decline.'

Charlie looked out to the seafront, catching a passer-by's eye. They waved excitedly at him as he turned his attention back to Jane.

'A pretty girl like you belongs on the telly, you know. I can make that happen, how do you fancy that? People running up to you in the streets, asking for your autograph?'

His mention of possible career prospects calmed her — maybe this was a genuine meeting.

'I've never wanted to be famous,' she said. 'But I would like to earn more money and maybe travel.'

'Oh aye, who'd want a big pot of money and the best seat in the restaurant when they could just settle for a life of struggle and years of hard work?'

She wanted to argue with him, but he was right. She didn't like her job. It wasn't what she really wanted to do, she wanted to go to college and have a career. The waiter returned to the table and poured the wine in two glasses. Jane took a tiny sip, the velvety liquid warming her throat. Charlie ordered food for both of them, which Jane was thankful for. The menu was a list of French cuisine, on which she could only pick out certain words.

'Well, how would you like to be on TV? I'm not fooling around, I know a future star when I see one.'

'I can't sing or dance.'

Charlie laughed, a deep guffaw, making her feel foolish. 'If you can smile and do the odd turn, that's all you need.'

She wondered what TV job required just the ability to smile. Charlie leaned forward, placing his hand on hers. The diners at the next table turned and watched, eyebrows raised to each other.

'Listen, it's not been announced yet—' he tapped the side of his nose with his finger — 'but there's talk of a new quiz show in the autumn. I haven't officially been given the nod, but I've been assured it's a shoe-in. Once it comes to light, I'll need a couple of glamorous assistants.'

The food appeared before them, swirled creamy potato next to a piece of chicken smothered in red sauce and mushrooms. Charlie took a mouthful, continuing to talk. 'And let me tell you, no matter how much you like your current job, once you can afford to rent your own place in London and go to the best parties in town, you'll never look back.'

Jane cut a piece of the chicken as she tried to take in what Charlie was saying. He was right, it did sound a lot better than her life now, and what she wouldn't do to escape the clutches of her mum's displaced ambition. Zoe could visit in the holidays and maybe one day live with her. Charlie appeared genuine, so maybe it was big-headed of her to assume he just wanted his way with her. The chances of a tabloid picking up on something nefarious was likely, particularly as he couldn't go anywhere without being recognised.

'Would I have to audition or something?' Jane asked.

Charlie smiled as he chewed on a piece of meat, wiping away a blob of sauce from his chin with the white linen napkin. 'What I say goes. But obviously I'd need to send a photo to them, just so they can OK it. Official procedures and all that.'

'My mum has some, a local photographer took them and—'

'They need something a bit more . . . professional, you know, show you at your best.'

The photographs her mum had arranged had been all they could afford, a thirty-minute photoshoot in the shopping centre. The synthetic feather boa and taffeta dress did not shout 'style'.

'Perhaps the ones Dave the photographer will be taking of me tonight, then?'

Charlie shook his head and tapped his palm on the table. 'No, no, you'll be too dolled up at the contest. You're a natural beauty, Jane. They'll want to see that. You look at your best right now, youthful and natural.'

Jane put her cutlery down and took another sip of the wine. Charlie called a waiter over and signed the bill. He looked at his watch.

'I've to be over at Dunes for a chat with Len in an hour, shall we go now?'

'Go?'

'To my suite.'

Jane froze, her eyes blinking rapidly.

'You look like a rabbit in the headlights! Listen, it'll take ten minutes and then we can get you on the road to success. That doesn't sound too bad, does it?'

Jane glanced around the dining room, people just going about their day without a care in the world. What harm could a few photos do? If she said no then he'd be offended and the chances of her getting anywhere or winning money for her mum would be zero. She may as well just go home now.

'OK, but I can't be long, my mum will wonder where I've got to.'

Charlie stood up from the table, rearranging his shirt and straightening his jacket. 'You'll be back at your boarding house within half an hour, you have my word.'

Jane followed Charlie through the dining room, eyes furtively glancing up at her. As they reached the lift, a brief thought of running out of the hotel flickered through her mind.

'Come on, then,' Charlie said, his finger pushed against the lift button.

She walked in to join him, her stomach lurching as the lift began to rise to the top of the hotel.

CHAPTER 16

2022
Zoe

'Is he expecting you?' a woman with *June* on her name badge asked.

'No, it's a surprise,' said Zoe. 'I'm his granddaughter.'

'Oh, how lovely! Have you come far?'

'Sheffield. Not too far.'

'Well, I'm sure he'll be glad to see you. Bob doesn't get many visitors; in fact, I only remember one in the last year. Sad really, isn't it?'

'I really should make more of an effort, I just travel a lot with my job.'

'What do you do?'

'I'm a journalist.'

June beamed. 'How exciting!' She set off, gesturing for Zoe to follow. 'He's this way.'

Zoe followed June along the carpeted corridors, up a flight of stairs and to a door at the end of the landing. June rapped her knuckles on the door.

'Mr Previtt? Are you decent?' She opened the door and peered in as Zoe held back.

A muffled voice called from inside and June opened the door wider to let Zoe in.

'You've got a visitor, Bob.'

Bob sat in a high-backed chair by a window which looked out to the sea. His face was pale and what remained of his thinning hair was combed back neatly. He lifted an arm up from his knee, reaching out a hand towards Zoe, his brow creased in confusion. Zoe moved forward to take his hand, shaking it gently.

'Don't you recognise her, Bob?' June chirped, refilling his plastic tumbler from a jug on his bedside table. 'It's your granddaughter Zoe.'

'Granddaughter?' Bob said faintly.

'Yes, your granddaughter.' She shook her head and spoke in a whisper, her hand on Zoe's arm. 'Don't be upset, love. If he hasn't seen you for a while, it might be confusing for him. His dementia is quite advanced now.'

Zoe smiled. 'Yes, I'm sure it is a bit confusing, bless him.'

'Just press the buzzer if you need anything.' June left the room, closing the door softly behind her.

Zoe took a chair opposite Bob. 'Hi, Mr Previtt, my name is Zoe.'

'Granddaughter?' Bob repeated.

Zoe leaned in. 'I wondered if I could ask a few questions?'

Bob Previtt looked even more confused than when she had been introduced as his non-existent family member.

'I'm trying to speak to people who were around in 1982—'

'1982?' he repeated as if trying to understand what the numbers meant.

'Yes, when the beauty queen went missing.'

Voices began talking in the corridor outside as Zoe continued.

'Here's a picture of her, do you remember her? Her name was Jane Delway.'

Zoe took a photograph of Jane from her bag and held it out to Bob. Bob squinted at the picture, taking it from her and holding it closer to his face. Zoe watched the wrinkles around his eyes soften as his eyes widened in recognition.

'Mr Previtt?'

His hand trembled as he handed it back to her, his mouth clamped shut. Zoe took it from him, her eyes still fixed on him as the voices in the corridor grew louder.

'Do you know what happened to her?'

He blinked rapidly, fingers tapping the arms of his chair.

'Mr Previtt, Jane was my sister. I want to know what happened to her.'

'The mayor will help you,' he said. 'Speak to Len, I've got his number somewhere.' He tried to push himself up out of his chair.

'No,' Zoe said, encouraging him to sit down again. 'Len Erwitt died years ago.'

'Died?'

Zoe nodded, her hand resting on his arm. 'Did . . . did Len do something to her?'

'Should never have gone to that damn boarding house.'

'Who shouldn't have gone to a boarding house? Len? Jane?'

'She'll take them all, you know. She will.'

'Who will? Dolly?'

'Photographs lie,' he mumbled, spittle gathering at the corners of his mouth.

His eyes met hers, his mouth relaxing as he tried to get the words out. Zoe waited, watching his lips attempt to shape the words. The door handle to the room clicked down and June entered with another woman wearing a suit. Zoe turned, flapping her hand to silence them before they spoke.

'I won't be long.'

June ignored her, marching forward. 'I don't know who you are, but I've just been told Mr Previtt doesn't have any children, so therefore, no granddaughter.'

Zoe gripped Bob's hand. 'Please, do you know what happened to her?'

His voice was soft and cracked, a small smile forming on thin lips as he ran his finger over the photograph and started to sing, '*She was a young beauty—*'

'Out of here now,' the suited woman commanded.

Zoe kept her eyes on Bob as the woman placed a hand on her shoulder.

'If you don't leave now, I'll have to call the police.'

'What happened to her?' said Zoe, her words slow and clipped.

Bob looked up to the women from the home and then back to Zoe, his eyes watery, then clamped his mouth shut again and looked out to the pier, humming gently.

'Do I have to call the police?' the woman asked.

Zoe rose from her chair and put the photograph back in her bag. She looked down at Bob, not with sympathy for a man who was sick and frail, but with anger. He knew what had happened and somehow he was a part of it, she was sure. She was also angry at herself, for not pursuing this sooner, before his and others' memories had faded. On the table by the door she noticed a photograph of Bob receiving a medal of some kind from the mayor, Len Erwitt. She took out her phone and snapped a picture of it as the women shouted across the room.

'Out, *now*.'

CHAPTER 17

1982
Zoe

A donkey plodded towards Jane as she walked barefoot in the shallows of the sea. The animal's head was down and watery gloop gathered at the corner of its eyes as bells tinkled across its bridle. A young girl sat atop, too tall and too old for the poor beast. Its owner held tight to the reins, nodding solemnly to Jane as they passed, his face crinkled and worn from years of sun and saltwater.

Jane put her head down, wiping away a tear from her eye with the sleeve of her top and sniffling. The small stones and shells in the wet sand dug into the soles of her feet but she felt nothing, she was numb. Her body did not feel like her own, she had given it away and displayed it so freely in the hotel room and had been unable to do anything to stop it happening.

She had always been such a bright girl, not by her own admission but by teachers and relatives who fawned over her high grades and prize-winning essays and poems. That was academics though — her mum had always sneered at those with degrees: '*Education is no match for good old common sense and ambition, Jane.*' And her mum was right: for all the As and *Excellent work!* she had received in reports, she felt as stupid as they come.

Stupid for agreeing to come to Sunshine Sands, stupid for letting her mum bully her into wearing clothes that she didn't like, but most of all, stupid for meeting a strange man in a strange place. It wasn't Charlie's fault really, she thought — girls who wanted to be on the telly probably wouldn't blink an eyelid at having their photo taken like that. Jane suddenly shuddered as her mind flashed back to the hotel room. A voice broke her thoughts.

'It's not that cold lass,' a man chided, holding his young child's hand as he ventured into the small waves. 'Tha's nesh!' he chuckled as he ran past her, splashing icy water up her rolled-up jeans.

There were only two choices now. Leave and go back home and face the wrath of her mum, or grow up and accept that sometimes girls had to do things they weren't comfortable with in order to get on in life. There was a lot of money at stake if she did win and Charlie had said she was in with a very good chance now. Jane's hand reached instinctively to her chest to protect herself. '*Don't be shy, Jane, you've got a great figure.*' The memory of Charlie's words and the flash of the camera caused her to fall forward a little, almost losing her balance.

But the worst was over now. She'd done it, she might as well stay and keep everyone happy. Tomorrow she would be home and safe.

CHAPTER 18

2022
Zoe

Zoe drove into a space on the promenade, a car horn beeping wildly in front, his reverse lights on, ready to take the spot that she had just filled. She waited in the car until the irate driver gave up and drove away. Zoe took a deep breath, her fingers tapping the steering wheel. She watched the carefree tourists walking along the promenade, a part of her feeling resentment for their happiness. She gathered her bag from the floor and took out her box of pills, prescribed for anxiety. She freed one from the blister pack and swallowed it down with a gulp of the warm Diet Coke that sat in the cup holder.

Dave Cooper crossed the road in front of her. He was wearing indigo jeans and a pale blue short-sleeved shirt. He looked like he had made an effort, like this *was* a date. Zoe pulled down the sun shield and the tiny light illuminated the mirror. She searched for a concealer in her bag, then gently swept it across the dark circles under her eyes. Then she drew a lipstick across her mouth, grimacing at the brightness of it, and wiped it away with a tissue pulled from the side pocket in the car door.

* * *

Luciano's was nicer than she'd given it credit for when she'd seen the prefabricated exterior and wooden cutout chef holding up a pizza, thumb and forefinger lifted to his MDF lips. Inside, the walls were dark flock wallpaper and the chairs finished in red velvet. Shining silver cutlery rested on crisp white tablecloths, with tealights illuminating the room. Zoe spotted Dave, already seated at the back of the restaurant, unaware of her presence as he typed on his phone. A waiter approached her.

'I'm meeting him.' Zoe pointed in Dave's direction.

The waiter smiled and led her to the back of the restaurant, the smell of freshly baked garlic bread making her mouth water. Dave looked up from his phone, beaming when he saw her. He stood as the waiter pulled her chair out, before sitting down again.

'Nice place,' Zoe said.

'A bit of a gem in Sunshine Sands, tends to attract a different clientele.'

Zoe raised an eyebrow, amused at his snobbish implication.

'I just mean it's a bit of a change from fry-ups and chips soaked in gravy.'

'I've been craving good old-fashioned chip-shop chips since I got here, if only Dolly wouldn't hold me hostage for meals.'

'She's quite a character, isn't she?'

'Do you know her well?'

Dave thought for a moment, his fingers touching the edge of a wine glass before him.

'Not really, well . . . as well as anyone can know her. She's not a fan of mine, that's for sure. I don't expect rave reviews.'

'Oh?' Zoe said, part of her relieved she wasn't the only one that Dolly seemed to have taken a dislike to.

'Without meaning to be unkind, she . . . well, she was always a little strange as a young woman. She would follow me. I think she had a bit of crush.'

Zoe couldn't imagine Dolly fawning after anybody, not then and certainly not now.

'And now?'

He laughed. 'Well, I'm not here very often and let's just say I think she's over it.'

'But you didn't get on with her back then, I mean when the beauty contest was on?'

'She would get very jealous if I showed any other woman attention. As you can imagine, that got very difficult during the beauty contest when my job was to do just that. Dolly would turn up wherever I was and just, well, glare.'

The waiter glided to the table and poured a little red wine into Dave's glass. He lifted the glass to his nose and swirled the liquid around before taking a sip and nodding at the waiter. The waiter filled both glasses.

'Thank you,' said Zoe, meeting his raised glass in the middle of the table.

'Anyway, enough about landladies with grudges, here's to the contest tonight.' Dave clinked her glass before taking out reading glasses and glancing at the menu.

The waiter took their orders and left them in peace in the near empty room.

'Have you managed to get enough content for your article?'

'Once I've seen the show tonight, it'll be easy to finish and send off.'

Dave reached down to his bag and pulled out a wad of photographs.

'I found these in my studio last night. Sunshine Sands over the years.'

He placed them on the table and fanned them out, a range of black-and-white and colour snaps. Zoe sorted through them, somehow surprised by their artistry. Gorgeous images of the sun setting behind the pier, an elderly couple laughing raucously on the benches by the beach.

'They're very good.'

He laughed. 'You sound surprised.'

Zoe felt her cheeks redden. He was right, she was surprised. He was clearly a great photographer, she wondered why he would bother to come back all this way and cover two-bit talent shows — but then again, so had she. Albeit she had an ulterior motive.

She sifted through them, trying to give each one a respectable view while also keen to find the ones she really cared about.

Dave sorted through them and took out a photograph, pushing it towards her.

'Is this what you were looking for?'

Zoe looked at the photograph of her sister wearing a jewel-encrusted crown and holding a giant bunch of flowers.

'Yes,' she said, the word sticking. She cleared her throat and repeated, 'Yes.'

'There's another here somewhere.'

Dave took all the photographs back and flicked through them, before pulling out another and handing it to Zoe. She looked at the more informal gathering taken after the beauty contest, her sister beaming, surrounded by dignitaries and fellow contestants. Another face caught her attention, a young woman stood in the background, her posture stiff.

'Is that Dolly?'

Dave took the photograph from her, put his reading glasses back on and peered closer.

'Yes, you could always rely on old sourpuss to spoil a good photo.'

He handed it back to her as the waiter reappeared with their food. Zoe put the photo to the side and dug into her spaghetti arrabbiata, twisting the pasta around her fork.

'She won't talk about the contest.'

Dave smirked. 'No, she wouldn't. You know about her dad being questioned, right?'

Zoe nodded.

'Dolly followed that Jane girl round like a spectre.'

'During the contest?'

'The whole time she was here. There are more photos there somewhere. Completely unusable because every one I got of Jane, Dolly was in the background, arms crossed looking daggers at her. I tried to blur her out, but I couldn't.'

He leafed through the photographs again, pushing one towards Zoe. Another of Jane, resplendent and as beautiful as Zoe remembered her, Dolly looking on morosely in the background.

'How's the pasta?' Dave asked.

Zoe brought her attention back to her food, her appetite now non-existent.

'It's great, thank you.' She swirled the spaghetti around her plate. 'You don't think . . .'

'What?'

Zoe took a deep breath. 'You don't think that Dolly had something to do with Jane's disappearance?'

Dave shrugged, 'Who knows? She certainly wasn't a fan of hers, or any of the other girls.'

'I know, but it's a leap to do something so awful for the sake of jealousy, isn't it?'

'People do bad things for all kinds of reasons; we might never know the motivations.'

Zoe didn't like Dolly, and there was certainly something odd about her and the Forget-Me-Not.

The rest of the meal passed in easy conversation. Dave told Zoe about his travels, his ambitions, those fulfilled and those left wanting. Zoe filled him in on her life as a war correspondent and the decision to halt her career to look after her children.

'This story then, the beauty queen, would be a career coup if you got somewhere?'

Zoe hadn't thought about it like that; the last thing she was looking for was recognition.

'True crime is a big seller,' he said, motioning for the waiter to come over.

'I'm not really—'

'There you go, sir. I trust you enjoyed your meal?'

'I'll get this,' Dave said, putting his hand over hers as she attempted to take the bill.

'Halves at least, I insist.'

Dave shrugged but didn't argue as Zoe took her purse out, retrieving her card and hoping there was enough money in her account to cover her half. She exhaled as the reader pinged its acceptance and the waiter tore off and handed her the receipt.

They exited onto the promenade. The street was packed with bodies and the noise of arcades and street hawkers selling boat trips and tours of the town. Zoe turned to Dave.

'Thanks for that, the food was lovely.'

'My pleasure.'

He put his hand on her upper arm and gently kissed her cheek. Any thoughts she had that he felt more than friendship were confirmed when his lips lingered there. He stood back, regarding her before she took the initiative and leaned forward, kissing him on the lips. The moment was broken by a loud honking of horns, causing Zoe to jump back.

'Jesus!' she said, her hand on her chest.

They both looked to the road where a brightly coloured transit was passing, a loudspeaker on top announcing a clown show later that day.

'Never a dull moment,' Dave said, before his phone buzzed. He took it from his pocket and looked at the screen. 'Sorry, I'm supposed to be at Dunes now. See you later?'

Zoe smiled, 'Yes, see you at the contest.'

'And after? Maybe grab a drink?'

'Yes, I'd like that.'

He kissed her on the cheek again and jogged away, weaving through the crowds. Zoe stood for a moment, taking in what had just happened between them. Whatever it was, it felt good, and even if it was only the shortest of 'holiday' romances, she would make the most of it.

CHAPTER 19

1982
Jane

'Miss Delway.'

Jane paused on the boarding house stairs, before making her way back down to Bernard in the small reception area. He lifted a bunch of pale pink chrysanthemums from the desk and handed them to her with the enthusiasm of someone presenting a dead animal.

'For me?'

Bernard nodded, his eyes resting on a small card wedged within the flowers. Jane took the card out and read it.

Leave before tonight.

'Who delivered these?' Jane said, her voice unsteady.

He turned towards the kitchen. 'Dolly!'

Dolly appeared at the kitchen door, a butter knife in one hand, a slice of limp white bread in the other.

'Who brought these flowers for Miss Delway?'

'The boy from Brannicks,' she said, avoiding eye contact with Jane.

'Our local florist,' Bernard added in explanation. 'Does the card not say who they're from?'

Jane looked back at the card and then at Dolly, who scuttled back into the kitchen. She put the warning card into her pocket, suppressing an urge to scream in frustration. She was here to please her mum — she had never wanted to set foot in Sunshine Sands, let alone this godforsaken boarding house. She didn't care about Charlie Bailey and his promises of fame anymore, and she didn't care about the contest. If she could leave now, she would.

* * *

'Oh my word! What beautiful flowers, wherever did you get those?' her mum said as soon as Jane walked into the room.

Jane threw them on the bed and sat next to them, her arms crossed. Her mum marched over and picked through the blooms.

'Wasn't there a card with them? Who are they from?'

'I don't know.'

'Are they definitely for you? How do you know if there's no card? I might have a secret admirer.'

'You have them, then.'

Her mum glared down at her, but quickly changed tack and smiled gently, a mood manoeuvrer to placate her daughter. She sat down on the bed next to her as Zoe inspected the flowers, pulling out a stem.

'Don't do that, you'll ruin the arrangement,' Marion said, her brow creased in annoyance.

Zoe's face dropped as she tried to push the flower back into the bunch, its stem bending and snapping.

'Now see what you've done,' Marion scolded.

'You can have them,' Jane said, scooping up the flowers and handing them to her little sister. 'From me to you.'

Zoe beamed, taking the flowers and carrying them around in her spaghetti-like arms.

'I'll bet they're from Charlie Bailey or the mayor. You can thank them later.'

'But—'

'No buts, I'm not having a daughter of mine snub such a kind gesture. If nothing else, I hope I've brought you both up with good manners. Now, I'll run you a bath and you can have a nice soak before the manicurist arrives. I'll put the heated rollers on too and see if we can't liven up that perm a bit, eh?' Marion gently pinched Jane's cheek as she always did when she wanted to lighten her daughter's mood.

CHAPTER 20

The girls were all told to wear 'elegant and sexy' dresses for the pre-competition reception which was being held at a Chinese restaurant on the promenade, a short stroll from the pier. Jane's mum had spent most of her savings on a wardrobe that would never see the light of day again once they got home.

Jane could barely walk in the stilettos her mum insisted she wear again. They pinched at her feet, making her wince each time she put a foot down.

'For goodness' sake, Jane, you look like a constipated penguin,' Marion said.

Zoe giggled until her mum shot her a look and the girl instantly quietened, tapping the nose of the fuzzy teddy bear she carried with her.

'I can't help it, Mum, they're so tight and the dress keeps riding up my legs.'

'You've got to show off what you've got — you won't have that figure forever, you know. The minute you were born, my body . . .'

Her mum's words faded as Jane shuffled ahead, trying with each step to escape the familiar story of her part in her mother's downfall. It was a well-worn tale, one that ended in her mum's disappointment, regret and decade-long addiction to diet pills.

* * *

A golden dragon curled around the red walls of the restaurant foyer, and a vase of silk lilies sat aside a golden cat, its mechanical arm swinging back and forth.

As soon as she caught up with her, Marion scrambled in her handbag and took out a comb, softly digging at Jane's curls.

'There, that's better.'

'Look at the cat!' Zoe said, reaching out to it.

'Don't touch,' scorned Marion.

'It's a lucky cat,' Jane explained to her sister.

'Why?'

'Never mind why,' snapped Marion. 'Let's get in there before the whole thing's over and we've missed our chance to mingle.'

She ushered her daughters through the doors and into the restaurant. Faces turned to see who the new arrivals were, then returned to their conversations. A waitress approached them holding out a tray of cubed cheese and pineapple, speared with cocktail sticks. Jane took one, eating it before her mum had a chance to stop her.

'Not too many, Jane,' said her mum, taking one for herself.

Jane recognised lots of the faces, all the girls looking older with their heavy make-up and back-combed hair. Dawn, who had been at Charlie's hotel, looked over and then whispered to the others. They shook their heads and shot dirty looks her way. Her stomach dropped when she spotted Charlie Bailey. He caught her eye and waved, instantly making a beeline for her.

'Now, be polite, Jane.'

Charlie held his arms out to the sides, a wide smile exuding TV charm.

'Ladies, what a sight for sore eyes you all are.'

He took Marion's hand and kissed it; Jane sickened as her mum swooned in his presence. Charlie bent down to address Zoe. 'Now then, who have we got here?' he asked, pointing at the teddy.

Zoe hid it behind her back, lowering her face. Charlie put a finger under her chin and lifted her gaze to him. 'No need to be shy, little one, Uncle Charlie won't bite.' He immediately stood up and whispered in Jane's ear, '*Much.*'

Jane gulped, but her throat was dry. She reached out to a passing waiter, who swung his tray in her direction. She took a glass of fizz and knocked it back, the bubbles easing her throat.

'Blimey, steady on, girl,' Charlie laughed. 'You've a long night ahead.'

Jane's mum scowled at her, her eyes widening in a silent warning.

'Thank you so much for the flowers, Mr Bailey,' Marion said.

He frowned. 'Flowers?'

'The lovely flowers you sent to the hotel.'

He shook his head. 'I'm afraid that must have been someone else.'

Jane glanced across at Dawn again. If anyone looked like they wanted her to leave, she did. She could afford to stay at the Grand, so could afford to play such an expensive trick.

A bespectacled woman holding a glass of whiskey appeared, extending the drink to Charlie.

'Len wants you to make a speech.'

Charlie took the drink and had a sip, making an appreciative *aahh* sound. His eyes fixed on Jane's, causing her to inwardly recoil.

'Good luck, Jane.'

He winked and turned, his assistant following him as he made his way through the party.

'Such a lovely man,' Marion said.

Jane took another sip of the fizz, before her mum swiped it from her and plonked it on a passing tray. Dolly stood at the edge of the restaurant with her dad, Bernard. He wore a suit that hung like a wet blanket, the trousers an inch too short. Dolly was dressed in her familiar cotton dress and baggy cardigan.

'Why ever are they here?' Marion said. 'I wouldn't have thought this was their kind of thing.'

'Who?' said Zoe, pushing between her mum and Jane and peering around. She spotted Dolly and Bernard. 'I like her.'

'You do?' said Jane.

'Yes, she let me help her in the kitchen today. When you were out and Mum was having a nap.'

Jane glared at Marion, annoyed she had let Zoe out of her sight and with Dolly.

'What?' Marion said. 'She might be a bit *odd* but she's harmless. And besides, you were off gallivanting somewhere, so you can't talk.'

'*I'm* not her mum.'

Marion gritted her teeth, her eyes blazing. It wasn't the time for this conversation, Jane knew that. She also knew that her mum would not argue here, a place where she was so eager to impress, wearing her best costume jewellery and 1950s cocktail dress given to her by Doreen, the sister she envied so much.

Marion took a gulp of champagne and changed the subject. 'We should be over there with the mayor, you don't want the others currying favour with him.'

'I'd rather stay here,' Jane said, noting Dawn was now within the circle surrounding Len Erwitt.

'Well, you can't, you've got to network.'

'I don't want to go over there, I don't want to speak to the mayor. I don't want to do this stupid contest.' She pushed past her mum and stormed off to the toilets, the guests parting in her wake.

* * *

Jane blew her nose and threw the scrunched-up tissue down the toilet, flushing the chain.

'Jane, are you in there?'

Her mum tapped gently on the cubicle door as Jane sat down on the toilet, her head in her hands, trying to settle the pounding headache that had suddenly come on.

'You're just a bit overwhelmed, that's all. Come out and have a nice cup of tea. Are you hungry? Perhaps your blood sugar's low. Come on, let's get you a biscuit or something. They've just brought out some very fancy-looking cakes.'

As much as she wanted to, Jane knew she couldn't stay in the toilet cubicle all night. She'd already made a show of herself, and everyone was probably talking about her. She stood up and straightened her dress, looking down at her feet, swelling in the tight shoes. She slid open the small bolt and opened the door. Her mum smiled encouragingly.

'There we go — you've just had a little wobble, that's all. It's nerves, only to be expected. Come on, let's make you respectable again.'

Jane followed her mum to the sink. Marion took a small make-up bag out of her handbag and unzipped it. She squirted a tiny blob of foundation onto her fingers and dabbed at Jane's face.

'There we are, better already.'

She took out a lipstick and ran it over Jane's lips, a fresh layer of a frosty pink colour. When she had finished, she stood behind Jane, urging her to look in the mirror.

'See? All better.'

Jane looked at her reflection. She looked like a woman, but inside she longed to go home, put her pyjamas on and curl up in front of the television.

Her mum gave another encouraging smile. 'Now, let's go back out there and show them what you're made of.'

Jane followed her mum back into the restaurant, where Charlie was now in full flow from a raised platform.

'I said to the wife, "How many men does it take to open a bottle of beer?" She looks at me all quizzical and says, "I don't know, Charlie, how many men does it take to open a bottle of beer?" "None!" I says. "It should already be open when you bring it to me!"'

The room erupted into peals of laughter, tears running down Len Erwitt's cheeks as Charlie paused to take in the crowd's appreciation. Standing nearby, Dolly watched the comedian stony-faced.

'He knows how to work an audience, that's for sure,' Jane's mum said brightly.

Charlie let the gathered throng know about his own seaside show and urged them to buy tickets before his final performance in a week's time.

'And as a special treat, I'll be giving two free tickets to the winner of Miss Sunshine Sands, followed by a slap-up meal here at the Lotus Flower, courtesy of Mr Chen.' Charlie held his hand out towards the proprietor, who nodded in thanks as the room applauded.

Zoe was playing with her teddy bear by a water feature at the back of the restaurant. Jane went to her, glad of the excuse to leave the adulation of Charlie Bailey.

'What are you up to?'

'Do you have a coin?' Zoe asked.

'What for?'

Zoe pointed to the well beneath the gently cascading water, where small change glinted beneath the lights. Jane reached into her handbag and scraped her hand across the bottom, gathering a handful of change.

'Here you go.'

Zoe picked out a two-pence piece and turned to the fountain. She closed her eyes, tossing the coin in the air, then opened them as the coin splashed into the water and settled at the bottom.

'What did you wish for?' Jane asked.

'Can't tell,' said Zoe, her finger tapping her nose, 'or it won't come true.'

Jane leaned forward and began tickling her little sister, who giggled and squirmed, trying to get away. Behind them, Len finished a speech and applause trickled around the room, followed by the attendees gathering their belongings and making their way outside.

'There you are,' Marion said. 'Time to go over to Dunes and get ready for the main event.'

Zoe clapped her hands together in excitement as the other contestants and their guests passed by, animated chatter and an air of tension surrounding them. She watched as Dolly passed by with her father, blinking to take a second look as his hand moved from her waist and patted her behind.

CHAPTER 21

2022
Zoe

Outside Dunes, Zoe watched as men in overalls wheeled boxes into the venue, a flustered woman with a clipboard counting them in. A man in a cowboy outfit leaned against a bin, drawing on a cigarette and staring out into the distance while a woman in a sequinned dress gestured animatedly at him. Outside the fortune-teller's booth, Madame Eloise was being hugged by a woman who had clearly been told of a great future as others queued to hear if their respective love lives, careers and finances would also improve in time.

It was four hours until the talent show, the celebration of a town at odds with its past. She thought about Bob Previtt, probably sitting up there on the hill looking down on them. '*Photographs lie*' — what did that mean?

The next few hours would be her final chance to find anything out, and if nothing came to light, she would try to come to terms with not knowing and be at peace. Try to find a new way forward and erase this place from her memory for good.

Zoe thought about the images of Dolly scowling in the shadows. A woman who appeared to love her boarding house and to some extent the resort, but who then had appeared deeply unhappy and resentful, but of what? And who was she berating last night? A speaker blasted out a ghoulish *mwuhahaha* and Zoe looked over at the Ghost House.

Something about the place spiked in Zoe's memory. It hadn't been a ghost house then, it was a 'freak show', something that would never be allowed today. She remembered the exhibits and her sister's horror at it all. She ventured closer as a woman dressed as a vampiric wench moved theatrically towards her. Zoe was too late to avoid her hand, which took hers.

'Come, my pretty, don't be afraid.'

'No, I—'

'My master would like to invite you to eat and drink with him, the Count insists!'

'I've just eaten and—'

She led Zoe to the small entrance, past a waiting queue who gave her stern looks but said nothing.

'One victim — sorry, *guest*, Igor.'

Zoe raised an eyebrow as 'Igor', dressed as a zombie, looked up from his mobile phone and opened the door.

'How much is it?' Zoe asked.

'Five pounds of your devilish money,' he said, putting his phone back in his pocket.

Zoe looked up at the prefabricated wooden house and saw a face at a window, the features obscured by a tangle of cotton web. She had begged to go in the Freak Show that day when Jane had brought her to the pier, but now she had more than enough terrors of her own to deal with.

Zoe followed Igor through the door and into a small dark hallway, where they were met by an actor wearing a long velvet cloak and sporting unnervingly realistic fangs. He wore one of those earrings that stretched the lobe so wide you could stick a finger through it. Her son Dylan had asked for one last year, sulking when she said no.

'Welcome to our home, I hope you enjoy my family's generous hospitality. Stay as long as you like . . . an hour, a day—' he leaned close to her face — '*forever.*' He feigned a passable Eastern European accent, most likely learned from watching old vampire films. 'Have fun, my pretty . . . and keep your neck covered at all times!' He opened his mouth wide as if to bite her as she hurried past him.

A door flung open, and she was ushered through to the next room. An elegant table was set with a half-eaten synthetic feast, the room eerily quiet. Zoe jumped as giant stuffed rats scuttled around the floor and the door to a grandfather clock burst open. She screeched as a pale-faced actor jumped out, chains dragging along the floor behind him. Running through cotton cobwebs, she spat stray strands from her mouth. Next, she found herself in a fairground-themed room, a robotic clown laughing maniacally above her, a maze of distorting mirrors ahead.

She laughed as her image morphed from squat and ball-shaped to stretched-out giant as she moved through the mirrors. After the novelty of her ever-changing image had waned, she tried to leave the room, each time halted by a false exit. Another couple somewhere else in the maze of glass appeared and disappeared in reflective splices. She tried to reach them but each time she felt she was close, they disappeared again into an echo of giggles.

'Hello?' she called out, pulling at the neck of her T-shirt as heat rose in her body. 'Can somebody let me out? I'm stuck.'

Common sense told her that she would get out eventually, that this was just a fairground attraction and the 'monsters' just actors, waiting for their big break in television. All common sense seemed to be lost as she began to bang on each mirror, waiting for one to give way and lead her to another room, or even better, an exit where she would be thrown into the room offering tacky gifts by which to remember this godawful sideshow.

Zoe tried to control her breathing as she felt it shorten, her chest tightening with each inhalation. She looked up at a small camera in the corner of the ceiling, a tiny red light flashing.

'Hello? I think there's a malfunction here somewhere, I can't get out, I—'

A door slid open, and Zoe felt a rush of relief to be out of the mirrored room, even if it led into yet another dark, cobwebby place. This time the theme was theatrical, a small stage on which marionette skeletons danced. A distorted rendition of the 'Dance of the Sugar Plum Fairy' bled out of the speakers as she sat for a moment on a row of red velvet chairs, plastic spiders hanging from thin cotton above her head. Just as her breathing was starting to settle again, a screen at the back of the stage crackled to life —a Super 8 film of black-and-white scenes spliced together, images of the sea, blurred figures wandering across a dark beach. The camera turned and panned up to Sunshine Sands pier. Zoe felt the blood drain from her face as she recognised some of the slightly out-of-focus figures. A crown lifted high by Len Erwitt, intercut with a cheering audience. She tried to see if she could spot herself or her mum but it was too quick, moving back to the stage and her sister.

A close-up of Charlie Bailey, then Bob Previtt beaming as they clapped, surrounding the winner, her sister. She scrambled for her phone, but let it fall into her pocket again as the film cut to the sea crashing against the sand. Photos of other women appeared, spliced together in short succession and then back to Jane as she waved and smiled triumphantly before the film glitched and Zoe was left in darkness.

* * *

'Can I see the owner?'

The vampire wench and Igor the zombie stopped giggling at something on his phone screen and looked up to Zoe and then to each other.

'I think she left about ten minutes ago,' the girl said, shrugging her blood-spattered shoulders.

'Do you have her contact details? When will she be back?'

Both looked confused.

'What do you want her for?'

'The film that plays in the circus room, I need to know who filmed that.'

They exchanged unknowing looks with each other before Igor spoke.

'The one about Sunshine Sands?'

Zoe could feel irritation rising in her body having to explain to the *gatekeepers*.

'Yes, I don't think it's appropriate to have things like that in a seaside attraction. The beauty contest stuff. It's not for other people's amusement, you know. Those women have families.' She gulped back tears, not wanting to get upset in front of two teens dressed in Halloween costumes.

They both looked contrite, glancing at each other as if expecting the other to explain.

'We will certainly pass your feedback on to our boss,' vampire girl said in her best scripted voice.

'Look, can I just have the owner's number? I'll speak to her myself.'

They waited a moment, before the boy scrolled through his phone and held it out to Zoe, a number displayed under the name BOSS.

'What's her name?'

'Eloise Delano.'

'The fortune teller?'

'She works between the two. It's a family business — this used to be some kind of freak show. The Delano family used to own most things on the pier until they were hounded out.'

Vampire girl shot Igor a warning look.

'Hounded out by who?'

Igor ignored the girl, seeming excited to share the story. 'The mayor at the time, him and his cronies. They wanted to take over all the leases here, but they'd been in her dad's family since the pier first opened in the eighteen hundreds. Anyways, they had friends in high places and money to burn and took most of it off him cos of some loophole, unsigned paperwork or something.'

'How do you know all this?'

Igor laughed. 'Eloise mentions it at least once a week, how this was all stolen from her family. You should talk to that photographer bloke, though he might tell it a different way, if you know what I mean?'

'Dave Cooper? Why would he know?' Zoe said.

'Thick as thieves back in the day, him and the mayor. My gran used to be a secretary on the council. Len even left him his house when he died, a fancy place on the hill.'

CHAPTER 22

Zoe walked away from the funfair. The crowds began to warp and stretch in front of her, as if reflected in the hall of mirrors she had just left. Her head felt as if it might explode with thoughts of her sister, that night, this place full of secrets. She reached into her bag and took out a blister pack of painkillers, her hands trembling as she drew her fingers across the empty foil pockets. She stumbled forward, passing a mechanical clown encased in a glass box. It span in its seat, laughing maniacally as its head moved backwards and forwards. Zoe banged at the glass.

'*Shut up.*'

Its laugh seemed to get louder, its movements more exaggerated as if mocking her. Zoe banged her fist against the glass harder, and still it laughed.

'*Shut up!*'

The glass rattled with yet another blow, followed by footsteps across the wooden pier behind her.

'Oi! Stop that.'

Zoe turned to a man wearing 'North Pier' branded overalls and wielding a sweeping brush.

'You'll damage it,' he scorned.

Zoe stopped, suddenly aware of the small crowd that had gathered, looks of concern and bemusement across their faces.

'Sorry, I . . .' She didn't know how to explain her behaviour.

The man shook his head in disgust and Zoe turned to leave, embarrassed by her outburst. As she walked away, a woman touched her arm.

'I don't blame you, love. Creepy buggers, those things are. I hate clowns.'

As Zoe headed towards the boarding house, she considered packing up and leaving. She didn't need to go to the talent contest. She could call Clark and get his take on things, and there would be enough posts on social media to string together the bits she needed for the article. It had been foolish of her to come expecting anything, but at least she had, and if nothing else it would give her therapist something to dissect in the next session.

CHAPTER 23

1982
Jane

'Ladies and gentlemen, boys and girls, welcome to Miss Sunshine Sands 1982!'

Len Erwitt basked in the applause of the seated audience before him. Kids with candyfloss-covered faces ran about down the aisle and in front of the stage as mothers tried to coax them back with desperate promises of sweets and fizzy drinks. The bar was two deep, with men wrestling to get pints in before the show began.

Jane peeked from behind the curtain, scanning the seats before spotting her mum and Zoe. Her mum was entranced by Len, her hands clasped on her lap as she looked admiringly up at him.

'And it is my great honour tonight to introduce our head judge, who is going to treat you to a little performance for your eyes only!'

Jane felt a hand clasp her backside, causing her to gasp. Charlie leaned forward and whispered into her ear, his breath thick with whiskey and cigars.

'Please . . . don't,' she said.

'Knock 'em dead tonight.' He squeezed his fingers together, holding her tighter.

Before she had chance to wriggle away, he let go and walked through the curtain and onto the stage. The cheers and whoops of excitement echoed through the venue, those who had been unable to get tickets to see him at the theatre now party to a special performance.

When Jane turned to go back to the dressing room she came face to face with Dolly.

She felt embarrassed by what she must have seen, as if somehow it were her fault that Charlie had felt it OK to touch her like that, as if she had invited it. Maybe she had — she had gone to meet him, posed for the photographs, and now here she was, dressed like a hooker.

'He shouldn't have done that,' Dolly said, her voice low and angry. 'You shouldn't let him.'

Dolly wore a plain blue dress, a small flower brooch pinned to the collar. Her hair still hung in curtains, held back from covering her face entirely by two brown kirby grips.

'It's OK, I can handle it.'

'Didn't look that way to me,' said Dolly.

'Yeah, well, I'll be fine. Thanks for your concern.'

Jane passed Dolly, who grabbed her upper arm, holding it in place.

'Watch out,' Dolly said sternly, before releasing her grip and letting Jane go.

The threat didn't scare Jane. She couldn't fight her way out of a wet paper bag, but Dolly was hardly Giant Haystacks either. She could ignore her, call her names, whatever she felt like, Jane would be gone soon and had no intention of ever coming back to Sunshine Sands and its strange residents. There was no need to have a freak show here, its residents were a living, breathing one.

* * *

The first round was cocktail party dress. The girls were lined up backstage, their chaperone Veronica on hand to rally them into their correct places. Cries of 'No, not there, *there*!' and 'Smile and heads up!' shot at them like bullets as they gathered like nervous children on the first day of school. Each girl was numbered like cattle at a market. There had been some arguing over who would take number thirteen, resolved when it was pointed out that a) the judges already had the numbers assigned to names and b) it would place them in near centre stage for any line-up. Jane had been assigned number six, precisely the number of times she had had to go for a nervous pee in the last hour.

'And go!' Veronica screeched.

Veronica pushed the first girl through, and the rest followed in single file onto the stage, to the applause of proud parents and happy holidaymakers. The judges' eyes travelled up and down each girl as they were paraded in front of them, Charlie licking his lips and tapping his fingers rapidly on the judges' desk. The first girl stepped up to a microphone at the front of the stage as Len leaned into one on the table before him.

'Here we have the lovely Leanne, aged nineteen, travelling all the way from sunny Hull. Measuring a perfect 35-25-35. Now then, Leanne, tell the audience what you do for a living and what your hobbies are.'

As Leanne reeled off a variety of hobbies from roller-skating to volunteering at an old people's home, Jane ran through her answers. Her hobbies were an embarrassment of lack. Her mum had helped her come up with something beyond reading magazines and playing with the family cat.

One by one the girls stepped forward to have their measurements announced and their jobs and hobbies scrutinised by the judges. When it was Jane's turn, she caught sight of Zoe in the audience, who waved frantically. She stepped into the spotlight, trying to keep her legs from giving way as her knees started to shake.

'And here we have seventeen-year-old Jane, a gorgeous girl hailing from Sheffield, just waiting to *steel* the show!' He paused for the appreciation of his regional reference. 'She measures in at 32-26-33. Now, tell us a bit about yourself, Jane.'

Dave was crouched at the front of the stage taking photographs, each flash taking her back to Charlie's hotel room. She looked around the roomful of faces staring up at her, her stomach spinning. Her mum watched her, eyes no longer adoring, but glaring as she mouthed, 'Say something.'

Jane took a deep breath. 'I . . . I work at a supermarket and my hobbies are swimming, reading and helping out at a local playgroup.'

The truth was she had once spent a morning at Zoe's old nursery tidying up the toys and making orange squash for break time, but her mum said it was as good as true, just a matter of how she worded it.

'Very good,' Charlie said, leaning into the mic. 'You can ring up my weekly shop any day of the week.'

Jane blushed as the audience chuckled, her mum looking pleased at the extra attention. Len leaned forward.

'Thank you, Jane. It looks like you might have a new customer visiting you soon.' He turned to Charlie, who nodded enthusiastically.

More laughter rippled around the room as Jane tried her best to hold the fixed smile she had learned from the Miss World videos her mum had made her sit through and study. '*It could be you, Jane, if you work hard enough, the world's your oyster.*'

When the round had finished, Veronica stood in the wings urging them all off and sending them back to the dressing room to get changed. Jane pulled out her swimming costume from the small case her mum had lent her, thankful she had agreed a bikini might be a little too much for a teen to parade around in. She hadn't, however, relented on the addition of bows she had sewn onto the shoulder straps. Jane looked down to a pair of scissors on the table next to hers — it would just take a second.

A gaggle of the other contestants were reapplying their make-up as they chatted about the judges, their reactions and who they thought would be out next. Then talk turned to Dolly.

'Gives me the willies,' Miss Doncaster said, with a dramatic shudder. 'Always giving us dirty looks.'

Miss Burnley chipped in: 'Never says a word, just follows her dad around like a lost sheep. A right weird—'

She stopped when Miss Doncaster poked her and nodded at the door. Dolly stood still, her eyes down as she clutched cartons of apple juice. The room fell silent as she moved through the narrow space, dumping a carton in front of each mirror. Miss Burnley clamped her lips tight, trying not to let a giggle escape. When Dolly left, the room let out a collective sigh of relief as the awkwardness evaporated.

Miss Doncaster brushed coral blusher on her cheeks. 'I'd watch your back if I were you, Kelly, you might find she gives the corridor floor an extra polish with grease now.'

'Right, girls, are we all ready in our swimsuits?' Veronica called from the doorway.

The contestants fell into line once more and followed each other out of the door.

* * *

Wolf whistles pierced the room as they paraded onto the stage wearing swimwear more suited to St Lucia than Sunshine Sands. Wives glared at their husbands as for the first time that night they found something more interesting than the pint glasses they clutched.

Jane resisted readjusting her swimming costume to free it from her bottom and put her best foot forward.

'Oooof, what a sight for sore eyes,' Charlie said into the mic, Len returning a satisfied smile.

'Now then, ladies, let's treat everyone to a second view. Round you go, girls.'

The contestants did as they were told, coming to a halt in a line at the front of the stage. Jane looked down at Dave, who lowered his camera when he reached her, giving her an encouraging thumbs-up, but she averted her eyes, concentrating on keeping her stomach sucked in. Dolly stood in the dimness at the side of the room, watching Dave as he continued along the line.

Len got up from behind the desk holding a piece of paper, concealing it from the girls as he stood before the microphone and turned to address the crowd.

'I'm sure you'll agree that we've been spoiled tonight with all the beauty here at Sunshine Sands, haven't we, ladies and gentlemen?' A murmur of agreement rippled through the room. 'Sadly we only have one crown, and we have to narrow it down a little. So, going on to our *talent* round are the following numbers.' He turned back to the contestants. 'If your number is called, can you please step forward.'

Some of the girls held hands, others their stomachs. For the first time since they had arrived Jane hoped her number would be called, because then she'd be in with a chance of winning the money for her mum, and what happened that morning at the hotel wouldn't have been for nothing.

'The six lucky ladies going through to the next round are . . .' Len looked down at the paper, teasing them with a dramatic pause. 'Number seven!' A girl in a red swimsuit clasped her hands to her face and jumped up and down before stepping forward. He called out four more numbers, each grinning with joy and relief as they stepped into the spotlight. 'Now then, our final contestant going through is . . . number six!' Jane felt dizzy under the lights, as the girls not chosen gave her begrudging words of congratulations.

Len took her hand. 'Come on then, love, step forward.'

She took her place by the others, all basking in the glory of being the chosen ones. In the audience Zoe was bouncing up and down, her mum on her feet clapping wildly.

'There'll be a fifteen-minute interval to give these ladies time to change into evening gowns and for the thirsty among you to get some refreshments.'

Before he had even finished the sentence, chairs were scraping back across the floor and a line had begun to form at the bar.

* * *

Marion looked at Jane's dress in horror.

'Who would do such a thing?' she gasped.

She held out the torn pieces of purple satin, clean cuts criss-crossed down the bodice and skirt.

Zoe looked like she was about to burst into tears, her eyes fixed on Jane, who peered over at the other girls, whispering among themselves.

'I could wear the cocktail dress again, Mum, it doesn't matter,' Jane said, trying to keep calm for Zoe's sake as much as her mum's.

'You'll do no such thing,' Marion snapped. 'It says evening wear, and besides, everyone will think we can't afford a proper dress.'

Marion played with the pieces as if trying to find a way to make the dress whole again. She turned to the room and shouted, 'Who did this?'

'Mum!' Jane hissed. 'Stop it.'

'Who vandalised my daughter's dress? Who has a knife or scissors?'

The room fell silent as her screams cut across the room. The other contestants and their families turned, looking from the dress to Marion in confusion. Veronica burst through the door.

'Whatever's going on in here, you can hear it from the stage.'

Marion grabbed the dress and marched over to Veronica, holding it out in her arms.

'Someone has sabotaged Jane's evening dress. It's been cut to shreds.'

Veronica looked suitably concerned as she eyed the garment, pulling at the torn material.

'What size is the dress?'

'Pardon?' Marion said.

'Size,' Veronica demanded. 'We'll have to borrow another, there's no time to fix this.'

'Ten,' Jane said.

Veronica made her way up and down the mirrors, speaking to all the girls who hadn't made it through to the final. Marion called after her, 'She can't wear someone else's dress! It won't look right.'

One of the contestants handed Veronica a yellow taffeta dress, which she brought over to Jane.

'Try this, I can always pin it if need be.'

'Yellow washes her face out!' Marion cried.

'Thank you,' Jane said, taking the dress back to her mirror and thanking her fellow contestant.

As her mum zipped her up, Jane felt strange flutters in her gut — not nerves, but fear. She glanced around the room at the other girls, wondering who would hate her enough to do this. Dawn hadn't made it through, but then all of the other girls were on stage with her at the time. Her mum stood behind her looking into the mirror.

'Well, I suppose it'll do.'

The dress fitted perfectly, and although she wouldn't dare tell her mum, it was much nicer than the one that now sat in a shredded pile on the floor. Marion turned Jane around, fussing with the puff sleeves.

'You look a picture, Jane. Now, you go out and win that crown.'

'Mum, I might not win.'

'Rubbish, you shine up there on the stage. We'll have to get some copies of the photographs that man's taken, he couldn't stop snapping you.' She looked to the door. 'Talk of the devil!'

Dave entered the room, his eyes hidden behind fingers. 'Are we all decent?'

'I'll ask him now,' Marion said.

'No, Mum, don't,' Jane begged.

Marion shook her head, but for once listened and stayed with Jane and Zoe. Zoe was putting lipstick on in the mirror.

'Pretty as a picture.' Jane smiled, stroking Zoe's hair.

'Have you run through your poem again?' Marion asked.

Jane's stomach lurched at the thought. She rifled through her bag, furiously pushing a book, her keys and an array of pamphlets aside.

'I've forgotten it!' she cried.

Marion tutted, shaking her head as she pulled out a copy from her own bag.

'It's lucky I'm more organised then, isn't it?'

She handed it to Jane, who took a deep breath and scanned the lines about spring bringing new life to the world in time for summer.

'Five minutes!' Veronica shouted through the door, causing a flurry of activity and more ozone-depleting hairspray to be blasted through the air.

Dave photographed the girls as they made final preparations.

Veronica appeared again, her cheeks red and hair stuck to her sweaty forehead.

'Girls, girls, come along now. Hurry up, single file. Have you all got your numbers on?'

Marion grabbed Jane's swimming costume and unpinned the number, attaching it to the yellow dress. She patted it and then gave Jane a brief hug before taking Zoe's hand and leading her past the girls and back to their seats in the audience.

Number seven stood behind her nervously pulling at her necklace, which split, causing tiny silver beads to spill and scatter along the linoleum floor. The girl scrambled across it, trying to retrieve them as Veronica shouted for them to 'Move! Move! Move!'

Jane felt a crunch under her shoe as she stumbled over the stray beads, number seven giving up and following behind. Jane sped up, trying to keep up with the line as they approached the stage curtain. Dolly sat on a stool in the wings, reading a magazine. She glanced up at Jane, staring at her dress.

'I've left the tag on!' Miss Wakefield cried.

Veronica huffed and marched forward. She tried to pull at the thread of plastic, but it wouldn't snap. 'For heaven's sake, Dolly!'

Dolly put her magazine down and scuttled over.

'Give me the scissors,' Veronica said, holding her hand out.

Jane froze as Dolly took a huge pair of dressmaking scissors from her pocket, the silver blades glinting under the lights.

* * *

'And now, ladies and gentlemen, girls and boys, please welcome our finalists for Miss Sunshine Sands.' Len turned and held his hand out towards the curtain, which Veronica opened to allow the six girls to walk through.

'Hurry,' Veronica said, pushing Jane, whose eyes were still fixed on the scissors back in Dolly's hand.

They stood in a line across the stage as the audience *oohed* and *ahhed* at their evening dresses.

'Well, what a picture we have here, eh? Ladies, you have done Sunshine Sands proud tonight — all worthy winners. Before we make that difficult choice, you have the opportunity to display your special talent for three minutes. There'll be no trying to hog the limelight as a bell will sound when your time is up. So, step forward number seven.'

Number seven sang 'Memory' from the musical *Cats* a capella, managing to hit most of the notes even when she stumbled over the second verse. Number twenty-one valiantly tap-danced on the spot despite the 'taps' not carrying much further than the front row. One of the judges' heads kept jerking up each time he fell asleep, an empty glass of wine before him. He woke up at the clapping as each girl finished.

Jane was the last to be called forward, the spotlight causing her to squint slightly. The audience were in the shadows, barely recognisable shapes before her. Charlie Bailey sat forward in his chair, leaning on the judges' table. Len, next to him, watched her, narrowing eyes waiting for her to speak. Through the silence came the clink of bottles being thrown in a bin behind the bar.

Much to her own surprise, Jane not only remembered the poem and the cadence it required, but the audience seemed to be listening. When she finished with the reflection that although winter brought an end, it came with the promise of spring, applause rang out through the room.

'Well then,' Len said, 'brains as well as beauty! What a talented bunch we have here.'

Relieved the night was all but over, Jane joined the other girls at the back of the stage where they were asked to wait while the judges deliberated in hushed tones as music filled the room. Len and Charlie gave the occasional look over as they nodded and conferred with the others, then Len stood and made his way to the stage to address the audience.

CHAPTER 24

2022
Zoe

Zoe swallowed a pill with a glass of tepid water poured from the bathroom sink, musing that if anxiety didn't get her first then cholera might. The garden gate to the boarding house clinked shut and she went to the window, watching as Dolly and Trevor walked down the path, towards the front door. Trevor carried a bundle of shopping bags as Dolly led Princess on a lead.

Zoe lifted her case onto the bed and began to fold clothes into it, wishing the kids could come home a day early. There were many times she had longed for a quiet house, faced with Dylan's love of music played at ear-splitting volume, Alice's habit of asking questions throughout any television programme and Belle's newfound love of impersonating zoo animals. But the truth was, when the children weren't around, the silence at home was crippling.

She opened the scrapbook and began to slide the loose photographs back in, making a silent promise to herself that once home she would burn all of this on the rusting BBQ in the garden that had only been used once in the past three years.

Zoe was about to zip up her case when she heard raised voices downstairs. She went onto the landing, recognising Dan's voice as he breathlessly tried to relay something to Dolly. Zoe ran down the stairs to see Dolly's arm around an ashen-faced Dan.

'I'm sure she's just gone off to the shops, probably to buy some make-up or tights for tonight,' Dolly said.

'She wouldn't, not without telling me. We tell each other everything.'

'What's happened?' said Zoe.

Dolly appeared irritated by Zoe's presence. 'Everything's in hand, you just go about your business.'

'Sophie's gone missing,' Dan said, his face distraught.

Trevor appeared from the kitchen, his forehead creased in concern. He eyed Dolly, who met his look with an equally grim expression.

'When did you last see her?' Zoe asked.

'She was meant to meet me at the entrance to the pier after rehearsals. We were going to go into town to get something to eat. She never showed up.'

'Not answering her phone?'

Dan held a mobile up. 'I have her phone because she couldn't use it in rehearsals, and she didn't want to leave it lying around.'

'How long ago was it since you were supposed to meet her?' asked Zoe.

Dan put a hand to his head. 'An hour ago. I went into Dunes to look for her and they said she'd already left. She wouldn't just go off without telling me.'

Zoe had only known them a couple of days, but instinct told her that that was true. Sophie and Dan had been attached at the hip since she first saw them in the dining room.

'Have you called the local hospital?' Zoe asked.

Dan's eyes widened. 'You don't think—'

'Just precautionary,' Zoe said. 'To rule it out more than anything. It's what the police would ask.'

'The police?' Dan cried.

'Stop it, you're upsetting the boy with all this talk of hospitals and the police. Common sense says she'll walk through that door any minute now having lost track of time.' Dolly attempted to usher him away from Zoe and into the dining room, but Dan shrugged her away and started scrolling his phone, searching Google.

'Hello, yes, could you tell me if you've had a Sophie Ashcroft come in? Third of September 1993. Yes, I'm her husband, Daniel. Are you sure? Could you try Sophie Bellamy, her maiden name?'

He ended the call relieved but dejected, turning with a hopeful smile as the boarding house door opened, only for it to fade away as Clark entered.

'Who died?' Clark said.

Zoe raised a warning eyebrow.

'What?' Clark said, confusion in his voice.

'Dan hasn't seen Sophie for a while — she was supposed to be meeting him after rehearsals. Did you see her?'

'In rehearsal, yes, then I had a meeting with the sound guy so didn't see any of the others leave.' Clark put his bag down in the hall. 'Shall we go and look for her?'

'I've tried everywhere. I should call the police.'

'Don't be daft, it's far too soon,' Dolly snapped. 'Why don't you let Zoe and Clark have a drive around first?'

Zoe knew that past experience had made Dolly wary of the police, but even she couldn't hold them off indefinitely.

'OK, you coming, Clark?' Zoe said, then to Dan, 'You wait here in case she comes back before we do.'

* * *

'Lovers' tiff?' said Clark.

Zoe peered under the windscreen shield, scanning shop windows for any sign of Sophie. 'I doubt it, they're far too lovey-dovey for that. The misery doesn't kick in until at least five years.'

Clark smiled. 'Speaking from experience?'

'Possibly.'

Zoe drove through the main street of the town, which was set back from the promenade and beach. Once busy storefronts now formed a line of charity shops and the odd grocery shop or vape store. She pulled up in a small budget supermarket car park and watched as a young blonde woman walked away in the distance.

'Is that her?' Clark said, his hand already reaching for the door handle.

Zoe shook her head. 'No, Sophie's much slimmer and her hair longer. You wait here and keep a look out, I'll go in and ask here. She might have got hungry and just gone to get snacks or something.'

Zoe gave a cursory glance up each of the aisles, making her way from one end to the other. She stopped at the lottery and cigarette counter and waited for a red-haired assistant to grapple with a card machine.

'Excuse me, you haven't seen a young woman with blonde hair, about my height but slimmer?'

The assistant looked solemnly out to the crowds of customers battling with trolleys in the aisles. All ages, all hair colours, all indistinct. Zoe mumbled thanks to the girl, turning towards the exit.

She spotted Dave in the distance at a checkout. He was balancing several bottles of wine and other shopping in his arms. He glanced over in her direction, not seeming to see her, and she turned back again, hoping he hadn't. She would have to contact him and make her apologies for later. Once Sophie was back, she would be on her way home and away from Sunshine Sands.

'Any luck?' Clark asked.

Zoe shook her head and slumped back in her seat, putting her seat belt on. 'Right, we'll drive along the seafront, then head back. Let's hope for Dan's sake she's returned by then.'

'You think she'll come back?' Clark said, shifting in his seat. 'This isn't the first time a woman has gone missing here, after all.' He stared out of the window. 'I thought it was over.'

'What do you mean you thought it was over?'

'Oh, nothing. I mean, it's been so long since the last one, the beauty queen. If there had been a killer stalking the streets back then, why would he come back now?'

In all the commotion of the past hour it hadn't registered with Zoe that there was a possible connection between Sophie and Jane.

'No,' she said, 'it can't be connected, not after all this time. I mean, Jane was out of the blue. There one minute and then she was—'

'Gone,' said Clark. 'Like Sophie.'

'Look, let's not get ahead of ourselves,' Zoe said, trying to calm the situation, despite feeling a sense of rising panic. 'She's only been gone a couple of hours at most — and she might already be back at the Forget-Me-Not for all we know.'

'I suppose so.'

Zoe watched a couple filling their car boot with shopping, a small child taking sweets from the bags and running around the car to escape the clutches of the mum.

'Do you have any other reason to think they might be connected?' She turned to Clark, wanting to gauge his reaction.

'Like what?'

'Well, two girls go missing, both staying at the same boarding house, and as you well know, Dolly can have a temper at times, to say the least.'

Clark laughed incredulously. 'Are you asking if I think Dolly is responsible for seeing off the beauty queen and now Sophie?'

It sounded ridiculous when he said it. 'Well, no . . . but you've got to admit it's odd. Plus the fact that she's so averse to discussing Jane, and doesn't want to involve the police.'

The smile disappeared from Clark's face, his tone suddenly serious. 'Dolly is protective. She's suspicious of people because of the past, that's all. And she doesn't like the police sniffing around because she doesn't trust them.'

It was like a shutter coming down, the atmosphere in the car suddenly tense and awkward. Dave appeared from the supermarket entrance, carrying a box of groceries. Zoe started the engine and drove away, the rest of the journey completed in silence.

CHAPTER 25

1982
Jane

The other three contestants swamped Jane as the audience erupted into applause. Arms pulled her into a perfume- and make-up-hazed embrace until she was gasping for air. She felt a hand grab hers and pull her free, out to the centre of the stage.

'Ladies and gentlemen, boys and girls, may I present the winner of Miss Sunshine Sands 1982, Jane Delway!'

Len let go of her hand and moved to the side, clapping in her direction as the audience continued to cheer. Jane's mind was a whirl of surprise, confusion and, if she was completely honest with herself, happiness. Though she couldn't wait to be home and have the whole thing over with, it was a nice feeling to be chosen. She looked down at her mum, who had tears running down her face, and Jane was glad for her. The money would be very welcome — as Marion had made patently clear — but it would shrink into comparison to the joy of telling her sister Doreen that Jane was Miss Sunshine Sands.

Jane's pleasure was short-lived when she felt a hand skim her backside as Charlie Bailey slithered behind her to take a crown from a pillow and place it on her head. She managed to smile throughout, aware all eyes were on her. He then placed a pink sash over her head and across her body and kissed her cheek.

'Congratulations, gorgeous,' he breathed into her ear, stepping to the side as he clapped his hands, making way for the triumphant photographs to be taken.

CHAPTER 26

2022
Zoe

A policewoman sat with Dan at the window table in the dining room of the Forget-Me-Not. Dan looked like all of the life had drained out of him as he went over the last time he saw Sophie. Zoe knew that if anything untoward was suspected, he would be the main person of interest, being her husband. It was impossible to know what went on behind closed doors, but as far as Zoe had seen, Dan was as unlikely a suspect as anyone she had ever met.

Dolly hovered by the dining room door, her arms crossed and face taut. Zoe suspected she was having flashbacks of the suspicion on her dad when Jane went missing. He had never been fully exonerated in the disappearance of her sister, but he had left the town, never to be seen again, and that spoke volumes as far as she was concerned.

'Why are you looking at me like that?' Dolly said.

Her ex-husband had once told Zoe that she had a transparent face — anything she was thinking was reflected in her expression to those around her. It took a lot of effort for her to appear neutral during interviews, but today she wasn't a journalist and the mask had slipped.

'Nothing, I'm just worried about Sophie, that's all.'

Dolly's face remained still, her eyes cold, causing a shudder to crawl up Zoe's spine. The knowledge that Dolly had as much reason as anyone to do harm to her sister was fresh in her mind. The telephone rang in the hallway and Dolly left to answer it. The policewoman stood up, putting a hand on Dan's shoulder.

'The likelihood is that Sophie will be back none the wiser of the upset she's caused. In the meantime, I'll head back to the station and let you know if anything has been reported.'

'Is that it? Aren't you going to look for her?' Dan asked. 'A search party? Helicopter?'

'I'm afraid it's a bit early for that, Mr Ashcroft. Sit tight and inform me the minute you hear anything. Sophie isn't vulnerable and you said she had her purse with her. If there's nothing by the morning, then we'll start a search.'

She left Dan at the table, who began scrolling through his phone, clicking on social media profiles and searching hashtags.

'Why don't you go and have a lie-down for an hour?' Zoe suggested. 'I'll let you know if I hear anything.'

'I can't sleep,' he said, not looking up from his phone.

'Did she speak to anyone at all at Dunes, might she have made plans to meet up with someone and got waylaid?' Zoe knew it was unlikely and she'd have told Dan, but sometimes people under a lot of stress forgot the obvious.

He shook his head. 'Only the other dancers and crew. They had a photo call and I was supposed to meet her outside after.'

Clark brought in a mug of coffee and placed it on the table before Dan. Zoe knew Clark would have to leave shortly to prepare for the show. If Sophie hadn't returned by then, Zoe had a terrible feeling that she wouldn't return at all.

CHAPTER 27

1982
Jane

'Jane, if you stand a bit more to the right . . . that's it . . . lovely.'

Dave Cooper attempted to gather various groups together for the post-pageant photographs. Len Erwitt was keen to speak to anybody of importance and bask in the success of the beauty contest. Marion and Zoe stood patiently on the sidelines, Marion brimming with pride as people fussed around her eldest daughter.

Jane's feet began to burn, her skin now red. It had been an hour since her win and there was no sign of the event dying down. Len was going to squeeze every last opportunity for publicity. A hand tapped her on the shoulder.

'Hi, Jane, I wonder, could I just grab you for a quick chat?'

Jane recognised Dave's friend Jeremy from the ghost train. She slid away from the group, relieved to get a break. Nobody seemed to notice her absence as Jeremy led her away to the side of the room. A small dance floor in front of the stage was now filled with partygoers who, free from the confines of their chairs, jumped up and down to the disco music.

'Can I get you a drink?' said Jeremy.

'No, thank you,' Jane said, relieved to finally sit down.

She slid her stilettos off and kicked them under the table as Jeremy took out a small notepad and pen from his jacket pocket.

'Well, I guess the first question is, how does it feel to be Miss Sunshine Sands?'

Jane exhaled, the fact that she had won still not sinking in. 'I can't believe it, really. I didn't think for a minute I'd even make it to the final.'

Jeremy scribbled in his notebook as he continued. 'So, now you go on to Miss Seaside Resort UK. That must be exciting? Quite a big cash prize, to say the least!'

The mention of another beauty contest made Jane's feet throb harder. 'Yes, I'm very excited for that, of course.'

'And I hear whispers that Charlie Bailey has asked you to audition for his show, the chance to be on television?'

Jane looked over to Charlie, who was chatting to some of the other contestants. As if feeling her gaze, he looked over and winked. Jane brought her attention back to Jeremy. 'No, I don't think that will happen.'

Jeremy asked her about her home life, about her job on the deli counter and dreams for the future. All the questions which she had practised answers to time after time with her mum over countless meals and last thing at night, when she'd rather have just slept.

'What are your plans now, tonight?'

'Sleep, I hope.' Jane caught sight of her mum, who was merrily chatting to Len Erwitt.

'A few of us are heading out for something to eat once this dies down, if you fancy it?'

All Jane wanted to do was go back to the boarding house. Her adrenaline was depleting by the minute and the thought of dragging out the night even further was not appealing in the slightest.

'I think my mum will want to get back.'

They both looked over to Marion, who was now dancing with Charlie Bailey in a tight hold. Her mum had never looked happier, in her element and drunk on Asti spumante and the overflow of Jane's win. She scoured the room for Zoe, but she was nowhere to be seen.

'Excuse me, I just need to go and make sure my sister is OK,' Jane said, squeezing her feet back into her shoes and limping across to the dance floor.

It took a few spins before Jane caught her mum's attention. As soon as Jane looked into her eyes, she knew she had gone beyond a couple of gin and tonics.

'Where's Zoe?' Jane said, trying to be heard above the music.

'What, love?' Marion shouted, shaking her head as she remained glued to Charlie.

'Where is Zoe?'

Charlie spun Marion around again until he was next to Jane. He shot her a grin, sweat gleaming on his forehead. Jane moved round, back to her mum.

'Muuum.'

'Oh, for goodness' sake, Jane, what?'

Marion loosened her grip on Charlie, and he kissed her hand and shimmied away to another woman, who fell enthusiastically into his arms.

'I can't see Zoe.'

'She's over there,' her mum said, her voice laced with agitation.

Jane strained to see Zoe sitting at a table holding a hand of playing cards. She leaned further, trying to look beyond a line of three dancing women to see who her sister was playing with. She saw Dolly holding cards and laughing as she put one on the table.

'Dolly has been looking after her, see? She's fine.'

Jane watched as Zoe giggled at something Dolly said, the two of them thick as thieves.

'Mum, can we go now?'

'Go? Don't be daft, Jane, you're Miss Sunshine Sands! We can't just leave, it'd be rude. You should be celebrating!'

'Nobody cares if I'm here or not now, they're all too drunk. Besides, it's way past Zoe's bedtime.'

Jeremy appeared again and held his hand out to Marion. 'Jeremy Lowden, *Sunshine Sands Echo*. I just wanted to extend my congratulations to you as the mother of the winner. I expect you're incredibly proud?'

Marion clasped one hand to her chest and the other on Jane's cheek. 'The proudest night of my life, Mr Lowden.'

'A few of us are heading out for a meal shortly, would you and your daughter like to join us?'

Jane mentally willed her mum to say no, to think about Zoe and their early departure tomorrow. When she saw the glee wash over her mum's face at the invitation, she knew it was a lost cause.

'We'd love to! How kind of you to ask. Isn't it kind of him to ask, Jane?'

Jane gave a tight smile.

'Excellent,' Jeremy said. 'I'll let you know when we're leaving. It's a place just up the road so no need for taxis.'

Someone called him over, and once out of earshot Jane chastised her mother. 'What about Zoe?'

Marion waved her concern away. 'Dolly can take her back to the boarding house and put her to bed. She'll be quite safe there.'

'She shouldn't be with Dolly, I don't trust her,' Jane said.

Marion frowned. 'Don't be daft. She might not be the full ticket, but she's harmless. Zoe will be perfectly safe with her.'

'I saw Dolly with some scissors.'

Jane waited for the penny to drop, but Marion remained confused.

'My dress. I think it was Dolly that did it.'

'Rubbish,' Marion laughed. 'She's not bright enough to do something like that, and besides, if she did — well, it meant you got to wear a more expensive dress, didn't it? And you won. Zoe's taken a shine to her and that's fine by me.'

Without waiting for a reply, Marion marched off the dance floor and over to the table where Dolly and Zoe were playing cards. Dolly listened to Marion and nodded steadily before looking over to Jane. Marion marched triumphantly back to the dance floor.

'There, that's that sorted. Now, go and freshen yourself up. I'll see you back out here in five minutes — we don't want to miss them if they leave.' She waved at Jeremy.

Jane stormed off towards the backstage area, as Dolly watched her.

CHAPTER 28

2022
Zoe

Princess yapped incessantly as if sensing the tension in the boarding house. Dolly picked her up and ruffled the fur on her head, the dog refusing to quieten. Zoe felt her headache returning, each yap like a splinter of glass in an open wound. Trevor had disappeared when the policewoman had left, mumbling about having to go and see his sister, who needed help with her evening meals.

Zoe retreated to her room to escape Princess's bark and to check online if there had been any mention of Sophie or updates on her sister. As soon as she hit enter, a photo of Sophie came up on a profile post that Dan had made public.

> @DanA
> *MISSING! My wife Sophie hasn't been seen for five hours. It's not long but she never goes off without me knowing. Please share if you're in the Sunshine Sands area. Staying at the Forget-Me-Not boarding house. Contact me with any sightings. This is not like her, I'm worried!*

@PennyJune
Isn't that the same place that the beauty queen stayed at when she went missing??

@DanA
I didn't know she stayed here??

@TommyGates
Mate, so sorry. Do you want me to drive up and help look? I'm sure she'll be back soon.

Zoe scrolled down the comments, Dan's friends and family offering support and words of sympathy.

@MarnieParker
I know that place, my grandad was there when it was some kind of residential place in the late 80s/90s. Hope she's home soon, Dan xxx

Zoe had assumed that the Forget-Me-Not had remained a boarding house since her sister left. Beneath the comment, Marnie had posted a link to an article written five years ago on the decline of the British seaside. Zoe scanned the words until she reached a paragraph pertaining to the Forget-Me-Not.

Many of the landlords and landladies of the north had to think outside the box as visitor numbers dwindled. Some became private residences, others housed those in social care and one in Sunshine Sands, the Forget-Me-Not, became a boarding house providing housing for the elder residents of the town.

Beneath was a black-and-white photograph of the boarding house, a temporary sign placed above the door: *Forget-Me-Not Residential Home.*

Councils welcomed the extra housing becoming available and were happy to fund refurbishments. Former Mayor Len

> *Erwitt was so taken with it, he moved in himself until his death in the early nineties.*

Jane had been under the impression that Dolly couldn't stand the old guard of Sunshine Sands, so why would she take one in, not least the most influential? A part of her admired the indomitable landlady for her business acumen in the face of potential ruin.

She remembered something Colin had said and got out her notepad, then typed *Boddington Club Sunshine Sands 1980s* into the search engine. Among results for the famous Manchester beer and the infamous and infinitely more influential Oxford University 'Bullingdon Club' appeared a small article written by a woman in the mid-2000s.

> *The desire for men's-only clubs has always been there. Where women's organisations are for chatting over tea and cake, listening to talks about books and building communities for support, men's clubs tend to be about influence and helping each other out with a secret handshake for financial gain. Women look for support and friendship, whereas men look for ways to move up the social ladder or get off a parking ticket (should the local policeman be a member). One such example of this was the strangely named 'Boddington Club' in the northern seaside town of Sunshine Sands, a town that has suffered economically since the early eighties. Not much is known about the secret society, but one of its members, Bob Previtt, was a serving police officer at the time when a young woman went missing in 1982. It was felt that due to his influence, the ranks of the club closed in and protected possible suspects within the town.*
>
> *Few photographs exist from that time, but one of the last taken before its disbandment due to falling members is below. From left to right: Jeremy Lowden (journalist), Len Erwitt (mayor), Charlie Bailey (entertainer), Bob Previtt (police inspector). Photo credit: Dave Cooper.*

She heard Dan speaking to someone on his phone as he walked across the landing, his door closing and voice disappearing. At least the police now appeared to be interested in his new wife's sudden disappearance. A voice called up from the stairs.

'Hello? Is anybody there?'

Zoe opened her bedroom door and looked out to the landing, where a man wearing a yellow boiler suit stood, a grey metal case in his hand.

'I'm here for the boiler.'

'Oh, right. Is Dolly not around? She was in the dining room a little while ago.'

He shook his head, an exasperated look on his face. 'I've knocked on every door and nobody's here. Listen, I've got another appointment to get to in an hour.'

'OK, hold on.'

Zoe grabbed her key and left her room, following the plumber down the stairs.

'This is where the boiler is, I expect,' he said, yanking at the cellar door. 'Do you know where the key is?'

Zoe rang the reception desk bell, hoping Trevor or Dolly would appear and take over. When nobody appeared, the plumber gave her a half 'told you so' smile. She scanned the hooks on the wall for a key, but there were only keys to residents' rooms.

'I suppose it's locked for health and safety reasons,' he said, leaning against the wall as his eyes wandered over all the old celebrity photos. 'I used to love Larry Grayson. *The Generation Game* was on our telly every Saturday. Did he stay here?'

'No, apparently only the Grand was good enough,' Zoe said, opening filing cupboard drawers and rifling through various compartments.

'I didn't think someone like that would stay here,' he chuckled. 'Not exactly the Hilton, is it?'

'It might be one of these,' Zoe said, holding a small bunch of keys aloft that she'd found in the bottom drawer.

She took them to the cellar door and tried them one by one. The sixth key slid into the lock with ease and turned with a click.

'There you go,' he said, opening the door and turning a light on.

'It's a bit dingy,' Zoe said, as the chemical dampness wafted up.

'Always the way with cellars,' he said, walking carefully down the narrow stairs. 'I spend half my life coughing and sneezing.'

Zoe followed him as he strolled down the stairs, whistling as he went. He switched another light on at the bottom, which illuminated a single pendant bulb that hung from the ceiling.

'Afternoon, madam.' He chuckled in the direction of a mannequin in the corner.

As he laid his case down in front of the ancient boiler, Zoe walked over to the life-sized shop doll. Her painted eyes stared straight ahead, a small chip in her left cheek, an arm bent. She wore a blonde acrylic wig that had tipped slightly so that the fringe covered half of one eye.

She was clothed in a half-made dress, pins still holding the waist together. On a table beside the mannequin was a sewing machine and, on the floor, a box filled with reels of cotton and needles.

'This thing must have been put in when the ark was built,' the plumber grumbled, as he turned valves and tapped at the pipes. 'I expect they won't want to be forking out for a new one, mind. Looking at a few thousand quid.'

The mannequin stood in front of a wooden wall partition. Zoe opened the door and peered in. The floor was damp and dusty, on it a stack of cardboard boxes filled with old paperwork and magazines, their contents speckled with mould. In the far corner there were five large wooden crates. Bright yellow stickers with skull and crossbones on them warned of toxic contents. Dolly shouted from the top of the stairs, 'Who is down there?'

Zoe rushed back to join the plumber, closing the wooden door as Dolly stomped down the steps, her eyes blazing when she saw the two of them.

'Leaky valve,' the plumber said, seemingly unaware of her anger.

'Pardon?'

'Won't take much to fix it, I think I've got one in the van. That's what will have been causing the pressure to drop.'

'Sorry, Dolly, you weren't here and . . .' She looked at the plumber.

'Barry.'

'And Barry needed to see to the boiler, or you'd have had to make another appointment.'

'Well, I'm here now, so you can be on your way.'

Zoe was relieved for the opportunity to leave Dolly and Barry to it. As she passed Dolly, the landlady put her hand out. Zoe paused for a moment, not understanding at first, then reached into her pocket and handed her the bunch of keys. Dolly took them from her without a word, as Barry proceeded to talk about quotes and old pipework.

CHAPTER 29

1982
Jane

The small restaurant was thick with cigarette smoke. Marion, now lubricated with even more gin, waltzed past the tables, her head held high as Jane followed behind. Under much protestation, Jane had taken off her bejewelled crown, though agreed to keep the pink *Miss Sunshine Sands* sash on as a compromise.

'Over here!' Sitting alongside Jeremy Lowden and Len Erwitt, Charlie Bailey waved his hand in the air, motioning for them both to join their table. Charlie pulled a chair out for Marion, and Jane headed for a chair next to Jeremy.

'No, no,' Charlie called out, 'you sit over here, Jane, we've got a lot to discuss.' He pulled a chair out for her to sit next to him.

'Come on, Jane,' Marion said, 'don't be a sourpuss.'

The wine and whiskey were already flowing. Fellow diners looked over, keen to get a look at Charlie and the newly crowned Miss Sunshine Sands. Jane wasn't used to so much attention; it should have felt good, but—

'Wine?' Charlie asked Marion, already pouring the liquid into her glass.

Jane glared at her mum, who ignored her.

'And for you?' Charlie said, the bottle hovering above Jane's hand, which protected the top of her glass.

'No, thank you, I'll just have water.'

Charlie shrugged and put the bottle down as Jane reached over to a jug.

Dave Cooper appeared from the bathroom, weaving his way past the tables, his camera still hanging from his neck. Jane took a gulp of her water, avoiding his cheery 'hello' as he sat down next to her.

He took a glass of wine and lifted it into the air. 'To our new queen.'

The others followed suit and raised their glasses. A couple of the other contestants were in the restaurant also, but now, away from the lights and cameras, chose to ignore Jane.

A selection of starters arrived, placed around the table. Garlic bread, olives, bruschetta and salad.

'Dig in,' Len offered, reaching over and spooning some olives onto his plate.

Marion, who only ever ate what she called *simple food*, eyed the dishes with suspicion, before giving in and taking a piece of bread doused in olive oil. Jane, who was starving by now, piled her plate with bruschetta and garlic bread, her mum too enamoured with the attention of the men to chastise her for it.

'Mind you don't let yourself go now, telly puts on a few pounds, you know,' Charlie quipped.

'Telly?' Len said.

Charlie continued, 'Aye, you could be sitting with my new assistant on a television show I've got coming up.' He tapped at his nose as if he had been discreet somehow.

Dave took a sip of wine. 'And why not? I mean, you've beaten a whole load of beautiful girls tonight.'

Jane didn't care that all eyes were on her as she bit into the bread, tiny cubes of tomato and onion dropping to her plate. The small plates were gathered and replaced with large bowls of spaghetti as the wine flowed and mid-meal cigarettes and cigars were stubbed out in cut-glass ashtrays.

'Parmesan, madam?'

A waitress hovered by Jane's side, a silver spoon brimming with powdered cheese. Jane inhaled and held back a gag at the pungent smell before her.

'No, thank you.'

'We'll need to have a meeting in the morning, Marion, to discuss promoting Jane as much as possible,' Len said above the chatter.

Jane sucked in a strand of spaghetti and looked to her mum, who nodded as she sipped her wine.

'Of course,' Marion said.

'Our coach is at ten in the morning,' Jane said.

Len waved his fork in the air. 'I'm sure we can arrange a later train back to Sheffield. You'll be back in time for *Coronation Street*, don't worry.'

Jane put her cutlery down and pushed her plate away, her appetite now gone. She sat and watched them eat their food, all still high on the success of the night and her win. Outside, the lights of the pier still glittered across the promenade, the big wheel slowly turning in the distance. Then she noticed a figure walking slowly by the window. It was Dolly.

'Mum,' she called across the table, then more urgently, '*Mum.*'

'What is it?' Marion slurred, annoyed at the interruption of her chat with Jeremy.

'Isn't Dolly supposed to be babysitting Zoe?'

'Yes, she'll be fine, stop fretting.' Marion waved the concern away and continued chatting to Jeremy.

Jane pushed her chair back and ran out of the restaurant, letting the heavy door close behind her. In the distance she spotted Dolly walking away and ran after her. She bent down to take her shoes off, the risk of standing on a stray stone or discarded ice lolly stick less worrying than the constricting leather that rubbed and burned her feet. She called after Dolly, who kept moving through the crowds on the backstreets of Sunshine Sands.

'Hey! It's the beauty queen,' a drunk slurred, walking zombie-like towards her.

He grabbed at her waist, pulling her back as she attempted to wriggle free. His friends jeered and laughed, glasses of beer held aloft. When his grasping hands slipped up her body she grabbed at his arm and bit the bare skin as hard as she could, dropping her shoes to the ground. He cried out in pain and released her, his friends laughing even harder as he retreated to them for sympathy.

Jane ran away, leaving her shoes behind her. Dolly had disappeared from sight, lost in a gaggle of hens and stags. She wandered up the side street, not wanting to give up, but not wanting to go back to the restaurant. She decided to return to the boarding house. She'd get flak from her mum for leaving like that, but she needed to know that Zoe was OK. As she turned to go back, she spotted Dolly in the living room of a small, terraced house.

She was sitting beside a gas fire, the raven-haired girl from the Freak Show kneeling next to her, with a hand on Dolly's. Dolly was upset about something — no tears, but angry and shaking. The two girls, locked in a secret once more. Dolly's fists were clenched on her lap and her mouth taut as she spoke. The other girl listened, and then suddenly put her hands on Dolly's shoulders, shaking her head as Dolly spoke.

Jane wondered if her anger was about the contest, about her. The two girls rose and left the room. She stepped back into a café doorway and waited as they exited the house and made their way up the street and turned left. She crouched down by a car when they stopped at a door a street away from the boarding house. A young man appeared, rubbing his eyes and yawning. As they spoke his eyes sprung open and he retreated into the house, returning seconds later carrying something in a black bin bag and leaving with the two girls.

Jane's pace quickened to keep up with them, a deep fear for her young sister now swirling in the pit of her stomach. She should have stood up to her mum, not let Dolly take her sister away. She turned the corner to watch as they entered through the front door of the Forget-Me-Not. When Jane reached it, she pushed the handle down, but it was locked. She pushed the bell, listening as it echoed down the hall inside, but nobody came. Jane pushed open the brass letterbox and peered through. There was faint rustling coming from the dining room.

'Hello? It's Jane, I forgot my key. Can you let me in?'

There was no reply.

She shouted, 'Zoe! Can you hear me? I'm locked out.'

Jane hobbled over the small rockery by the doorway, knocking over a gnome which fell to the ground with a thud, a small chip of plaster falling from his cheek. She put her hands against the window and looked into the gloom of the dining room through the net curtains, rapping her knuckles on the glass.

'Is someone there? Can you let me in?'

A figure approached the window and pulled the curtains shut. Jane crouched to the ground and scooped up a handful of small stones and began throwing them up at the window to the bedroom where her sister should be. When the hall light clicked off, she ran back to the door, opening the letterbox again. Through the darkness she watched as the three of them pulled something heavy across the tiled floor and disappeared down into the cellar, a dull repetitive thud as they descended.

The window above opened, and Jane heard Zoe calling out. 'Hello?'

Jane ran from the door and back to the window. Zoe waved at her, the arm of her Snoopy nightdress falling back to her elbow. Relief at seeing her sister rushed through Jane.

'Are you OK?' Jane said, her voice just above a whisper.

Zoe yawned. 'Yes, I was asleep. Are you coming in?'

'Can you do something for me?'

Zoe nodded.

'There's a bolt on the bedroom door, can you slide it across to lock the room and stay inside until I come back?'

'Why?'

'Never mind why, can you just do it now?'

Zoe disappeared back through the curtains, returning a moment later and poking her head back out of the window.

'You've locked it?'

Zoe nodded.

'Now, don't answer the door to anybody but me, OK? Not Dolly or . . . or Bernard. OK? *Nobody* but me.'

'Pinky promise,' said Zoe, hooking her little finger in the air.

Jane lifted hers up. 'Pinky promise. Now close the window and try and get back to sleep. I'll be back soon.'

Jane watched, waiting for the window latch to click shut before heading off down the street. She opened the phone box door, the stench of ammonia taking her breath away. She looked up at the list of useful numbers and dialled the local police station.

'I'm staying at the Forget-Me-Not and . . . well, I'm locked out and I saw something odd. My sister is in there and—'

'Sorry, madam, what do you mean by odd, exactly?'

She thought for a moment, her eyes drifting over the multiple business cards for plumbers, taxis and 'female company'.

'I don't know. These people — Dolly, the daughter, and two others . . . and the woman from the freak show on the pier. They were dragging something in a bin bag.'

'Rubbish?'

'No, it wasn't rubbish. It was . . . I don't know what.'

'Give me the address and I'll have someone pop along in the morning.'

'In the morning? I'm locked out.'

'Do you know anyone that has a key?'

A woman knocked on the glass of the phone box, tapping her watch impatiently. Jane turned her back to her, listening to the operator.

'*We've been very busy tonight, there's a beauty contest on.*'

Jane clutched her sash, 'Yes, I know.'

The woman knocked on the glass again.

'*Now, what was the address? The Forget-Me-Not, you say?*'

Jane slammed the receiver down and pushed open the heavy booth door. The woman brushed past her and into the phone box, uttering expletives to no one in particular. The waft of gin and cigarettes on her breath was a momentary relief from the one of urine Jane was now pushed out of.

She rushed down the promenade, ignoring the attention her bare feet were now attracting and flew into the restaurant to find the table her mum and the others were at was now empty. A waiter was clearing half-empty glasses and a napkin stained by her mum's coral lipstick.

'Where did they go?'

The waiter shook his head, continuing to clear the table.

Jane went back outside to the promenade. A guffaw of laughter rang out from across the road, the group leaning against the iron beach railings. Car horns beeped and revellers called out as she dodged moving cars, running to meet them.

'Where are your shoes, Jane?' her mum said, seeming more lucid out in the cool air.

'I lost them, someone grabbed me and—'

'Grabbed you?' Dave said.

'It's fine,' Jane said sharply. 'Mum, can I have the key please, I want to go back to check on Zoe.'

Marion rolled her eyes. 'She's fine, I'm sure Dolly's got everything in hand.'

'Why don't we all go back to the boarding house?' Charlie suggested. 'Bernard never minds a cheeky after-hours drink.'

'Yes, and he'll be glad of the extra money,' Len said. 'Us locals stick together.'

'Can't we go dancing?' Marion pleaded, spinning around.

Len caught her as she stumbled forward. 'I think you'd be better nearer to your bed.'

Marion playfully slapped him. 'Ooh, Len, what are you saying?'

Len shook his head. 'You women are a law unto yourselves. Now then, let's go and knock Bernard up.'

As they walked back along the promenade, Jane wondered if Bernard would be there to even mind at all.

CHAPTER 30

2022
Zoe

Gary stood outside Dunes talking on his mobile phone.

'No, we can't delay or cancel tonight, don't be ridiculous. It's one dancer gone off in a strop, we can't let it ruin the whole talent show.'

It was two hours before curtains up and there was still no sign of Sophie. Her family and friends had been contacted and nobody had heard from her since that morning. Gary began to pace the wooden boards of the pier, fingers locked in his hair as he shouted into his mobile phone. Holidaymakers glanced in his direction with each expletive he spat, ushering their children away.

'I don't care about what happened forty years ago, I care about tonight. If we cancel, all this hard work will be for nothing.'

Zoe passed him to go into the bar; when he saw her he grimaced. Dan had wanted to come down to Dunes in the hope that Sophie would turn up as if nothing were amiss and resume her part in the show. They had managed to persuade him to wait, and they would let him know if and when she returned.

Inside, Dunes' crew and talent milled around, an electrician was securing cables on the stage and a stage manager was checking the microphones.

'Hey.'

Zoe jumped and spun around to see Dave. She flushed as if he might have known she was planning to leave as soon as she could and forget about the drink later.

'All OK?'

'Yes, just one of the residents at the boarding house who's supposed to be in the show has gone AWOL.'

'So I heard. It's not unusual, first-night nerves and all that.'

'No, I don't think it's that.'

Dave looked at her questioningly. 'What *do* you think?'

Zoe shrugged. 'I don't know, she just didn't seem the type to leave her husband like that. They were so close, or at least they looked it, to me.'

Dave began fiddling with his camera, clicking through the photos he'd taken and studying them. Gary came back in, clapped his hands together loudly as he smiled triumphantly.

'Can I have everybody's attention, please,' he shouted.

Bodies appeared from backstage and the seating area and joined him at the front. Zoe took out her notepad and pen and found a seat a little way back, slinking down in her chair.

'As you may have heard, one of our dancers has pulled out of the show tonight, leaving us one down.'

A couple of the dancers turned to each other, eyebrows raised in incredulity. Clark, who was in full drag, kept his head down, a clipboard clasped to his stomach.

'Fortunately, it isn't too much of a disruption, just that you, Rob—' the dancer looked up at Gary — 'you'll have to improvise a little on the short duo segment. Can you manage that?'

He nodded.

'Excellent, and I'd thank you all to keep your chins up and keep it positive. And whatever you do, please don't post anything about this on social media, we want the focus to be on the show.'

Zoe scribbled in her notepad and underlined the words *insensitive knob*.

One of the cast members' hands shot up. Gary looked flustered, keen to move on.

'Yes, what is it?'

The girl looked nervously around before speaking. 'Erm, well, what if she didn't just pull out, what if—'

'There is nothing to suggest anything else and I'd thank you all to stop with any conspiracy theories.'

The girl slumped back like a wounded puppy as Gary clapped his hands vigorously in the air, calling an end to the meeting.

'Right, I want everyone ready to go in one hour. Stay backstage now and get ready for your calls.'

The dancers and singers pulled themselves up and walked silently out of the room towards the backstage door. Clark waved at Zoe, who gave him the thumbs-up as Gary marched over to her.

'That was a private meeting, you shouldn't have been here.'

'Sorry, I didn't know, I didn't want to disturb you by walking out.'

He eyed her notepad as she slid her hand over it, hoping he hadn't managed to read her opinion of him.

'I don't want anything about this in your article. We've worked very hard to make tonight a success and I refuse to let a two-bit entertainer with stage fright cast a shadow on proceedings.'

Zoe stood up to face him. 'That's a little harsh, don't you think? You have no idea why Sophie isn't here, and to be frank, I don't think you care as long as everything goes well tonight.'

Gary ground his teeth, his cheeks reddening. 'It was a mistake to have you here. You aren't interested in writing anything to promote Sunshine Sands, you're more interested in digging up dirt to make your name.'

'I can assure you I already have a name in journalism, I don't need a girl going missing to make my time here worthwhile, and I find that deeply offensive.'

'I know who you are,' he said, his eyes narrowing.

Zoe tried to keep her cool despite her hands starting to tremble. Gary folded his arms and leaned back a little.

'You're that missing beauty queen's sister. Quite a coup to be here now — you're probably hoping Sophie goes missing so you can write a Netflix documentary.'

'How do you know who I am?'

'You're not the only one who's been doing some digging, Miss Kincade. I've got friends in the media too, you know, journalist friends.' He held up his phone. 'Plus, these days, it takes about ten minutes to find out anybody's history. I know you've been sniffing around.'

A woman carrying brushes and a handful of make-up called Gary over; he held a hand up to her and turned back to Zoe.

'Write one word out of place and you'll have me to deal with. I'll discredit your whole story as a bitter rant from a grieving journalist with a grudge.'

He sauntered over to the woman, leaving Zoe shaken. If he knew who she was, who else did? She looked over to Dave, who mouthed, *All OK?*'

She nodded, putting her bag over her shoulder and leaving.

CHAPTER 31

As soon as the doors opened at Dunes the public began to swarm in. There had been talk of a TV station covering the event, which had brought even more people onto the pier, hoping to be on camera and wave to their families back home. As it was, there were just two other journalists present alongside Zoe, each bringing with them a photographer to snap the reality TV celebrity judges. Gary had had a red carpet put down, running from the entrance to the end of where the pub benches sat outside. Dark clouds gathered in the sky, the rain still holding off as guests arrived, bottlenecking as they stopped to take selfies on the carpet.

Gary had withdrawn Zoe's press privileges. He had asked her to stand with the other journalists outside and informed her that when she did come in, she wouldn't be allowed backstage under any circumstances. She took out her phone to message Dan, to see if there had been any news on Sophie.

She put her phone back in her pocket and made herself busy interviewing attendees on the red carpet, which was now strewn with sand and grey footprints from the damp pier. There was little that would be of use to add to her article, but people were happy to be out and maybe spot a celebrity or two. The rain began to fall in tiny, occasional drops as the last of the audience left the carpet to go into the venue. Zoe sensed a shift in the excitement around her. Holidaymakers began to nudge each other, with whispers of '*Is it him?*' and '*Get a picture, quick.*' On hearing those outside, people began to come back out of the entrance to see what the fuss was about.

Dave, who was busy snapping the arrivals in front of where Zoe stood, lowered his camera and stared ahead as droplets of rain fell on him. Zoe looked to see what everyone was getting so worked up about, and when she spotted him, she froze.

Charlie Bailey took careful steps aided by a silver walking frame and a young woman, who walked at his pace, her hand on his back. His hair was still full and curly, his moustache still thick, but now both were white in colour. If anyone were in doubt it was him, his ubiquitous multi-coloured dickie bow and bright blue braces were there to confirm it. A slow hand-clap began to ripple, the crowds moving towards him. Teens who had no idea who he was started to take photos, gathering that it might earn them likes online.

Gary appeared at the entrance, trying to herd those that had left their seats to go back into the venue. When Gary spotted Charlie, he put his hands to his head, rubbing his temples. Charlie approached where Zoe stood, his eyes that were once bright now slightly red behind thick-lensed glasses, and stopped right in front of Dave. When his female companion checked he was OK, he brushed her away.

'Hello, Dave,' Charlie said, his voice cracked with age and cigarettes. 'I'm surprised to see you're still around these parts. Thought you were long gone.'

Dave said nothing and didn't raise his camera, despite being offered the perfect opportunity to get a newspaper-worthy shot of the one-time star.

With all the cameras snapping and fans shouting, Zoe couldn't hear what Dave said as he leaned forward and spoke to Charlie. Charlie's expression darkened, his teeth grinding behind tight lips. Dave kept his eyes on him as the old man shuffled away, switching his celebrity smile back on for the holidaymakers and the requested selfies.

* * *

Zoe wriggled through the group of people surrounding Charlie in the venue and found her seat. Every other step he held a hand in the air, waving at the audience, each time a cheer rippling around the room. Gary stood in the wings, looking at his watch and then the audience, whose attention was no longer on the show. He marched forward onto the stage, tapping the mic, sending a loud *duff-duff* sound into the room.

'Good evening, ladies and gentlemen, welcome to Dunes Bar and . . .' He trailed off as nobody other than a young couple at the front appeared to be paying attention to him.

'Are you going to do a turn, Charlie?' a man in his sixties called out across the room, his wife and their friends egging him on. 'Go on, Charlie!'

Charlie laughed and nodded his head towards the small staircase leading up to the stage. 'I wouldn't be able to get up those steps.'

A gentle '*booo*' carried around the room, and Charlie, clearly enjoying this moment of adoration, blew kisses to all, as his companion helped him into his seat.

'Charlie — how's your father?' a man called, causing Charlie to grin widely as more cheers rang out.

Any hopes Charlie had of prolonging his moment in the spotlight were dashed when Clark waltzed dramatically onto the stage to 'Disco Inferno'. He wore skyscraper sapphire-encrusted heels, a body-skimming silver evening dress and a long auburn wig. His theatrical make-up had transformed him beyond recognition and his presence turned all attention to the stage. Zoe looked over to Charlie, who shook his head at the spectacle before him.

Clark welcomed the audience to the talent show, and told stories heavy with innuendo that the children didn't understand but giggled at anyway. He finished with a version of 'I Am What I Am', before introducing the dancers to the stage to perform a number from a West End musical. Zoe wondered where Sophie would have been within the group, and where she was right now. Was she somewhere alone, wishing she hadn't left and missing her husband? Or had she never wanted to leave?

Gary appeared before the mic, clapping along with the audience as the dancers spun and sashayed off stage right.

'What a fantastic start to our celebration, I'm sure you all agree. We will now introduce the first three acts of our grand talent show. At the end of the evening it will be up to you who goes home with the Sunshine Sands North Pier Talent Trophy and a fortnight in Turkey, courtesy of local travel agents, Fly Away Travel.' He gave a speech about the history of the pier, ending abruptly when the audience became bored and began to chatter among themselves. A woman got up to go to the toilet or get a drink, trying to exit discreetly.

'Don't go anywhere now, you'll miss the best bit!' Gary called, his tone verging on desperation.

The woman sat back down, red-faced as her friend giggled next to her.

'Now then, all the way from sunny Bradford, the fabulous singing duo Cuts Both Ways.'

The couple walked onto the stage, parting hands as they took their respective mics. Their outfits matched in purple sequinned splendour, he in a suit and she in a tight stretchy minidress. Zoe was taken aback by the quality of their voices, though she knew that you could go into any working men's club in the UK and find talent that would never see the light of day. Fame took more than talent, it was a lot of luck and, more often than not, contacts.

A few of the audience near the door turned to the entrance when they heard the doorman having a scuffle with someone, as Cuts Both Ways valiantly continued. Zoe glanced over to see a forlorn-looking Dan trying to push past the suited man, whose biceps were bigger than rugby balls. She excused herself, trying to stay low down as she made her way along the row of seats, past the audience members who tutted and groaned as she temporarily blocked their view. By the time she reached the doorway she was relieved to see the bouncer consoling Dan rather than manhandling him. He patted his shoulder as Dan stood with his head in his hands.

'Dan, what's going on?' Zoe said.

'They shouldn't be going ahead without her, everyone should be looking.'

The bouncer gave her a look that said he had no idea what was happening. Zoe put her arm around Dan and led him away from the entrance.

'Have you heard anything at all?'

Dan shook his head, leaning against the railings as seagulls circled above.

'Is there someone you could call to come up here and be with you?'

'Sophie's parents are on their way. I felt like such a failure telling them.'

'Failure?'

'A week ago, I stood at the altar and promised them I'd look after her for the rest of her life, and now she's gone.'

Zoe inhaled the sea air. 'You're her husband, not her keeper. If she wants to go off and take some tim—'

'Why is nobody listening? She hasn't *gone off* for some space. She would never do that. Something bad has happened to her, I know it, and I think you do too.'

His face was drawn, but he appeared to be all out of tears now. He was right, the part of Zoe that hoped Sophie just needed space had faded. But how likely was it that forty years after her sister had disappeared, another woman had gone missing under similar circumstances *and* while staying in the same boarding house. The links might be tenuous, but they were links all the same. She thought about the people that tied

Jane and Sophie together, the people they had both met. And one face had been here the entire time: *Dolly*.

* * *

'Wait here a minute,' Zoe said, leaving Dan by the fish-and-chips stand.

Eloise was talking to the actors outside of the Ghost House. They were now in their own casual clothes, ghosts of chalky make-up still visible on scrubbed skin. Eloise waved them away, her long black skirt flapping in the wind. She looked anxiously at her watch, then into the people milling about on the pier.

Dolly appeared like a spectre through the crowds. She looked out of place among the young revellers that now overtook the pier in search of alcohol and good times away from their everyday lives. Dolly approached Eloise, both women talking animatedly. Dolly was carrying a bag, which Eloise peeked into. As they were about to go into the horror house, Zoe called out.

'Eloise.'

Dolly spun round, agitation washing over her face when she spotted Zoe. Zoe walked over regardless, determined to speak to Eloise while she had the chance.

'I thought you were going to the talent show,' Dolly said.

Eloise shifted on the spot, eyeing Zoe and then Dolly nervously.

'Dan came down to Dunes.' She turned to where he stood, anxiously scrolling on his phone. 'He was upset, and I didn't want him to make a fool of himself. Did you know Sophie's parents are on their way here?'

Zoe noted Dolly's pupils darkening as she spoke. 'He should just wait until the morning, we have this in hand.'

Zoe let out an exasperated laugh. 'Dolly, you can't believe Sophie just disappeared like that. It's quite a coincidence, isn't it?' Zoe waited to see if there was any recognition in Dolly's eyes, perhaps guilt. 'He's worried, and rightly so.'

Dolly raised an eyebrow, as if losing your partner was no more than missing a bus. Zoe turned to Eloise.

'I came to the Ghost House earlier.'

Eloise glanced nervously at Dolly.

'Why do you show that film of the beauty contest?'

'It's just old footage, dear, could have been anything.'

'I don't believe you,' Zoe said. 'You two know something about Jane's disappearance.'

Dolly's eyes were blazing, Eloise retreating into herself as if Dolly might explode at any moment.

'Of course we don't,' she spat. 'Do you think we'd stay quiet if we did?'

'Yes, if you were involved in it.'

The words hung in the air between them, Zoe fully prepared for the anger that would come her way, possibly even a baseball bat if there was one handy.

'We know nothing about it,' said Eloise. 'Like Dolly said, if we did, we'd have spoken up.'

Dolly stepped forward and whispered into Zoe's ear, 'Leave this place Zoe, we will be fine. It will all be fine.'

The landlady stood back, her eyes boring into Zoe's. Zoe looked to Eloise, who was nodding slowly, her hand resting on Dolly's shoulder.

'She's right, Zoe, go home.'

CHAPTER 32

1982
Zoe

Zoe threw the bedclothes off, kicking her legs free from the pile of blankets she had cocooned herself in. The room was stuffy and her throat was dry and scratchy. She wandered sleepily into the en-suite bathroom and read the small hand-scribbled sign saying *Not drinking water* above the sink.

Her nightdress clung to her body, sweat drawing the thin cotton to her skin and sticking. She padded back into the bedroom and looked in the cupboards for a can of pop or maybe even little milk sachets left for tea, but there was nothing. Her eyes fell on the bolted door, then flickered to the window and back. She remembered seeing a big bottle of lemonade in the dining room and suddenly nothing seemed more tempting than drinking down those sugary bubbles. Jane would understand, she wouldn't mind her getting a drink — she'd only be a minute, five minutes tops.

Zoe tiptoed onto the landing and into the darkness, disoriented by the lack of lights that normally illuminated the way. She heard voices downstairs and recognised Dolly's. She sounded cross and then sad. She wished she could just ask Dolly for a drink, but then Jane would know she'd left the room and she'd be in trouble. When she reached the top of the stairs, she paused to hear that the voices had quietened. She crept down the carpeted stairs, flinching at each squeak and creak, before scuttling across the hall and into the dining room.

She spotted the large bottle of lemonade on the table in the corner and licked her lips, already anticipating the pleasure of drinking it. Lights and shadows passed by the bay window as cars made their way back and forth along the seafront. Zoe gripped the plastic bottle top in her hand as she clamped the bottle against her body, attempting to open it. She heaved dramatically, her thirst not allowing her to give up and go back to bed.

On the fourth attempt she felt the lid ease and the first rush of fizz escape the bottle with a hiss. The lemonade began to expand and foam, spilling over the lip of the bottle. Zoe held it to her lips, keen to drink and not to leave a trace of her having been there when she should have been tucked up in bed. She gulped greedily and the relief was instant, her thirst quenched. She took the bottle away from her lips, gasping for the breaths she'd just missed while drinking. A large burp escaped from her mouth; she held her hand to her face, hoping she hadn't been heard. A key jangled in the front door and there were voices outside, laughter and overly loud requests to '*ssshhh*'.

Zoe quickly replaced the lid, twisting it tight and placing the bottle back on the table. She heard the door open and the voices became louder and more clear, four men and then the familiar voices of her mum and sister. Her mum's voice sounded funny, like she was speaking in slow motion, and much happier than she normally was. The handle on the dining room door moved down and Zoe ran to the table by the window, scrambling on the floor and underneath it, pulling a chair back as she crouched, watching.

The famous man with the moustache entered the dining room first, the one that everyone was always shouting funny things to. She had laughed too when he shouted, 'How's your father?' even though she didn't know why. The man put his finger to his lips as he led them to the table in the middle of the dining room. Her mum was clinging onto the man who wore the heavy gold chains and seemed in charge of everything. Zoe scowled as she watched Marion stroke his arm and laugh at everything he said, before she let go and slumped heavily onto a chair, still laughing. She didn't recognise this happy, carefree version of her mum and she didn't like it.

The man who took photographs and his friend the journalist, were talking to Jane and she looked sad. Zoe always knew when her sister was worried about something, even though she tried to hide it from her. It was Jane who provided the cuddles and fun for Zoe, her mum the rules and dinners. Zoe wanted to jump out and run to her sister, but she had promised to stay in her bedroom and she had broken the promise — she never broke her promises to Jane.

'I'll need to go and check on Zoe,' Jane said to the man with the camera.

Zoe's face crumpled when she saw him touch her sister's back; something about his familiarity with Jane worried her, but then, Zoe worried about everything. Worry gave way to fear when she realised that soon Jane would know she hadn't done as she was told. Zoe scanned the room, trying to work out how she could pass everyone without being seen and go back to her room and pretend she had been asleep all the time.

The laughter and talk quietened when Dolly appeared at the door. Zoe watched as everyone at the table turned to her. Len's eyes flickered to Charlie and then back to Dolly.

'Dolly, dear, we've just come for a few late-night drinks to celebrate. I'm sure your dad won't mind?'

Dolly picked at her fingernails, her eyebrows stitched in annoyance. The front door slammed shut and Dolly glanced back. Zoe heard footsteps disappearing down the path and the gate opening and closing.

'Is Zoe alright, Dolly?' Marion said. 'Jane's worried something terrible's happened!'

Dolly shot Jane a disgruntled look. 'She's fast asleep, I just checked on her.'

Marion smiled at Jane, but her sister didn't look convinced. Did she know already that she wouldn't stay in the room? Didn't Jane trust her? That upset Zoe, but then again, here she was, stuck under a table because she hadn't done as she was told.

'Is Bernard around? I'm sure he'd like to join us for a drink,' Len said.

'He's away for the night,' Dolly said sharply.

'Away? He was at the contest,' Charlie piped up.

'My aunty called half an hour ago, his mum's very sick. He's gone up to Carlisle to be with her.'

'At this time of night? Couldn't he have waited until the morning?'

'No, it was urgent. They don't think she'll make it much longer.'

'Oh right, well . . . I'm sure he wouldn't mind us being here. We'll clear up after ourselves,' Len said.

Charlie whispered something in Marion's ear, and she let out a raucous laugh. Jane shot her a disapproving look.

'Mum!' she scolded. 'You'll wake the whole street up.'

Marion instantly quietened, putting her hand to her temple in salute. Len got up from his chair and wandered over to the door, his arms held out wide towards Dolly. He pulled her into him, her body stiff and unyielding in his embrace.

'Why don't you join us, Dolls, have a bit of a break, eh?'

Dolly wriggled away. 'Leave me alone.'

Len flushed. 'Don't be like that, Dolly.'

Zoe peered up at the faces in the room, now all serious. Jane seemed worried about something. Zoe didn't like it. She didn't like any of it. The way her mum was being silly and childish, the way the men touched her and her sister. She was glad Dolly had said that to the important man.

'Now then, Dolly,' Charlie said, rising from his chair, 'no need for that, Len was only being friendly.'

As he walked towards Dolly, she retreated back, her hands in front of her as if protecting herself. She reminded Zoe of a feral cat they had once found on their road and tried to capture. The faint scars still lined Zoe's forearms where she had tried and failed to grab it and it had drawn its claws across her skin.

'Leave her,' Jane said.

Charlie stopped and turned to Jane. 'Leave her? You make it sound like I'm going to hurt her.' He smiled. 'Nothing could be further from the truth — we love our Dolly, don't we?' Charlie placed an arm around Dolly's shoulder and brought her further into the room. 'Now, come and sit down and have a drink with us, enjoy yourself. You're putting a dampener on the party. Jeremy, get a drink for Dolly.'

Marion grimaced as Dolly was placed next to her, the young girl staring straight ahead. Jeremy poured wine into a glass and pushed it towards her.

'Why don't we put some music on?' Charlie said. 'Have a little party, eh?'

Jane went to the door.

'Where are you off to?' Charlie said.

'I'm just going to check on Zoe.'

Marion swayed to the radio playing hits from the sixties. 'You worry too much.'

Jane turned to her, unable to hide the spite in her voice. 'And you don't worry enough.'

CHAPTER 33

1982
Jane

Jane closed the dining room door behind her and ran up the stairs. The voices in the dining room echoed throughout the boarding house, but those behind the closed bedroom doors stayed silent. Jane knocked gently on their door.

'Zoe?' she whispered.

There was no answer, which given it was now the early hours wasn't a surprise. Her little sister could sleep through a thunderstorm. Jane went to rattle the handle to rouse her, concern spiking when the door opened. She had taken the bolt off.

The room was in darkness, just the faint glow from the streetlights illuminated the closed curtains.

'Zoe, are you OK?'

Jane tiptoed over to the put-up bed by the window. The bedclothes had been thrown to the side, the bed empty. She turned to the double bed, still perfectly made. She called out louder, 'Zoe?'

Walking over to the bathroom, she pushed the door open and turned on the light. Her make-up was still scattered around the sink, a damp towel hanging on the cold radiator. Jane ran out of the room and back downstairs, checking the kitchen and a broom cupboard. She noticed a faint light beneath the cellar door in the hall, the same door she had seen the three figures disappearing into.

In the dining room she could hear Charlie teasing Dolly about her make-up and dresses, her mum playfully chastising the comedian for being so mean.

The cellar door opened and she stepped through. A single lightbulb swung from a wire above. Beyond the bottom of the stairs, darkness. Surely Zoe wouldn't have come down here? She walked slowly down the steps; when she reached the bottom, she hesitated.

'Zoe?' she called out softly.

In the darkness she could only make out the shapes of boxes: a storage room. Jane was about to turn and go back when a hand clasped her mouth and a face leaned into her.

'You shouldn't be down here.'

CHAPTER 34

1982
Zoe

Zoe crouched under the table, waiting for her sister to burst back into the dining room and tell everyone she wasn't in her room. She was going to be in a lot of trouble. Her mum would blame her for spoiling the night, but worse than that, she had let her sister down. Jane was her best friend, better than Martha or Beverly in her school class. They would fall out with her if she didn't want to play chase or make daisy chains in the summer, but Jane never ever fell out with her or made her feel bad.

Zoe watched as Marion danced alone in the corner of the room by the drinks trolley. Dolly had left the room — to help Jane look for her, she suspected. Now just her mum and the others remained, the man in chains' head dropping up and down as he nodded off, his hand still clutching a whiskey glass.

When her mum turned her back to pour another drink and the men chatted among themselves, Zoe took her chance. She gently pushed the chair beside her out from under the table and crawled across the floor, stopping each time one of the adults looked like they might turn and notice her.

'Another whiskey, Len?' Marion said.

When she saw Len was sleeping, she shrugged and continued dancing, trying to sing along to the song on the radio but always a line behind.

Zoe scrambled to the door, almost making it, when she tripped over a ruffle in the carpet and fell to the floor.

'What are you doing in here?' Jeremy said. 'Shouldn't you be in bed by now?'

Marion turned to see what the commotion was about. 'Zoe, whatever are you up to?'

'I was thirsty, Mum, I needed a drink.'

'Leave her be,' Charlie said. 'No harm done.'

Marion tutted and took a swig of her drink. Zoe's cheeks flushed at the attention she was getting, and her palms were sore from the fall to the carpet.

The photographer offered her a glass of water. 'We'd best let your sister know you're OK, she was very worried about you.'

CHAPTER 35

2022
Zoe

Zoe's phone buzzed in her pocket; she took it out.

Dave: *All OK? Where did you go?*

'We should be getting on, Dolly,' Eloise said, nodding to two policemen who wandered by.

Zoe looked back at Dan, who spotted the officers and began to make his way over to where they had stopped by the entrance of Dunes. She glanced at her watch: it was 9 p.m. She messaged Dave back to say she was just getting some food.

Dave: *Phew, thought you'd done a runner for a moment!*

She could leave now and be back home in the early hours, but the journalist in her needed to wait, to see what had happened to Sophie. If her editor found out about the missing girl, she would expect Zoe to have stayed and found out what she could. Missing-women stories were all the rage, they had been since tabloid journalism had begun. Especially, she had learned early on, when the victim was young, blonde and female.

Zoe watched as Dolly and Eloise disappeared into the gloom of the Ghost House, cotton spiderwebs above their heads as the door closed and locked behind them. Gary had joined the policemen and Dan at the entrance, his face flushed and his brow creased in frustration. He led the police away from Dan, his arms gesticulating wildly. When the police turned to go, Dan followed them as they made their way back up the pier past Zoe.

'You OK, Dan?' Zoe called.

He ignored her, still pleading with the policemen, who appeared exasperated by his presence.

She turned to the Ghost House, where a gaggle of teenagers stood at the entrance, pushing at the door that was locked hours before closing time. Every other attraction on the pier was alive with flashing lights, spinning rides and music. Deflated, they left and made their way to the waltzers.

Applause rang out from Dunes, signalling an interval, and audience members appeared through the entrance for fresh air and nicotine. She walked around the rear of the Ghost House searching for another door. There was an emergency exit next to a wheelie bin that was overflowing with beer cans and fast-food cartons. Zoe looked around, making sure that she wasn't seen, before dragging an empty crate over and stepping onto it and then onto the bin, the lid collapsing slightly under her weight. She squinted into a window, wiping the sea-salt smears away with her sleeve. It was a museum storeroom, the limbs of disused mannequins and props scattered across the floor like a battlefield. A row of discarded waxwork heads sat on a shelf, waiting for their chance to be reunited with a body when required for an exhibit. A black spider crawled across a thick cobweb in the corner of the window — not all horrors in this room were pretend. Zoe gasped, steadying herself so as not to fall back onto the wooden boards of the pier in disgrace. A light flashed on in the room and Zoe ducked down slightly as Eloise entered, followed by Dolly.

The women were searching dusty shelves and boxes, occasionally taking something down to inspect it. Eloise pulled out a ball of twine, handing it to Dolly, who put it in a polyester shopping bag. The two women had the kind of synchronicity with each other which only comes with years of familiarity. Eloise, the eccentric fortune teller and funfair heir, and Dolly, the strict, suspicious landlady of a crumbling boarding house. Geography had brought them together, but something more bound them. Why had Dolly sought out Eloise today when one of her residents was missing, when the eyes of suspicion were likely to focus in on the Forget-Me-Not once again? Tea and a chat would be understandable, it was normal to seek out friendship, and perhaps she thought Eloise might have some insight, given her gift — but trawling the basement of the Ghost House for props?

Dolly had appeared fond of Sophie, pleased that she had chosen the boarding house, like her family before her. Sophie's nan had a connection to Jane as a fellow contestant, but nothing had spooked her enough to put off the rest of the family returning.

Eloise pulled out a box from underneath a table and spun the reels on a small combination padlock. She unhooked it and opened the box as Dolly looked on. There was some chat between the two of them before Eloise pulled out something heavy. A satisfied grin crept across the landlady's mouth as Eloise held up the gold mayoral chains and handed them to her.

***

Charlie Bailey appeared through the doors of Dunes, his companion carrying his coat and bags while still trying to navigate him down the wooden pier. Zoe straightened herself up, took a deep breath and made her way to meet him. There were no gawkers or fans following him now, the initial excitement of his presence now dissolved. Zoe looked at her phone: it was still only 9.45 p.m.

'Has the show finished?' Zoe asked, getting his attention.

He looked into her eyes, and she waited for some spark of recognition, her heart racing.

'Another interval,' he said in a gruff voice. 'My back's playing up, I couldn't take another minute sitting in those cheap chairs they use nowadays. Did you want an autograph?' He turned to his companion. 'Debby, there's some photos in that bag — get one out, will you?'

'No,' Zoe said.

Charlie turned back to Zoe as the companion let the pre-signed image fall back into the tote bag.

'I wonder . . .' Zoe started, not having planned for this moment, or even wanting it. 'I wonder, would you have a few minutes to chat?'

'Chat?'

'Yes, I'm a journalist with the *National Mail*.'

Charlie's eyes lit up, a hint of the former showman suddenly appearing before her eyes. 'In that case, yes.'

'Are you free now?' Zoe asked.

He looked to Debby, who shook her head. 'Charlie needs to get back to the hotel and take his painkillers.'

'I'll be right as rain once the horse pills kick in.'

'Of course,' Zoe said. 'I could always meet you there in half an hour or so, maybe the seating is better at your hotel?' She smiled hopefully.

'He needs his sleep,' Debby interrupted.

'I'm not dead yet,' Charlie snapped. 'Yes, why don't you meet me in the bar at the Parade in half an hour. It's been a long time since I had a drink with a pretty lady.'

Charlie took Zoe's hand, holding it as he bent slowly to kiss it. She watched, horrified as his wiry moustache brushed her skin. She took her hand back, resisting the urge to rub it dry on her trousers.

'Perfect, I'll see you at about ten fifteen?'

Debby rolled her eyes, clearly tired of chaperoning Charlie up and down all day.

'Aye, I'll see you there. Are you thinking of writing a feature on me?'

Zoe was taken aback by his assumption that forty years after his summer season was cancelled and his TV show canned, he might steal a full page of a national publication.

'Perhaps, let's have a chat and see where it goes.'

He turned slowly, almost going over his frame when one of the legs got caught in the slats of the pier. Debby rushed to help him, and he batted her away.

'*Stop fussing.*'

As they disappeared out of sight, Zoe was already beginning to run through the questions she might ask him. He was clearly eager to speak to anyone that would listen — why else trudge all this way to be in a pier-end audience? Then she remembered being told of this phenomenon regarding former stars. When the lights fade and the attention goes to newer talent, they will bring themselves to public places — a hit of recognition igniting and fuelling that deep desire to be loved and admired again. Charlie had certainly had that tonight; he had made more of an impression than anyone else in Dunes. She wondered why Gary hadn't encouraged him more, given him the spotlight he so desperately desired and the audience he craved.

One thing was for certain, whatever his involvement around the time when Jane went missing, he couldn't be anything to do with Sophie. He could barely move himself around, let alone another woman.

Zoe took out her phone and called Dan. There was no answer, but as soon as she hung up a message appeared.

No news.

A giant roar of cheers echoed from within Dunes, followed by whistles and shouts. Zoe made her way back, standing in the doorway just in time to see Cuts Both Ways jumping up and down on the stage, a cannon shooting metallic gold confetti into the air. Clark was attempting to separate the winners from the gracious hugs of the runners-up and corral them to the centre of the stage. A sickness rose within Zoe, as if some kind of forty-year alarm was ringing inside her body. Memories flashing of her mum jumping to her feet and clutching Zoe tightly, caught up in Jane's win. She had never felt that level of affection before or since from Marion. It hadn't mattered that it had been because of Jane, she was just happy to have had it.

The singing duo held the trophy aloft, as the *Passion Island* reality stars aimed their media-trained smiles at Dave, who stood in front of the stage taking photographs. The triumphant singers were ushered off to make way for the song and dance finale, Clark taking the lead. A few of the audience members had left their seats, dancing in front of the stage and clapping along to lip-synced Diana Ross and Tina Turner. Clark was in his element, and as much as Gary irked her, she had to admit he had put on quite a show for a small seaside town whose glory days were a distant memory.

* * *

Zoe sat in the Parade Hotel bar sipping her second Diet Coke.

'Can I get you anything else, love? Only, I'm shutting down in five minutes.'

Zoe glanced up at the clock above the optics: it was 10.20 p.m. Charlie had likely gone back to his room and fallen asleep. He was in his eighties, and he had come a long way, for barely half a night out. She paid for her drinks and left the bar, heading into reception. She wrote her name and number on a scrap of paper in her handbag and handed it to the receptionist.

'Excuse me, could you give this to Charlie Bailey, please?'

The receptionist took it and placed it in a pigeon hole on the wall behind the counter. 'Still a rum old bugger, isn't he?'

'Sorry?' Zoe asked.

The woman grinned. 'Charlie. He'd not been here five minutes and was trying it on with one of the housekeepers. Honestly, I hope I'm still that vital when I'm in my eighties.'

'I hope she put in a complaint.'

The woman looked at Zoe quizzically. 'Complaint? It's Charlie Bailey! She'll more likely be shouting about it all over her social media.'

'Could you just make sure he gets my number in the morning? I won't disturb him while he's asleep.'

'Asleep? He's still out, probably on the pull!' she cackled.

'Well, I doubt his companion will let him get up to too much,' Zoe said, trying not to be too put out that he'd stood her up for the interview.

'What companion?'

'His carer, Debby?'

The receptionist screwed up her nose. 'Oh, aye. Well, she was only helping him today. She normally works in the kitchen here, but does a bit of agency work on the side, you know, with the elderly. He offered a few quid for someone to help him out and she jumped at the chance. I saw her walking past about half an hour ago, back home to her kids, no doubt.'

The thought of Charlie Bailey out on the pull in the town on his own was bemusing but also concerning; he was frail even with a walking frame. She was sure though that Debby had not had a say in his decision to go on alone and was likely thankful that her night with the grumpy ex-star was over.

***

As the audience left Dunes, the fairground sideshow workers welcomed the new influx of customers with offers of *'three shots for one'* and *'ride twice, pay once!'* Zoe watched as ping-pong balls landed in wooden barrels, only to bounce straight back out to the groans of the customer. She walked around to the stage door, glancing in the windows to see the cleaners and Colin stacking chairs and wiping down surfaces sticky with beer and pop. Clark flew out, beaming, followed by several of the dancers and the talent acts. A small crowd of holidaymakers pushed their children forward, little hands holding out pieces of paper and pens towards the performers. Clark happily signed away, exchanging pleasantries and leaning in for selfies.

'I take it all went well?' Zoe asked when the last of the autograph hunters had left.

'Didn't you see it?' Clark said, a hint of disappointment in his voice.

'Some of it. I had to leave when Dan turned up, otherwise that might have become the show for the night.'

A couple of his fellow performers ran up behind him and hugged him. 'You were amazing! Coming for a drink in town?'

'Sure, you fancy it?' he asked Zoe.

She smiled apologetically. 'Maybe later?'

Dave walked around the side of the building and joined them. 'You ready?'

Clark looked from Dave to Zoe, a flash of confusion across his face. The two dancers tugged at his arm, before dragging Clark away as Zoe and Dave headed back down the pier towards the promenade. She paused for a moment at the Ghost House, the lights still on.

'Closed, I'm afraid,' Dave said, pointing at the sign.

'I wonder why, it's early for the pier.'

He shrugged. 'Who knows what goes on in the mind of that mad old bird.'

Zoe didn't like the way he talked about Eloise, that old-school terminology that belonged in the history books. He registered her face.

'Oh, I'm sure she's OK really, but enough years palled up with Dolly and anyone would go a bit loopy.'

They continued walking, weaving in and out of the night-time crowd, crop tops and short-sleeved shirts at odds with the chilly evening.

'I spoke to Charlie earlier,' Zoe said.

Dave came to a halt. 'What about?'

She laughed, surprised at the strange tone of his voice. 'Not a lot really, as it turned out. He was supposed to meet me in his hotel bar but didn't show.'

Dave's shoulders relaxed. 'Right, well, he was never known for his respect of other people's time. I guess not much changes.'

'It was just on an off-chance anyway, I doubt anything would have come from it.'

Dave was about to speak when he was drowned out by a police car and ambulance that sped along the promenade in front of them, the crowds of people oblivious to the noise and flashing lights.

'Here we are,' Dave said, pressing a remote and unlocking the doors of his car.

'Oh, I thought we were going for a drink?'

'Town will be rammed tonight, besides I've got much better wine than the cheap stuff they flog around here.'

He walked around to the passenger side and opened the door. Zoe paused, not wanting to seem rude, but also not wanting to be stuck somewhere miles away from the boarding house.

'I'll call you a taxi from mine, it's not far away,' he said, as if reading her mind. 'Honestly, Sunshine Sands on a Saturday night? You'll thank me for saving you from it.'

Zoe slid into the low seat of the Porsche. He glanced back down the promenade.

'Can you see anything?' Zoe asked.

'No, I suspect it's a drunken brawl in one of the bars, a regular Saturday-night occurrence, I'm afraid. There's more police cars than ice cream vans in Sunshine Sands.'

Zoe flinched as the door slammed shut. Dave walked around to the driver's side and slid in, putting his seat belt on. He looked at her, waiting.

'What?' She noted his belt. 'Oh, yes.' She pulled her own seat belt over her shoulder and clicked it into place.

A couple of young men were admiring the car, giving satisfied smiles when Dave revved the engine to pull away. Cars had never been one of Zoe's things — if it got her from A to B without a wheel falling off or the engine steaming, it was good enough. The attention of the crowds caused her to dip in her seat, hiding her face. Dave kept his eyes on the road, smiling as they sped away.

'Do you think it went well?' Zoe asked.

He turned to her, a look of confusion on his face.

'The show tonight?'

'Oh right, of course. Well, it's hardly *Britain's Got Talent*, but they did a fair job. With the reality TV stars in attendance, they'll be sure to get some coverage in the tabloids tomorrow. I've already sent the photos off to them, so we'll see.'

'Strange to see Charlie turn up, why do you think that was?'

She studied Dave's face in the half-light of the night, multi-coloured hues reflecting on his skin.

'A last grasp at fame, I expect. Sad really, he should have stayed away, left the stage in his prime.'

'He seemed surprised to see you,' Zoe said, keeping her voice light. 'Annoyed, even.'

'He was annoyed alright, annoyed I didn't take his photograph. He knows it'll be mine that make the big papers.'

Zoe wondered what had happened in the intervening years, or maybe they had never seen eye to eye, not even back then. It was Len who was Charlie's friend; perhaps the mayor's closeness to such a sleazy entertainer had bothered him.

As they drove along the promenade and up into town, bright coloured lights were replaced by yellowish streetlights, which lit pavements littered with crisp packets and beer cans that rattled around the concrete.

'The nice part of town,' Dave quipped.

Further up the hill they passed the nursing home where she had met Bob — or rather, ambushed him.

'Where they put you out to pasture,' said Dave.

Zoe didn't mention that she'd been there. She took out her phone, to check if there were any messages from the kids.

'I'm afraid the signal's a bit patchy up here, the back of beyond,' Dave said, as Zoe watched the one bar remaining disappear.

He turned into a wide driveway, a strip of ornamental lights lining the edges of perfectly manicured lawns. The large Edwardian house looked like something from a movie.

'Nice digs,' said Zoe, looking over to a summer house and water fountain. 'I'm clearly on the wrong side of the newspaper business.'

As soon as the words left her mouth, she felt foolish. It made her sound bitter and resentful of any success he'd had.

'Well, it was left to me, but there's still quite a lot of upkeep. I've done OK, though.'

'Were you related to Len?'

The car came to a sharp halt on the gravel. Dave turned his body to her. His curious expression jolted her a little, but she continued.

'I mean—' she gestured towards the water feature on the lawn — 'it's quite an inheritance.'

'I suppose I was like a son to him; he had no children of his own. And besides,' he grinned mysteriously, 'I knew all his secrets.'

'Secrets?' Zoe said, feeling a spike of fear coursing through her body.

'Yes, the fiddling of the books and backhanders. He must have felt some kind of need to keep me sweet, even in death. Does it matter?'

'Not really, I'm just trying to piece together the history.'

A flash of amusement crossed his face. 'The town isn't that complicated really — aside from tourists, it's just the council and the businesses. My friendships with people in high places isn't something I think about. Besides, it's common knowledge around here. Everything is, that's why I spend most of my time in London.'

He turned the engine off and climbed out. Zoe would never normally wait for a man to open her door, but somehow, she felt this was de rigueur for Dave and she waited while he walked round and let her out. Before them was a warmly lit porch, topiary swirls in giant plant pots either side of the door.

'Come this way,' Dave said, taking her hand and leading her around the side of the house to a lawned area in the garden.

Zoe looked ahead to a panoramic view of the sea, Sunshine Sands twinkling in the distance.

'Not a bad view,' he said.

'It's beautiful up here,' she replied. 'Peaceful too.'

They stood in silence for a moment as a windchime tinkled behind them. Zoe wondered if this was some kind of romantic preamble, if he would slowly turn and take her in his arms.

'Right, a drink then,' Dave said, cutting her thoughts short as he walked back to the house.

'Will it be easy enough for me to order a taxi home later?'

'No problem at all, I have them on speed dial.'

Zoe followed him across the lawn and round to the front door, a lion's head knocker gleaming from the porch light above.

* * *

Dave switched on the radio, smooth jazz playing from expensive retro speakers. He poured two glasses of wine while Zoe scanned his bookshelves, hoping his reading material was better than his music choices. It was a habit she exercised whenever she was in somebody else's house, a literary DNA test that gave her a blueprint of the person who collected them. There were four shelves dedicated solely to photography, giant glossy books stacked on top of each other. On the novel front, his tastes were varied: James Patterson, Paul Theroux, Oscar Wilde and Lee Child.

'Who's your favourite author?' he asked, handing her a glass of wine.

Zoe thought for a moment, a voice inside her head toying with honesty versus the need to be seen as at least a little academic.

'Depends on my mood, but mostly dark thrillers — Mo Hayder, that kind of thing.'

'I thought you'd be more romcom.'

'Well, just goes to show you can never judge a book by its cover then, doesn't it?'

'I guess I thought you might prefer some lighter reads, given some of the dark things you've seen in your work as a journalist.'

Zoe took a sip of wine and shrugged. 'The serious stuff was a long time ago. I don't think seaside towns and the rise of rural living is exactly the stuff of nightmares.'

Dave smiled, his eyes meeting hers. They were bright blue, but in this lowly lit living room they appeared much darker. He leaned forward, as if he were about to kiss her, then reached past her.

'Here—' he handed her a hardback book — 'some of my work in print.'

It was clear to Zoe it had been self-published: the font was slightly dated and the publisher's logo on the spine matched his initials: D.C. She put her wine down and opened the book. Though the unprofessional font continued, the photographs, like all the ones he had shown her so far, were very good.

'Impressive.'

'Thank you. It sells quite well, probably for the wrong reasons.'

'Wrong reasons?'

'Well, Sunshine Sands is famous — or should I say, infamous — for *other things*, isn't it? People search the town and *hey presto*, my book appears.'

Zoe stopped flicking through the pages and closed the book, handing it back to Dave. She took another gulp of wine.

'I should probably think about getting a taxi back, I didn't realise how tired I was.'

'Really?' He looked like a little boy whose favourite toy had been taken away.

'You must be tired too?' she said, not wanting to offend him. 'It's been a long day.'

She yawned as an overwhelming tiredness enveloped her, a sudden need to sleep.

'Finish your wine and I'll call a taxi, they're pretty quick to come.'

He led her over to the lounge area of the open-plan room. She sunk into a plush velvet sofa with carved walnut arms. Dave put his book on the coffee table and sat at the other end, leaning against the arm.

'So, have you got what you came for, more answers?' he said.

She blinked, trying to rouse herself. 'More questions than answers, but at least I have enough for the article I need to submit.'

'That's great. Then back to your normal life?'

She nodded, and thought about her *normal* life. For the last day or two she had been drawn into the strange town again, its secret society of residents that held the past's secrets like prized gems. Normal life suddenly seemed very appealing.

'Are you OK?' Dave asked. 'Would you like some water?'

'Yes, it seems I can't take my wine tonight.'

Dave got up from the sofa and went to the sink, running the water, before filling a tall glass and bringing it back to her. He took a coaster from a stack and put it on the low coffee table in front of her.

'I suppose the only problem with being the photographer,' Zoe said, 'is that you're never documented in the story.'

Dave looked at her quizzically, sitting down again. 'That's fine by me. I want to tell the story, not be part of it.'

'Why did you move away for so long? Or more to the point, why come back here?'

'I left to make a name for myself, and London is the obvious choice for anyone in the arts. And to answer the second question, well, I still have this place and it's a bolthole by the sea. Yes, the town leaves a lot to be desired, but up here I could be looking down on any coastline in England. And I have my memories here, of course.'

'Good ones, I assume?' Zoe said, taking glugs of water to quench the sudden thirst.

He cupped the wine glass, slowly turning it back and forth. 'Yeah, mainly good ones. It's a different place now, but like I said, it's somewhere to take a break.'

'How often do you visit?'

'What is this, an interview?' he joked, taking a sip from his glass.

'Sorry, force of habit.'

He was right, she knew that. It was only when she had moved back north to bring up the children that her own career had floundered. Now everything was easier with video calls and social media. Back then, if you weren't meeting over a glass of wine in smoky pubs in Soho, then you weren't in the loop and your career ground to a halt.

'So, did you come back now just for a break? Or was the lure of the talent show too great to resist?'

Her laughter faded as his face darkened. She had made a fair comment, she wanted to know. He relaxed back into the sofa.

'Well, it's the first big event the resort has held in decades and post-Covid, it might just be the regeneration of the place. I wanted to be here to witness it. Photograph it. I do still care about the place, and I have this place, so a vested interest.'

Zoe looked around the room and out through the large bay windows to the water feature: an illuminated mermaid, water trickling down her fishtail and into a large pond. She estimated the house must be worth close to a million. The views were spectacular and the house itself was impressive by anybody's standards.

'And how does it feel? Coming back, I mean?' Zoe felt her head suddenly drop forward, as if she might fall asleep.

'Time to call the cab?' He smiled, not moving from the sofa.

Zoe rallied herself, shaking her head to rouse herself. 'Yes, if you don't mind. I don't know what's wrong with me.'

'It's the sea air.' He reached to a side table, taking a telephone from its cradle and dialling a number.

Zoe leaned forward and leafed through the book again as he ordered a taxi. There was a black-and-white image of a graveyard, a beautiful church high on a hill with the sea just visible in the distance. A vicar was standing by an open grave, his prayer book in hand as he appeared to preach to the mourners. There were many, but Zoe's eyes fell on a woman standing back, under a tree. A small boy stood next to her, holding her hand. The caption below read: *The funeral of Len Erwitt — former mayor of Sunshine Sands*. She turned the page, another familiar face before her.

'Oh my God, that's my mum,' Zoe said, her eyes fixed on a photograph of a dinner table in the boarding-house dining room.

'I remember her well,' Dave said.

'You do?' Zoe said, his words shocking her into consciousness again.

He was suddenly beside her on the sofa, his fingers stroking her arm. Zoe moved slightly, feeling his fingers fall away. She began to search her mind for more of that night, a night that was moving from the recesses of her mind, slowly revealing itself to her. She had been naughty. She had left her room and felt guilty, afraid, and then Jane had gone.

'I remember this, this night.' Zoe tried her best not to let her memory fail her as the images brought everything to the forefront for the first time in forty years. 'It's the last time I saw Jane. I was there, in the room.'

Zoe fought the fog of sleep that was pushing down on her.

'Yes, you were, I saw you hiding under the table.' Dave placed his hand on her back, fingers brushing up and down her spine. 'You thought nobody knew you were there, but I saw you.'

Zoe felt her phone vibrate in her pocket. She must have shifted into a spot with signal.

'Can I use your bathroom?' she asked.

He directed her to a small room in the hallway, the walls pasted with William Morris wallpaper and a candle filling the air with the scent of roses. Zoe sat on the toilet with the lid down and took out her phone. It was a DM from Carys, the girl who had contacted her through Friendbook.

Hi Zoe,

I spoke to Mum again this morning to see if there was anything else she could remember. She's going to try and dig out some photos for me. Here are some of the main things:

She remembers a photo call at the beach. They had to wear really tight shorts and T-shirts. She said the men were really pervy even though their wives were there! She doesn't seem particularly bothered by it TBH, said it was just the way things were.

She met a famous TV presenter called Charlie Bailey. They were all a bit starstruck and even though he was much older, a few were desperate to be seen with him. He actually invited my mum to his hotel room, but her boyfriend was there so there was no way that was happening. She saw Jane with him at his hotel — it annoyed her at the time and thought that's why she won.

My mum and the others were warned not to speak to the newspapers about the incident (Jane going missing). Apparently, they were told they'd be sued and wouldn't be able to enter the competition again or any others in the northwest. Basically, they'd ruin their careers.

There was a photographer there, she can't remember his name, but he was young. She caught him a few times taking photos of the girls while they weren't looking and complained about him to the organisers, but they didn't do anything. She saw him with Jane a few times that weekend and noticed on the day of the competition she seemed really uncomfortable around him. After she went missing, my mum did go to the police in Sunshine Sands and tell them this, but again, nothing came of it.

I hope that helps?
Carys x

'You OK in there?' Dave called from the hallway.

'Won't be a minute,' she replied.

Zoe stood up, pacing back and forth in the tiny space, trying to get her thoughts in order and buy some time. It wasn't only Dolly that had connections to the two missing women — Dave had too. She thought about her visit to see Bob Previtt, and the way he had seemed haunted when she showed him the photograph of Jane. She remembered his words, *'Photographs lie.'*

Photographs did lie, she knew that, you only had to look at social media. But his statement hadn't been anything to do with filters and fake lives. He had meant *photographers* lie.

'Zoe?'

She opened the toilet door to find him waiting for her. He looked down to the phone in her hand as the music on the radio stopped and the news cut in:

'A young woman has been found dead on Sunshine Sands beach tonight. The police have yet to confirm the identity, but there are concerns it is a dancer who went missing earlier in the day, a Mrs Sophie Ashcroft.'

CHAPTER 36

1982
Jane

The hand fell away from Jane's face and Dolly rushed her down the basement stairs, away from the others. On the floor in front of them lay a body partially obscured by the bin bags it was hidden in.

'What have you done, Dolly?' Jane cried, staring down at the arm that had fallen free from the plastic.

There was little else down there, but for a few crates filled with old newspapers and a broken chair from the dining room.

'When it's me he does it to, it's OK, I'm used to it.'

'What's OK?' Jane said, still trying to make sense of the terrifying situation she had suddenly found herself in. Dolly tilted her head as if studying the form of her lifeless father, no trace of emotion on her face.

Jane's thoughts returned to the reception in the Chinese restaurant, Bernard's hand on Dolly's backside. He was a strange man, Jane knew that. Lurking around without reason, treating Dolly like a slave, binding her to the boarding house. She didn't seem to have any life outside of the place and her only acquaintances appeared to be the men that her dad knew.

'I caught him going into your bedroom earlier tonight. He was standing over Zoe while she was sleeping.'

'Zoe? My God! What did he do?'

'He pulled the covers down, lifted her nightdress up—'

Jane felt the adrenaline coursing through her veins, a sickness rising.

'Did he . . . ?'

'No, I stopped him,' Dolly said coldly, staring down at her dad.

'Oh, Dolly,' she exhaled. 'How long has he been . . .' She trailed off, not wanting to say the words.

'Abusing me? For as long as I can remember.'

'And nobody ever suspected? Nobody helped you?'

Dolly crouched down, taking the lifeless arm and stuffing it back in the bin bag. 'Who was I going to tell? Half the town is at it.'

'Half the . . . you mean Charlie?'

Dolly regarded her, her dark expression confirming Jane's fears.

'And Len?'

Before Dolly could answer there was a knock on the door upstairs, footsteps moving along the hallway and the creak of the front door.

'Oh God,' Jane said, 'the police, I called the police. I was just panicking over Zoe, and you wouldn't let me in and—'

Dolly put a finger to her sealed lips as Charlie spoke.

'Evening, Bob, what brings you here? Fancy a drink?'

Jane tiptoed across to the bottom of the stairs, straining to hear.

'On duty, I'm afraid. We had a call earlier, a girl saying something about a bin bag in the cellar and being locked out.'

'Eh?'

'That's what I thought. Anyway, as it was the Forget-Me-Not, I thought I'd better check it out for Bernard's sake.'

'Looks like you've had a wasted trip, nothing to see here.'

Dolly and Jane both looked to the heap on the floor as the policeman said his goodbyes and the front door closed.

'What are you going to do with him?' Jane hissed.

'Don't you worry about that. I have a plan.'

The door at the top of the cellar opened.

'Is somebody down there?' Dave called out.

Jane ran towards the stairs before he came down. 'Hi,' she said, making her way up.

'What are you up to?' he asked, looking over her shoulder, amusement on his face.

Jane wiped down the dust from her dress. 'I was looking for Zoe and—'

'Zoe's in the dining room with your mother, the little scamp was hiding under a table.'

Jane felt a rush of relief, for a split-second forgetting what she had just seen. As she closed the cellar door, there was a muffled sneeze from below.

'What was that?' Dave said, stopping suddenly.

'What? I didn't hear anything.'

He looked at Jane, then pushed her to the side and flung the cellar door open, his footsteps disappearing into the darkness. Jane waited, unsure whether to run and tell her mum and try to get them all away from the boarding house. Before she had a chance to think further, Dave appeared again, his eyes blazing as he marched to the dining room, coming back with Charlie and Jeremy.

'What are you on about?' Charlie said. 'What body?'

'I told you there was something fishy about that call to the police.' Dave lowered his voice to a whisper. 'Dolly has *killed* Bernard. It's his body that was wrapped in the bin bag, that's what whoever called the police station was on about.'

'Jesus Christ!' Charlie gasped.

Jeremy looked ashen. 'What the hell are we going to do?' he whimpered.

'We?' Charlie exclaimed. 'We aren't the ones that are at fault here! It's that murdering nutcase Dolly.'

'But if we report this to the police, who knows what she'll come out with to defend herself? We'll all be in trouble. The stuff we've covered up, she knows everything! We'll all be finished.'

'Where's Dolly now?' Charlie asked.

'Down there,' Dave said. 'She's not going anywhere for the time being. I've made sure of that.'

The three men appeared unaware of Jane's presence for a while, voicing their options, justifying the reasons. Then Jeremy turned to her.

'And what about her?' Jeremy said. 'What does she know?'

CHAPTER 37

Zoe ran out from the dining room and into the hall and hugged Jane; her warmth soothed Jane's icy cold skin.

'I was worried about you,' Jane said, her body now trembling.

'I was thirsty, I—'

'It's OK, just go to your room now, alright?'

Jane stood before Zoe, her hand on her shoulder. Zoe looked like she was about to cry, tears welling in her eyes. Jane crouched down before her and held her hands tightly.

'I'll be up soon, I promise. Pinky promise.'

Zoe fiddled with the cuffs of her nightie. 'Why have you got dirt on you?' She pointed at the smears on Jane's dress.

'I went in the basement to look for you, it's very dusty down there, that's all.'

Zoe peeked behind her to where Dave, Jeremy and Charlie stood.

'Where's Dolly?' said Zoe.

'She's fine, Zoe. Now please, go to bed.'

The girl nodded, sniffing and using the arm of her nightie to wipe her nose and face. The three men watched Zoe as she passed them and continued upstairs.

'Night night,' Jane said, trying to keep her voice steady. 'I'll be up soon.'

Zoe's footsteps padded along the landing, the bedroom door opening and closing again.

'What the fuck do we do now?' Jeremy said, taking a cigarette out of a pack and lighting it.

'Go home, Jeremy,' Charlie said. 'Say nothing, and more importantly, write nothing.'

Jeremy signalled his understanding with a flick of his head. His face was pale and drawn. He caught Jane's eye as he passed her, looking as if he might say something, but instead continued out of the door.

Dave and Charlie loomed over Jane, Dave's arms folded and Charlie narrowing his eyes as he studied her.

'And what are you going to say about all this?' Charlie said, gesturing to the cellar. 'We're in a proper pickle now, aren't we?'

Jane heard Dolly shuffling her feet against the dirty floor, her voice muffled. She stepped towards the cellar door and Charlie stepped forward.

'What did she tell you, Jane? Torrid tales, no doubt, about how bad we all are to her.'

'Let her go,' Jane said, her fists clenched by her sides.

Charlie let out a raucous laugh. 'Poor Bernard wasn't exactly the best father in the world, but I don't think he deserved this.'

'*Not exactly the best father?*' Jane seethed. 'He abused her, and if she hadn't caught him in time, he might have done the same to my sister.'

Marion appeared at the dining room door, hanging on to the frame to keep herself steady.

'Has the party moved to the hallway?' She looked from the men to Jane. 'Oh, Jane, what have you done to that dress?'

She stumbled over, patting at the material with her palm. 'I don't think that will come out in the wash. Honestly, you look like you've been crawling through a forest.'

A charming smile spread across Charlie's face as he moved towards Marion, his arms out. Jane froze, afraid he was about to hurt her mum. She lunged forward, missing Charlie as he gently took hold of Marion's hand.

'Why don't we have another drink, Marion, and see what old Len's up to?' He turned to Dave. 'I'll leave this mess to you.'

Marion forgot all about Jane's dress and let him take her back to the dining room, the two of them chattering about music and dancing.

Dave remained by the cellar, watching Jane as if waiting for her next move.

'You've got to let her go, she's not the criminal here.'

Dave sighed heavily, leaning against the wall as if waiting for her to finish.

'I-I thought you liked me,' she said, trembling as she put a hand to his chest.

A smirk spread across his lips as she continued to try and make things OK, to pretend they were something.

'The photographs . . .' She tried to swallow but there was a knot in her throat at the memory. 'I thought after that . . .'

'I take lots of girls' photographs, it's my job.'

'But you said in the hotel room—'

'Oh, so *now* you're interested in me and what I think of you? Only, that day you scuttled out of the room like a frightened mouse, didn't want anything to do with me afterwards.'

'I'd never done anything like that before, that's all. Charlie didn't tell me that the photographs would be so . . .'

Dave raised his eyebrows, higher and higher again. 'What? Topless? You've seen Page 3, right? You're older than half of those girls.'

Jane's cheeks felt hot, the shame of letting those photographs be taken in the first place. She had been naive to go to Charlie's room, but the shock of seeing Dave there, complicit in the plan, had made her feel uncomfortable then, and now dirty and ashamed.

'Just let Dolly go, she'll deal with everything herself. She won't say anything about anyone else, why would she? And I won't, I promise.'

'*Pinky promise?*' he sneered.

The shame suddenly evaporated, his sly digs at her no longer relevant. She was involved in this now, and if she was, so was her family.

'You're all just a bunch of perverts.'

Dave stood up from the wall, his face darkening.

'You, Charlie, Bernard for sure, what about Jeremy and Len? Do they abuse and perv over young girls or do they just protect you? What secrets are they hiding?'

'Shut your mouth,' he hissed, glancing towards the closed dining room door.

'Perhaps I should go and call the police back, see what they think of it all?'

Jane turned to run to the front door as Dave rushed over, one hand over her mouth, the other on her stomach, dragging her back towards the cellar. She tried to wriggle free, kicking out her bare feet against the wall. He took her to the cellar door, his breath heavy as he fought to keep her from escaping.

'Calm down,' he growled, pulling his arm tightly around her. 'You call the police and you'll only get Dolly in trouble.'

She drew her leg up and kicked back at his knee. He groaned, falling forward and releasing his grip. Jane fell forward too, her ankle giving way on the top step and her whole body flailing as she hit each stair with a thud. A searing pain tore through her skull as her head struck the corner of a concrete step, the blow splitting the skin right to the bone. Her surroundings blurred and distorted, splices of a voice above her, not a comforting angel, but a devil cursing her for the inconvenience of her fall. She came to a stop on the dusty basement floor, her limbs splayed and bent at unnatural angles, a shard of shinbone piercing through the thin skin.

The door above closed and footsteps rattled down the stone stairs, then she felt a presence crouch beside her. Jane could just make out the outline of Dave's bent knees, her vision obscured by the blood that had trickled down into her eyes, a film of red as she slipped in and out of consciousness.

'Well, you have made this difficult, haven't you?' Dave hissed. 'I wasn't expecting it to come to this so soon.'

Jane whimpered and groaned as she felt the touch of his hand on her body, resting at her breast. He jumped up when a voice called out from above, causing him to scuttle back up the stairs and through the door. Jane opened her mouth to call out, but all she could manage was a weak '*help me*' that travelled no further than the end of her broken body. The pain sliced through her as she lay on the cold stone floor. She thought about Zoe, alone upstairs, and a single tear escaped her eye, leaving a wet pink trail as it diluted the blood. She blinked slowly as her life ebbed away, searching for Dolly in the gloom. The last thing she felt was relief when she saw the discarded masking tape and the rope that had bound Dolly's wrists. Dolly, at least, had escaped.

CHAPTER 38

2022
Zoe

The stark studio light hurt Zoe's eyes. She blinked rapidly, urging herself to wake up. She could hear the sound of clattering upstairs, as if Dave were casually clearing up the dinner plates after a meal. The walls in the studio were plastered with photographs, every available space taken. They were all women, some posed in the studio, others candid, those where the subjects appeared unaware of the presence of a camera.

She leaned over to the side of the mattress and threw up, the acidic fluid burning her throat. Once she had been sick, she felt a little better, pushing herself up from the floor. Once on her feet she paused a second, waiting for the dizziness to pass. She hobbled over to a large desk in the middle of the room, a standard lamp poised to illuminate a mass of photographs on the surface.

Bile rose in her throat again when she spotted a blown-up image of Jane. Her sister was sitting on the edge of a bed in a hotel room, not the Forget-Me-Not, but a much plusher affair. She was naked from the waist up, her eyes dead and mouth unsmiling as she looked into the camera's lens. In the background, heavy curtains were held back with gold brocade ties, and a chunky gold watch and tumbler of whiskey sat on a bedside table behind her. Zoe's eyes were drawn to a large mirror that hung over the bed, two figures reflected in the glass. Charlie's curly hair and wide frame alongside Dave, lean with his unmistakable wavy, shoulder-length hair.

She looked at all the others that included Jane — there were at least a hundred in all the places they had been in 1982. The arcades, the beach, the Chinese restaurant, Dunes. Multiples of the same scene, just slight variations on her expression as he had snapped away. There were other women too, some in Sunshine Sands, others in cities around the world. She wondered whether these women knew they had been the object of so much attention, particularly those who seemed unaware of the camera. She put her hands on the table to steady herself, trying to make sense of the situation and to figure out a way to escape. It was then she saw them: multiple images of Dan's wife, Sophie. Most were backstage, Sophie laughing and chatting with the other performers, getting dressed, getting undressed.

'How are you feeling?'

Dave stood at the doorway; he grimaced when he saw the vomit-splattered floor by the mattress.

'Oh dear, are you not well?'

'You killed Sophie.'

'Here, you need some water.'

Dave strolled over to a sink in the corner, taking a glass from a shelf and running the tap for a few seconds before filling the glass. He walked over to her, holding out the drink.

'Be careful of the photographs, I don't want to ruin any.'

Zoe swiped the glass with the back of her hand, the glass tipping and the water seeping into and around the prints.

'Thank goodness for negatives,' Dave said, calmly gathering up the photos and taking them to the side of the room where he began to peg them on a thin line, water dripping down onto the ceramic floor.

'Why did you bring me here? You knew I'd see all this,' Zoe said, her voice hoarse. 'Why didn't you just let me leave tomorrow none the wiser?'

'Don't undersell yourself, Zoe, self-deprecation doesn't suit you. I knew it was just a matter of time before you joined the dots.'

He held the corner of a photograph of Sophie.

'I expect Dan will appreciate a copy of this.'

Zoe felt her blood run cold. 'Who . . . who are all these other women?'

Dave ran his eyes over the room, his brow furrowed as if trying to remember and make sense of them. He walked slowly around the room, passing Zoe, who leaned back against the table. She glanced towards the door, wondering if she was strong enough to make a run for it.

'Some I remember, others—' he shrugged — 'slip my mind. So many of them, they come and go. You don't think I killed them all do you? Christ, I'm not that prolific.'

Zoe swallowed down the acid that rose again in her throat, her fingers crawling across the table where a discarded fork lay by a crumb-strewn plate. She pulled it behind her back as Dave turned to face her.

'I have no idea.'

'I forget most of them, just beautiful visions that I capture before they disappear again. I couldn't tell you most of their names, I never asked. But Jane — Jane I will always remember . . . and you.'

'I can't say the same about you,' she said defiantly. 'Nothing more than a momentary blur.'

'Ouch.' He grinned.

'They'll catch up with you eventually — DNA, cameras everywhere. If you kill me then that'll just make it worse for you.'

'Worse how? I'm in my sixties, a life sentence for one and I doubt I'd see sunlight again. It makes no difference what I do to you if I'm caught, but if I'm not . . .'

'Why Sophie? Why after all this time come back and do something that would risk being connected to Jane's death?'

He moved along the line to a photo of Jane. 'Your sister adored you, you know.'

It sickened Zoe hearing him speak in a way that suggested he knew anything about her relationship with her sister. He had only known Jane for a matter of days.

'Tell me what happened that night.' If she was going to die at the hands of this mad man, she hoped at least she would die knowing the truth. 'What did you do with her?'

CHAPTER 39

1982
The Men

Marion leaned against Charlie, her arm hooked in his, as he guided her back to her room.

'I've had a lovely night,' she said, barely able to focus her eyes on the stairs in front of her.

'Easy does it,' Charlie said, 'you'll have me over in a minute.'

Marion couldn't see the frustration on his face as he manoeuvred her up the stairs and across the landing. He opened the door and took her into the bedroom where Zoe lay sleeping.

'Seems such a shame for the night to end,' she slurred, falling onto the bed face first and instinctively clutching a pillow and closing her eyes.

* * *

Len had sobered up on hearing the news of Bernard's demise, and now stood in the basement over Jane's body. Dave lit a cigarette.

'For God's sake, son, not in here, there's chemicals on the shelf, we'll all go up like a rocket,' warned Len.

Dave took the cigarette out of his mouth and ground it into the floor with his foot. Charlie strolled down the stairs, joining them, halting sharply when he caught sight of Jane. His eyes darted from her body to Dave.

'Bloody hellfire, what have you done now?'

Dave said nothing as Charlie moved closer, reaching down and placing two fingers on her neck. He sighed heavily.

'Well, at least it's solved one problem — if she knows anything about us then she can't go squealing to the police.' He turned his attention back to Dave. 'I hope you've come up with a plan, lad. Tonight's turned into a proper shitshow.'

'I'll borrow Len's car,' Dave said, looking to Len.

'The Jaguar? It's only just been cleaned,' Len said.

'A mucky car is the least of our problems, Len,' spat Charlie. 'Christ, I'll give you the money for a valet myself, if you're that hard up.'

'I can't have any of this come back to me,' Len said. 'I'm the mayor.'

'You've as many skeletons in the closet as any of us,' Charlie hissed, his cheeks red and the veins on his temples pulsing. 'If one of us goes down, we all do.'

'*We* haven't just murdered a young woman,' Len protested, glaring at Dave.

'It was an accident. And let's face it, it's solved the problem of keeping all your dirty little secrets contained too, so you can both help me deal with this mess.'

There was a loaded silence. Then, 'What about Dolly?' Charlie asked. 'Where is she?'

'She ran out while I was trying to stop madam here blurting everything out in front of the old slapper upstairs,' Dave said.

'I can deal with her,' said Len. 'She's got her own reasons to stay quiet about tonight.' The three of them glanced over to the bin bag. 'Aside from the obvious, she relies on the likes of me and Bob to keep her licence here if she decides to carry on with the boarding house. And there's no way she could set us up for Bernard, because the police were called when we were all in the restaurant, on show for all to see.'

Dave nodded. 'Well, she'd better keep her mouth closed, otherwise—'

'Otherwise what?' Len snapped. 'You'll see her off as well?'

Dave squared up to Len, their faces inches apart. 'You're not so hostile when you're begging for photographs, are you? Don't think I won't squeal if you throw me to the lions.'

Charlie moved between them, a hand on each of their shoulders. 'Now then, fellas, let's calm down. Nobody is squealing and no one is getting thrown to the lions.'

He moved them apart and then held out a hand to Len. Len put his hand in his suit pocket and took out his keys, dropping them into Charlie's hand.

'Right, another hour and the pier will be deserted. Can you manage on your own?'

Dave nodded, and Charlie handed him the keys.

'OK then, Len, you deal with Bob. We tell him that the last person we saw Jane with was Bernard.'

'What about the mother?' said Dave.

'She'll barely remember her own name tomorrow, let alone who did what and when tonight. The suspicion lies with Bernard, and Dolly won't argue with that — it gives her an out too.' He gestured to Jane's body. 'Jeremy controls the stories, and if you've got any photos of Jane and Bernard together, we can leak that. It'll look like he had some crush on her, she was staying under his roof and—' he gave them a knowing wink — 'Bob's your uncle. Or luckily for us, the head of police in our pockets.' Charlie chuckled, the laughter dying quickly with the others' glares.

* * *

Dave pulled up alongside the pier in Len's Jaguar. It was 2 a.m. and the pubs and clubs were long shuttered up. He turned to face the sea when a bin lorry passed, the yellow lights flashing silently as it made its way into town. He opened the boot and checked the promenade again, before reaching in and lifting Jane's tarpaulin-covered body from the car. The sea crashed against the pillars below, muting the sound of his footsteps as he reached the funfair. The flag on top of the Freak Show snapped in the wind; he turned sharply to the deserted sideshow and carried on. He sped up, his arms struggling under her weight. He reached the end of the pier and took a deep breath, heaving her body up onto the railings, then paused, staring out to the dark sea, before pushing her over. He had already turned away when her body hit the water.

CHAPTER 40

2022
Zoe

'You bastard,' Zoe spat, lurching forward, the fork clutched in her outstretched hand.

Dave moved to the side and she stumbled, crashing into the wall and falling to the floor. The fork flew from her hand and bounced across the tiles with a clatter. Zoe gripped the hand she had used to cushion her fall, her wrist throbbing.

'So the Boddington Club was just a front for perverts?'

He raised an eyebrow, amusement across his face. 'Who told you about the Boddington Club?'

'It doesn't matter, but people talk and sooner or later you'll pay for all this. I won't be the only one "joining the dots", as you put it.'

He shrugged. 'I've had a good run, I think I could last a few more.'

'Jane was a threat, she knew what you were all up to, but why Sophie? She couldn't have known anything.'

Dave leaned back casually as he thought for a moment. 'Opportunity really. I mean, she did know something about the beauty contest that bothered me.'

'Sophie did? What?'

Zoe hated the fact that Dave looked like he was enjoying this exchange, the power to divulge what and when he wanted, but her desire to know before it was too late was all encompassing.

'I was chatting to her backstage, taking some *extra* photos of her, you know, something a little more racy. It's always the quiet ones . . .' He glanced over to a photograph of Jane.

Zoe's eyes widened.

'Oh, nothing too X-rated, not like your slutty sister.'

Zoe calmed her breathing, trying not to let him get to her.

'We were packing up and she started asking questions, as her mum had been a contestant back in the day. Yabbering on about the photographer being a bit weird back then and her suspicions about him and the missing beauty queen. Silly stuff really, but then she starting talking about this journalist at the boarding house and how she might tell her.'

'You killed her for that?'

'Well, that, and because I had the opportunity.'

Dave reached into his back pocket and drew out Zoe's phone, holding it up to show her.

'You've had quite a few messages pop through. Clark, wishing you a great night, with a wink emoji.' Dave raised an eyebrow. 'I can't think what he's implying. Oh, also several from Dylan — your son, I assume?'

Zoe's face crumpled at the mention of her eldest child.

'He wants to know what time you'll be back tomorrow as he's making lunch, so that's nice.'

A bell rung, echoing through the house. For the first time Dave looked panicked.

'Who's that?' Zoe asked.

Dave marched over to a set of drawers and yanked one open, pulling out a bundle of black silk scarves. Zoe's stomach churned as she imagined why they were there and what they might have been used for previously. She tried to scramble away as he wrestled with her, his knee across her legs halting her. She cried out as he grabbed her wrists, pain slicing through her body. He tied them together, before taking another scarf and wrapping it around her face and across her mouth.

'You shouldn't have come back here, Zoe, you should have stayed away,' he spat. 'The minute Gary told me who you were, all of this became inevitable. And before you ask, he knows nothing about what I did, he just asked if I could help steer you away from making a nuisance of yourself. Check you out, take you on a date and flatter you.'

The idea that these two men had conspired to charm and divert her was sickening, not least because it had worked. She had believed that Dave liked her. Christ, was her radar so far off now that she had fallen for the lies of an ageing psychopath?

'You didn't think I actually fancied you, did you? Christ, Zoe, I'm surrounded by models most days. I'm not exactly short of opportunity.'

The bell rang again. Dave held her phone in his hand, taunting her as he scrolled through notifications, a smirk on his face. So calm, so *smug*. He was a man that had gotten away with so much for so long, he believed he was completely untouchable, and so far his belief was justified. She thought about the other women he had brought back here, or met in hotel rooms to take 'professional' shots. Jane was never stupid, she was young and naive, and men like him preyed on that. Dave wasn't the kind of man that people suspected — he was educated, creative and good-looking. And he had that trait that keeps men like him free from suspicion for so long: charm.

The bell rang a third time. This time Dave sighed as if slightly annoyed at the intrusion. He put her phone in his back pocket and left the room, a heavy lock securing her in there. She dragged herself up from the floor, stumbling without the use of her hands. Zoe ran and threw the weight of her body against the door, wincing as pain sliced through her shoulder. She rested for a moment, her ear to the door. Dave had turned the radio up and beyond that there was little she could make out. She tried to call out, but the gag was so tight she could manage little more than a desperate gurgled plea.

As the music got louder, she sat down on the floor and kicked her legs against it until she thought her knees would give way — still nothing.

Whoever it was, she felt sure that Dave would be able to get them to leave. He had gotten away with so much for so long, there was no reason for her to believe anything would change now. She began to feel herself slipping back into a drug-fuelled sleep, but she tried to fight it, opening her eyes wide and shaking her legs back to life.

There was a crash upstairs, as if furniture had been thrown to the floor. Zoe climbed to her feet, her ear tight to the door. The music was off now, and she could hear the scraping of glass. She felt sick for the person he had just hurt — whoever had decided to visit him so late had made the worst decision possible. He was being careless now, and she knew that he wouldn't think twice about finishing her off next.

Footsteps padded down the steps. Zoe looked for somewhere to hide, to give her a moment to think, but think about what? It was useless: there was only one door in and out and he was about to come through it. She crawled back to the mattress and sat against the wall to await his return.

A key slid into the lock and turned, the door handle pushing down. Zoe thought about those 'final girls' in the horror films, walking from the killer's lair smeared in blood and sweat and glowing in their triumph. Those girls were in their late teens and twenties though; she could barely find the energy to lift her head as the door opened.

'Zoe!' Eloise cried, her full skirt swishing back and forth as she ran over. 'Dolly! She's down here!'

She crouched down to Zoe and pulled at the gag, managing to undo the tight knot. As it fell to the ground Zoe began to cough and splutter. Eloise untied her hands and Zoe rubbed at her wrists, the injured one now swollen and red.

'You didn't foresee this,' Zoe croaked weakly, her small stab at humour.

Eloise checked Zoe's swollen wrist and then the rest of her body for injuries. 'No, but I did tell you to go home.'

There was no time to argue. Eloise pulled her to her feet and Zoe rested her arm around her neck and shoulder, taking some of her weight.

'I think he spiked my drink, I passed out and was sick.'

Eloise dragged her through the doorway to the bottom of the stairs. She stopped suddenly.

'What?' Zoe said.

Eloise put her index finger to her lips. She crept slowly up the stairs, Zoe limping behind her, trying not to cry out in pain. The grand hallway was empty, but for the giant oil paintings of ancestors that looked ahead with grandeur and importance. Eloise walked carefully along the wooden floor towards the open-plan kitchen and living room. 'Stay here,' she turned and whispered to Zoe, pulling the door almost closed, so Zoe could peer through the gap.

Dave was barely recognisable as he stood by the window, holding a kitchen knife against Dolly's throat. Blood gushed from an open gash on his head, a shard of glass still protruding from the wound. The coffee table was smashed to pieces, more of his blood oozing into the carpet. His breath was laboured, his dark eyes on Eloise.

'I thought we'd put the past behind us, agreed to let each other get on with our lives,' he said.

Dolly watched Eloise, her body relaxed, almost accepting of this moment.

'Let her go,' Eloise said, holding out a hand. 'Give me the knife.'

'You're the same as me. You both have blood on your hands.'

'We are not the same as you,' Eloise said. 'We don't hurt the innocent.'

'You think you're some kind of vigilantes, do you? Is that how you see yourselves? Charlie's back in town tonight, I don't fancy his chances much.'

Eloise had her back to Zoe, her expression unseen, but Dave saw something in her face. His eyes narrowed as he spoke.

'That just leaves me then, doesn't it? Saving the best 'til last, I suppose,' he mused, twisting the knife against Dolly's skin.

Zoe stepped away, walking back down the hall and opening the front door. She crept around the house, ducking at windows in case her shadow or movement was seen by Dave. When she reached the living room window she faced Eloise through the glass. The fortune teller caught her eye and then put her attention back on Dave. Zoe looked around her feet, ornamental stones and rocks around perfectly manicured shrubbery. She crouched down and lifted a rock, light enough to manoeuvre but heavy enough to do what she needed it to do. To give Eloise enough time to take action. Zoe lifted her arm up and back — she had one shot at this. If she failed the first time, Dolly would be dead and likely Eloise soon after.

She took a deep breath and threw her weight forward, smashing the French window with the rock and catching Dave on the back of the head. It wasn't enough to bring him down, but the shock caused him to let go of Dolly as Eloise took her chance. In one swift movement she lunged forward, grabbed a piece of glass from the floor and drew it across his throat. Dave clutched his hands to his neck, the arterial blood spurting through his open fingers as he fell to his knees. His eyes were wide, fixed on Zoe, as she came through the broken door and stood over him, watching him collapse to the ground. Eloise watched too, the piece of glass still held aloft in her hand, should he by some miracle rise again.

When the last gurgle and splutter left his mouth, Zoe collapsed onto the sofa, the shock beginning to set in. She had come to Sunshine Sands to help solve a murder and now she sat here, complicit in one. Dolly turned to her, her eyes narrowing.

'You look like you could do with a cuppa.'

Zoe stared aghast at Dolly, studying her face, looking for the punchline. She let out a slow laugh at her matter-of-factness, shaking her head in disbelief at the insanity of her words.

'I think we've work to do first, Dolly,' Eloise cut in, already gathering the broken glass in her hands.

Dolly went to the kitchen, searching through the drawers and taking out a roll of bin liners and bottles of detergent and sprays. She tore off two bags and handed one to Eloise, before turning to Zoe.

'Go downstairs and clean up any trace that you've been there. Eloise and I will deal with all this,' she said, gesturing at Dave.

All this was now completely lifeless. His eyes were wide and haunted, limbs splayed at angles. The two women busied around him, moving his body to the side of the broken coffee table. It was clinical and practised.

'Was it you that invited Charlie Bailey tonight?' Zoe asked. 'Was Dave right? Did you . . . ?'

The two women paused mid-clean, then Dolly motioned for Eloise to keep going as she spoke on their behalf.

'Never mind all that, we need to be out of here soon. You get going downstairs.'

Dolly marched over to a large cupboard in the kitchen, returning with a vacuum cleaner, continuing her task to remove all traces of the night. Zoe pushed herself up from the sofa, collected an armful of cleaning products and made her way downstairs.

She tried not to dry heave as she scrubbed at her own vomit on the floor, the small sponge not fit for purpose. She walked over to the line of wire on which Dave had clipped the water-damaged photographs. Part of her wanted to gather all the images of her sister and rescue her from this place, but she didn't want to take any memory of the house or its owner with her. From the side of her eye she noticed her own blood on the wall, where she had fallen. She took the sponge and rinsed it in a small sink. On a shelf above the taps there was a glass jar filled with odd bits of jewellery and metal.

Zoe dropped the sponge in the basin and reached for the jar, sifting through its contents. Earrings, a silver bracelet made up of small, connected hearts. She tipped the jar onto the edge of the sink and pulled apart the tangled chains and links until she found it. Carefully she unwound the tarnished chain and separated it from the rest. She dangled the small silver dolphin pendant in front of her eyes, her small gift to Jane that day.

Dolly appeared at the door and Jane quickly pushed the necklace into her pocket.

'All done?'

Jane grabbed the sponge. 'Just a little more over here.'

She marched to the wall and crouched down, wiping the blood away.

'Don't worry too much about that, but check there's nothing personal left of yours? A handbag or purse?'

Zoe shook her head. 'They're upstairs, I think.'

'Very well,' Dolly said, walking over to the mattress with a five-litre plastic container.

She poured the contents over the mattress and around the floor. She took an ashtray that had been upstairs on the coffee table and placed it on the floor. She winced as she lit a cigarette, spluttering the smoke into the room, before dropping it onto the mattress. The mattress ignited almost instantly, fire spreading wherever the flammable solution led them. The orange flames reflected in Zoe's eyes as she watched, transfixed.

'Come on, it's time to go,' Dolly said.

As the flames spread further, Zoe rushed to Dolly, who guided her through the door and up the stairs. The open-plan kitchen and living room were immaculate, as if nobody had been there for a week. Zoe looked to the floor.

'Where is he?'

'In the car.'

'What? Why don't you leave him here? In the fire?' She felt shocked by her own thought process. It seemed there was only a hop, a skip and a fire between playing detective and becoming a criminal.

Dolly handed Zoe her handbag. 'They would know he'd been injured; it would start a fuss. We don't like *fuss* in Sunshine Sands.'

Zoe felt sick, the sudden realisation of the questions, the police, the interrogations and suspicion. Dolly marched out of the living room and through the hall, Marigolds keeping her fingerprints off the door handles and surfaces.

'Quickly,' Dolly ordered, 'unless you want to go up in flames yourself.'

Smoke and licks of fire began to seep from the basement into the hallway. Zoe clutched her bag and ran, following the landlady out of the house.

* * *

'How did you know I was here?' Zoe asked as Dolly helped her into the back of a car and sat beside her, reaching over her and securing her seat belt.

'Clark. We saw him in town and he said you went off for a drink with Dave. When we couldn't find you in any of his usual crony haunts, we came here. He always did like to show off this place.'

Eloise started the engine; the radio came on automatically, more news of the body on the beach. She flicked it off.

Dolly patted Zoe firmly on her thigh. 'Don't you worry about a thing, Zoe. Eloise and I will see to everything. We always have.'

Eloise looked into the rear-view mirror, catching Zoe's eye, before driving away from the house, smoke and flames now visible through the elegant Georgian windows.

* * *

The promenade was thinning out now. Zoe spotted Clark, arm in arm with the dancers. They laughed and swayed, still high from the evening, seemingly unaware of the night's events.

'Is Dan still at the boarding house?' Zoe asked.

Dolly shook her head. 'No. Her parents arrived and have taken him home.'

Zoe was relieved. She didn't think she could face him, at least not tonight. She knew his pain, she understood loss and she also knew how it felt not to have answers. Worse still, they were answers that she had but couldn't give, at least not yet.

'Will you tell him what happened, about Dave?'

Dolly pursed her lips and looked out of the window.

'You can tell them if you want,' Eloise said. 'We can't stop you writing about this, about your sister and the other women who suffered at his and the other men's hands. Or about Dolly, her childhood.'

Zoe looked at Dolly, her face drawn, a slight twitch in her cheek. The story would be a long timeline of corruption, abuse and murder. It was everything that the public craved from their TV documentaries, office water coolers surrounded by people the day after airing, keen to discuss the latest episode in wide-eyed horror and gratuitous delight. What would they call it? *Dark Sands*? *Murder & Ice Creams*? *Snapped! The Killer Photographer*? Zoe had been an onlooker until tonight; now she was a participant, a name that would appear on the end credits, an update of her life and expected parole date.

The car pulled up outside the Forget-Me-Not and Eloise turned the engine off.

'I think I need a drink,' Zoe said.

As they reached the gate, Clark ran up behind them. 'Ladies!'

'Hi,' Zoe said, forcing a smile as he approached.

He flung an arm over Dolly's shoulder, and she allowed her icy demeanour to thaw. 'How did you do, Clark?'

Clark beamed. 'The best, Dolly. The *best* night.'

'I'm very pleased for you,' she said. 'Perhaps now we can wind the season down, have a rest and get this place ready for next year.'

Zoe was surprised to hear Dolly speak of the next season. How could she be so confident that nothing would come of the last twenty-four hours? For a woman who seemed so weary with the town, it was odd to witness this sudden enthusiasm for the future.

'Good night?' he asked, nudging Zoe's arm with his elbow.

'Surprising,' she said.

'Excellent!' he said, struggling to put the key in the lock. 'I've always told Dolly Dave's not that bad.'

The theme tune from *E.T.* began to play. Zoe patted her pockets trying to find her phone and then reached into her handbag, shuffling through the contents. Then she remembered and her eyes fell on the boot of the car.

'Is that your phone?' Clark asked.

Zoe rushed after him as he went to the car, opening the back door and patting his hand around the back seat. When he couldn't find it, he searched the front seat and glove compartment as the ringtone continued to play.

'It's probably under one of the seats,' Zoe said. 'Not to worry, I'll get it tomorrow when it's light.'

She guided Clark away, but he stopped at the back of the car, leaning down and putting his ear to the metal.

'It's in the boot!' he exclaimed as he tried to prise it open.

The three women watched, their eyes wide as he tried again, cursing when one of his inch-long false nails pinged into the air. He scrabbled around the pavement, rising again and holding the nail aloft.

'Found it.'

Dolly rolled her eyes. 'Come on, you. I'll put some water by your bed and a little snack to mop up some of that alcohol.'

Clark appeared to forget all about Zoe's phone and walked over to Dolly, planting a kiss on her forehead.

'What would I do without you?'

'Go on with you, off to bed,' Dolly said, opening the door to the boarding house and guiding him through.

He walked in, waving a hand in the air. 'Goodnight, all.'

Zoe followed Eloise to the boot as she clicked her key fob and released the lock. Zoe was relieved to see that Dave's body was covered with a heavy tarpaulin. Eloise looked at her expectantly, then seeing that Zoe wasn't going to do it herself, reached under the sheet.

'I think he put it in his back pocket,' Zoe said.

Trying to keep his body as covered as possible, Eloise fumbled around, before taking out the phone and handing it to Zoe. There were twelve missed calls from her son Dylan. She quickly messaged him; he must have been worried when he couldn't reach her.

Sorry, left phone at hotel. All OK?

Almost instantly a message came back.

Yeah cool, was just wondering if you were going to the supermarket on your way home. Need snacks.

'For fuck's sake,' Zoe muttered to herself.

'What?' Eloise said with trepidation.

Zoe typed back.

Send a list of requests, hollow legs.

She put her phone on silent and left Eloise to lock the boot.

* * *

In the light of the hallway Zoe noticed blood trickling down Dolly's neck, the skin bruised and cut where Dave had held the knife so closely.

'You should get that looked at,' Zoe said.

Dolly put her hand to her throat, lightly touching the wound and studying the smears of blood on her fingers. She took a tissue from her pocket and wiped her hands.

'Eloise can sort that, she's a dab hand with a needle and thread, if it comes to it.'

Eloise nodded impassively, clearly resigned to taking a needle to her friend's throat and stitching up the skin that Dave had cut. Once again, Zoe was in equal parts fascinated and horrified by their clinical indifference to what would be unimaginable to most.

'Have the police been back here to talk to you about Sophie?' Zoe asked.

'We were at the pier when they called round,' Dolly said. 'Trevor spoke to them, told them he'd seen her with Dave earlier in the day.'

'And had he?' Zoe asked.

'Of course not,' Dolly snapped, in her usual agitated tone. 'If we'd have known that, we could have stopped it.'

'So you didn't know until tonight that it was Dave that killed my sister?'

Dolly shook her head. 'We knew he was involved, somehow.'

'How?' Zoe said.

'The night it happened I escaped from the cellar and ran to Eloise at the old Freak Show. We saw him as he was walking back from the end of the pier, then her sash washed up on the beach the next day.'

'But that didn't mean much,' said Eloise. 'They were all so intertwined with each other. I believed he was just doing somebody else's dirty work.'

'I think I'll leave that drink,' Zoe said. 'I need to lie down.'

As she went to leave, a key turned in the boarding house door. Trevor appeared, sleepy-eyed and yawning. Zoe's eyes darted to Dolly and Eloise, certain they'd be agitated by his presence.

'Go to bed, Zoe,' Dolly said, still facing Trevor. 'Everything will be fine in the morning.'

Zoe left them in the hall and made her way to her suite, passing Dan and Sophie's vacant room. She couldn't imagine how Dan was feeling right now. She considered messaging him, but thought better of it. Her head was fuzzy with everything that had happened, her body hurt from being knocked around. It could wait. She took out her pills, medication that numbed her feelings and helped her calm down. Jane spun the tablet around in her palm before putting it back in the bottle and throwing it into her handbag.

She lay on the bed and took out her phone, several messages from earlier now filling the screen in a series of frantic beeps. Her editor asking how things were going, her children asking what was for dinner tomorrow and Clark asking how her 'hot date' was, along with a blurred selfie of him and other revellers. The discovery of Sophie's body was all over the news apps. The articles were dotted with amateur phone footage taken by curious holidaymakers, though thankfully there were no macabre images, just police and ambulance workers milling around a white tent on the beach.

She clicked on a short video of a news reporter speaking to a policeman, urging those with any information or knowledge of Sophie's movements that day to come forward. She lay down in the dark room, listening as the boot of a car slammed shut and the garden gate to the boarding house opened.

CHAPTER 41

Zoe's head pounded as she opened her eyes, the events of last night flickering into her mind like a terrible nightmare. For a split-second she allowed herself to believe it had all been a bad dream. She listened as pots and pans rattled in the kitchen downstairs, just another day at the boarding house. She reached over to the bedside table and took some headache pills from her make-up bag, slugging them down with a gulp of lukewarm water.

She messaged her children to say she would be back a little later, but not to worry, it would be in time for dinner. She rattled through the contents of the freezer in her mind, and decided on what to cook them, which she already knew would be rejected in favour of a takeaway.

Zoe winced as she stepped out of bed, her body still aching as she put on a pair of sweatpants and a hoodie. There was no time or inclination to shower or bathe, just a need to get out into the air and take a walk to settle her mind. She packed her suitcase and laptop bag, ready to go on her return.

Downstairs, the family from the Crowther Suite were checking out, the children as wild as the day they had arrived.

'I trust you have enjoyed your stay? You must have your breakfast before you leave, I insist,' Dolly said, eyeing Zoe as she passed by.

Outside, it felt like the town itself was suffering from a hangover. A row of bunting fluttered along the pavement as a streetsweeper moved slowly down the road, its driver dead-eyed and solemn. A shopkeeper pulled up heavy metal shutters, revealing hundreds of sticks of rock and red candy dummies hanging on ribbons. Zoe considered buying some for the children, before noticing a dying wasp wedged in the display, its legs slowly moving back and forth before it gave up and lay still.

Zoe walked up the steps and into the lobby of the Parade Hotel. The reception was filled with suitcases and holidaymakers checking out. The woman on the desk last night had finished her shift and, in her place, a slick young man took keys and gave buoyant farewells to departing guests. When she reached the front of the queue he smiled, his teeth perfect and startlingly white.

'How can I help you?'

'I wondered if you would call Charlie Bailey's room for me. I was supposed to interview him last night, but he couldn't make it.'

'Of course, madam, do you know which room he's staying in?'

She shook her head. 'I'm afraid not, we were due to meet at the bar.'

The man tapped away at the keyboard in front of him, narrowing his eyes as he scanned the information.

'It seems he checked out last night. That's strange.'

'Strange?'

'He was due to give a little talk in the Pearson Room this morning.' He gestured over to a sandwich board by a giant rubber plant.

Coffee & Cake with comedy legend
Charlie Bailey
The Pearson Room 11 a.m.

A publicity photo of Charlie was pinned underneath. Zoe guessed it had been taken thirty years ago, as it bore little resemblance to the frail white-haired man she had seen last night. From the little she did know about Charlie, she didn't believe he would miss an opportunity to talk about himself to his fans. She went back to the reception desk, getting the attention of the man once again.

'Do you know who organised this talk?'

He disappeared into the back office, returning after a moment with a slip of paper. He handed it to her. 'A local company, been around for years. They used to own most of the pier attractions.'

Zoe read the piece of paper: *Delano Entertainment*.

CHAPTER 42

The vampire girl held her dress over one arm, the other unlocking the back door to the Ghost House.

'Here, let me help,' Zoe said, taking the dress from her arm before the girl had chance to reply. 'Where's your zombie friend?'

The girl looked perplexed, not understanding the joke.

'The guy dressed as a zombie, the other day?'

Something registered in her face. 'Oh, you mean Connor. Right. He's not in today, nobody is. I'm just here to do a stock take and return my costume. Can I help you with something?'

'I'm writing an article for the *National Mail*, Eloise said I could take a look around.'

'She didn't say anything.'

'I'm meeting her later for an interview. She said it was OK to pop in for a look.'

The girl shrugged, taking her costume back from Zoe, and walked into the gift shop, dumping her dress on the counter.

'I'll be here if you need anything,' she said, inserting earbuds in her ears and lining up music on her iPhone.

Zoe took a mug from a shelf, a decal on it of the old Freak Show tent, *The Delano Family* in fancy scroll beneath. Jack the

Ripper keyrings lined the walls alongside fluffy monster toys and skeleton fridge magnets. She paused at a jewellery rack, cheap silver necklaces hanging from a carousel. She turned it, stopping when she saw the row of tiny silver dolphins swaying from side to side. She held up the pendant, identical to the one she had given her sister, the one she had worn for the beauty contest.

'How much are these?' Zoe asked.

'Pardon?'

Zoe smiled and waited for the girl to remove her earbuds. 'How much are these?'

The girl eyed the necklace. 'Five pounds, I think. Only cheap tat, it'll probably go green in a week.'

'Can I buy one?' Zoe said, taking ten pounds from her pocket.

The girl looked surprised. 'Sure, I haven't got a key for the till though, so you'll have to come back for your change.'

Zoe freed a necklace from the stand and put the note on the counter. 'Just put the change in the tip jar.'

The girl looked down to the jam jar with a slit cut into the lid, a small pile of five- and two-pence pieces languishing at the bottom.

'I'll put the lights on for you,' she said, her mood suddenly brighter.

The girl opened a small cupboard on the wall and flicked multiple switches for each room. Strip lights lit up through the building to the buzz of electricity.

Zoe thanked her and headed through the first door, the place not quite as 'horrifying' in the glare of fluorescent white light. The tracks that the stuffed rats ran along were now visible, curling around the floor, and the painted face of a 'ye olde' barmaid was comical in its simplicity. The hall of mirrors wasn't so amusing to her in the harsh light, every self-perceived flaw exaggerated. She looked away and marched forward into the puppet room, stepping up onto the stage and standing beside the marionettes, their heads and limbs hanging limply to the floor.

Zoe continued through the door into the slim black corridor that circled round and led visitors into the gift shop. She noticed a crack in the plasterboard behind the mannequin of a luminous green witch. Zoe edged behind the figure and followed the line with her fingers, pushing at the thin partition until the crudely cut door creaked open. She looked back out to the corridor and peered around the corner to the exit, where the vampire girl was still sat behind the till, scrolling through her phone.

The door led to what at first appeared to be another storeroom, but as Zoe moved around, she could see it was another horror attraction in the process of being built. She pulled the partition door to and entered the room. There was a circular dining table in the centre, five empty chairs placed around it. Paint pots and brushes were strewn across it, next to plates of synthetic food waiting to have colour added, to make the grapes red and the apples green. On the wall there was a crude oil painting, a copy of the photograph she had seen in the foyer of Dunes: Len, Charlie, Jeremy and Bernard. Dave had been added on to complete the group, for once not able to hide behind his camera. She looked from the picture to the five empty chairs, when something in the corner of the room caught her eye.

She crouched down beside the metal walking frame, an NHS sticker on one of its legs. *Royal Surrey Hospital* and then in biro — *Charlie Bailey*.

Charlie must have come in here on his way back from Dunes. Her mind shot back to Dave Cooper, the ease with which the two women had dispatched him and the coolness of their demeanour afterwards. When Charlie walked past the horror house, Eloise and Dolly had still suspected him of Jane's death. But even innocent of that, he had been one of the men who had treated women and girls so appallingly back then.

In the corner was a plastic storage box on a pasting table. Zoe crept over and withdrew a notepad, filled with shorthand scribbles.

It belonged to Jeremy Lowden, his name and email noted on the first page. It was filled with local stories, from issues with refuse collections to the winner of 'best garden' in the town. It ended midway through, five years previously. She dropped it back in the box and rummaged through various items of clothing, a dickie bow, a man's handkerchief and a box of cigars.

In the corridor she heard footsteps and voices, wheels creaking along the floor. She rushed over to a boarded-up window, the glass painted as if looking out onto the night pier. Zoe stepped behind a heavy velvet curtain, dust pluming up into the air as she pulled it around her. She held a hand to her face, desperate to stifle a sneeze that tickled her nose.

'Put it over there for now.'

She recognised Eloise's voice, and then Trevor's.

'I still think we should have kept these at the boarding house until everyone's gone home.'

'Too risky,' Eloise replied. 'If anyone comes sniffing around, it might all be discovered.'

It sounded like a blade slicing through cardboard, then packaging being torn apart. Paper ripping and scrunching and bubble wrap popping. Trevor groaned as if lifting something heavy.

'This one,' Eloise said.

A chair scraped on the floor as Trevor exhaled. 'Awkward devils, aren't they?'

Zoe felt the pressure in her bladder growing; if she did sneeze now, the horror would surpass anything she had experienced so far in the Ghost House. For the next thirty minutes she listened as Trevor came back and forth with packages, each unwrapped and their contents placed according to Eloise's instructions. While he was absent, Eloise was sorting through something, jangling metal and stapling material.

Outside the pier was beginning to get busy with those making the most of the final weekend of the season. Screams and laughter as rides bumped, spun and rattled along sea-salt-worn tracks.

'Right, I think she'll like that,' Trevor said. 'Hey, don't get upset. Do you want a tissue?'

Eloise sniffed, then blew her nose. 'It's been a long forty years, you know, to get this far.'

'I know, love,' Trevor said. 'Almost there.'

The sneeze came without warning — a brutal, sharp *atchoo!* Zoe crossed her legs and held her crotch.

'What the . . . ?' Trevor said.

The curtain was snapped to the side, and Zoe sneezed again. She rubbed at her nose, feeling the heat in her face as Trevor glared at her. Eloise appeared by his side.

'What are you doing in here?' said Trevor.

He was no longer the meek sidekick to Dolly, fear and anger blazing in his eyes.

'I . . . I was just having a look around,' Zoe said.

Trevor scowled. 'Well, you've no business being in here.'

'I need the loo.'

Trevor looked to Eloise, who moved to the side, giving her room to leave the confines of the window. He stood aside and both watched her as she took careful steps forward, her eyes drawn to the table in the middle of the room. The need to use the bathroom dissipated as she walked around the chairs, three of which were now filled.

Though crude, their waxy faces were recognisable to her: Len, Bernard and Jeremy seated around the half-finished banquet. Len's chains had been placed over his shoulders and Jeremy held a biro in a half-clenched hand, the tip resting on a notepad where the word *Murderers* had been written. The clothes they wore looked authentic for their time, the style and colours as the ones they wore in the photographs.

Zoe walked behind the model of Len, noticing that where the chain had weighed down his clothing, the top of his neck was now visible.

She narrowed her eyes, leaning in to see the part of the mannequin where the wax head met the neck. The trunk of the body had been stuffed with a wool-type material, the head fixed in place with some kind of metal spike. As she reached out to touch him, Trevor stepped forward, but Eloise held her arm out and stopped him. Zoe put her finger into the wool, and ran her finger down the nubs of the bony vertebrae, but it wasn't plastic or wire supporting his likeness — it was a human skeleton.

CHAPTER 43

Zoe stood at the end of the pier, looking out to sea. She held the tiny dolphin pendant in her hand, the one she had taken from Dave's house. The other that she had bought, she wore around her neck. She had all the answers she had come for now. She knew her sister was never coming back and she knew that the person responsible would never hurt another. She closed her eyes and said a silent prayer, before throwing her palm up and releasing Jane's necklace to the sea.

An elderly man joined her, his bony fingers clutching the rail.

'Lovely day,' he said.

Zoe nodded. 'Yes, I suppose it is.'

'Twenty years me and the missus holidayed here.'

Zoe turned to him. His eyes were watery, skin drawn tight across sharp cheekbones.

'You must miss her.'

'She mithered me from morning 'til night — pick up your socks, put the seat down. If I managed to escape for a pint, she'd be at the pub door after an hour, tapping her watch. But by God, what I wouldn't do to have her bending my ear now. She was always there to pick up the pieces.'

'And the socks,' Zoe smiled.

'Aye, and the socks,' he chuckled. 'Worst day of my life, losing her. I didn't want to go on. Many times I've thought of taking one too many of my pills, or walking into a busy road.'

'You mustn't do that,' Zoe said, her voice urgent.

He tapped at his head with a finger. 'Memories might be all I've got, but I've got some great ones. Besides, now I can stay at the pub just that bit longer.'

They stood side by side for a moment longer, the laughter and squeals from the funfair filling the air around them.

'Take care,' Zoe said, turning to leave.

'Aye, you too,' he replied, still looking out to the horizon.

* * *

The family from the Crowther Suite were packing up the car when Zoe got back, the children already secured in their seat belts in the back. The dad tried to wedge the windbreaker back into the car, turning it one way and then another. After several failed attempts, he brought it down hard over his knee, snapping the frail wood in two, before throwing the bits in the boot. Her phone buzzed and Zoe opened the email from her editor.

Hi Zoe,

How did it go? Any celebrity gossip? I saw on the news about the poor girl on the beach, awful stuff. Did you dig up anything on that? I'm sure there'll be another commission from Mike if you find out more.

Don't forget that champers when you're home! Safe travels.

Amelia

Princess was in the garden, digging at the tufts of grass and soil around the wheelie bin, dragging up a stray piece of bacon and chomping on it greedily. The dog wagged its tail as Zoe approached, trailing her back into the boarding house. She followed the clatter of cutlery into the dining room, where Clark was attempting to eat a full English breakfast.

'Sore head?' Zoe asked, slumping down opposite him.

'What time did I get back?' he groaned, dropping his cutlery in defeat and resting his head in his hands.

'I can't remember. 2, maybe 3 a.m.?'

Clark rubbed at his temples. 'I don't remember anything after the eighth shot of tequila.'

'Probably for the best.'

He raised his head, his eyes wide. 'What do you mean? What did I do?'

'Nothing,' Zoe assured him, 'I didn't mean anything by it.'

'I heard about the body — I mean Sophie,' he said, slumping back in his chair. 'Terrible.'

'Yes.'

'How was Dan?' He shook his head. 'Silly question. He must be devastated.'

'He's gone home to be with his family.'

Dolly marched into the dining room and dropped two tablets by Clark's glass of water.

'Paracetamol,' she said.

'Thanks, Dolly.'

'You finished?' she said, her hand already on his almost full plate of puce bacon and sloppy eggs. 'I'll make you something later, when you're feeling more up to it.'

He nodded in agreement, the motion causing him to grimace.

'Are you planning to leave today?' she asked Zoe. 'Just so I can let the cleaner know.'

'Yes, in about half an hour.'

'Very well, just ring the bell when you're ready and I'll check you out.'

Dolly flicked at a chair with her hand as she left, a puff of dust rising in the air. She tutted and called out for the cleaner.

'I bet you'll be glad to get back to normality,' Clark said.

Zoe took a deep breath, the thought of normality — bills and endless requests for meals from her children — the best thing she could imagine right now. She studied Clark's face, his blue eyes and cheekbones most women would kill for. Her thoughts went to the image of the child she had seen in the photograph in Dave's book, Dolly clutching his hand.

'What?' he asked, amusement on his face at her sudden focus on him.

'You lived here when it was used as a halfway house, a care home of sorts?'

'Yes. I was very young, but I remember it being a bit gloomy.'

'Do you remember Len Erwitt staying here?'

Clark shifted around in his chair. 'Vaguely. I mean, I was only young then.'

'Why were you taken to his funeral?'

'Was I?'

She didn't know from his response if he genuinely didn't remember, or was trying to cover up the past, something most people in Sunshine Sands were adept at.

Clark took his hands away from his creased brow. 'I don't know, perhaps Dolly couldn't get a babysitter?'

'Perhaps, but I'm just trying to understand why a woman that despised him and all he stood for would not only go herself but take you.'

Clark appeared to sober up rapidly, straightening his spine and tapping his fingers on the melamine placemat.

'You told me that your mum had been through some bad things, that's the reason she turned to drugs.'

Clark's face darkened. It was the first time Zoe had seen him agitated.

'Was . . . I mean, was Len connected to your mum at all? Maybe he was the reason your mum turned to drugs?'

Clark ran his hands over his head. 'Does it matter?' he said, defensively.

Zoe thought for a moment, everything from the past two days slotting into place like a puzzle.

'Yes, yes it does matter.'

'Len was my dad.' Clark watched her, waiting for a reaction, but Zoe gave none and just let him talk. 'He hated the fact that Dolly was the one who got to have me. He couldn't publicly acknowledge me, otherwise he'd lose all the hard-won respect he'd somehow managed to garner. When he got older and frail and his wife died, he decided he wanted to absolve his sins, make peace with everything. He offered Dolly enough money to keep this place going for a few years in return for lodgings here, and he got to play at being a father to me. I suppose Dolly was desperate for money to stay in business and was able to put aside her hate for him. She's that kind of person, just wants to do what's best.'

Zoe didn't believe that Clark knew anything of what had really happened to Bernard, Len and the others. Dolly had protected him then and she continued to do so now. She knew that money was not Dolly's motivation for letting Len stay under her roof, her motivation was that he became easy prey.

'I'm glad you have Dolly,' Zoe said. 'She really does love you. Most mums aren't half as protective as she is of you.'

Clark nodded. 'Yes, I doubt I'll be leaving Sunshine Sands as long as the Forget-Me-Not is here.'

'There are worse places to be,' Zoe said, looking around at the faded wallpaper and framed pictures.

Princess bounded into the room yapping. Seeing Clark, she jumped on his lap. He grimaced with each bark as he stroked her fur.

'There's quieter places though,' he smiled.

Zoe rose and left Clark at the table, wandering through to the kitchen where she found Dolly drying some pots with a Sunshine Sands tea towel. The landlady didn't greet her with her usual barbed comments, but instead offered her a cup of tea.

'No, thanks,' Zoe said. 'I'll need to be getting off soon, loo stops and all that.'

'Right then, would you like Trevor to fetch your bags?' Dolly said, putting a plate on the draining board with a clatter.

'No. It's fine. I just want you to know something.'

Dolly narrowed her eyes and pursed her lips. 'Right then, you'd best come out with it. What is it to be? A grand exposé in the *National Mail*? Am I to make sure my hair's done for the pictures before I'm carted off to jail?'

'I want to thank you. I want to tell you I understand why you've done what you've done.'

The suspicion remained on Dolly's face.

'I'm not saying I agree with all your *plans*, but in a place where nobody seemed to care about my sister, you did. Not just her, but the other women who suffered.'

Dolly brushed off the sentiment. 'I just want to make Sunshine Sands a better place, that's all.'

'One thing I don't understand. Len was buried and I read online that Jeremy died in hospital, so how did you . . . ?'

'Will the interrogations ever stop?' Dolly said, hanging the tea towel over a rail. When she saw that Zoe was waiting for a reply she continued. 'Eloise's father was the town's funeral director as well as the owner of the Freak Show — their bodies were never buried. Just bags of stones. And between his and Eloise's taxidermy skills we were able to keep them . . . well, fresh, as it were.'

'When I heard you talking in your room . . .' Zoe barely dared have her fears confirmed. 'You were . . .'

'The finished bodies had to be stored somewhere and as you were snooping round the basement—'

'They were in the wooden crates?'

'Yes, Trevor brought them to my room. I quite enjoyed giving them a piece of my mind.' She gave Zoe a tight smile, a sign that there was no more to it.

Princess scampered into the kitchen and jumped up at Dolly's shins, digging at her skin. Dolly bent down and picked her up in her arms, the dog lapping at her cheeks.

'I want you to know I won't be writing anything about any of it,' Zoe said. 'You've done what you can to make things better, the only way you knew how. Oh, and not forgetting that I wouldn't be stood here if you and Eloise hadn't come to Dave's house. You saved me, Dolly — you couldn't save Jane or Sophie, but you did save me. And not just from Dave, but from Bernard all those years ago.'

Dolly put Princess down on the floor, brushing away Zoe's words. 'I'd best take this dog for a walk, all those scraps play havoc with her insides.'

Zoe nodded as Princess chased her tail in excitement at the promise of going out. Dolly unhooked a lead from a peg on the wall and went to leave, pausing when she saw the dolphin necklace. Zoe flinched as the landlady grabbed her shoulders, taking her by surprise as she squeezed her tightly and planted a kiss on her forehead.

'Safe travels, Zoe,' she said. As she reached the doorway, Princess tugging at the lead, she added, 'And don't be a stranger, you're always welcome back here at the Forget-Me-Not. Oh, and bring the kiddies, there's not enough youngsters in Sunshine Sands.'

Zoe went to get herself a glass of water, noticing an old photograph that was leaning against a biscuit tin. It was Dolly, Trevor and Eloise in their teens. Eloise was laughing, Trevor had a begrudging smile, and for once Dolly was smiling too, her hair blowing away from her face and cheeks glowing as they stood on the beach, all three full of secrets and plans for the future of Sunshine Sands.

CHAPTER 44

Summer 2023
Zoe

Dolly walked down the promenade, her kitten heels clicking along the pavement. She wore sunglasses, despite the skies showing no sign of sun, and her skin was mottled purple with the snapping winds that caused the dark sea to smash into the shore. A tram passed her, its bell ringing out. On its side a giant picture of the Ghost House advertised its new attraction. When she caught sight of Zoe standing by the Horror House door she held out her arms.

'There you are!'

Despite having revisited Sunshine Sands over the winter, Zoe was still not used to this new, warm incarnation of Dolly.

'And this must be Dylan,' Dolly said, holding her hand out to Zoe's teen son, who swapped his chips to the other hand and reached out.

'This is Belle and this is Alice,' Zoe said.

'Lovely to meet you all, I've heard a lot about you.'

Belle peered up to Dolly as she chewed on a sugary donut. 'You knew my Aunty Jane, didn't you?'

Zoe and Dolly exchanged glances, Zoe not knowing if she should change the subject.

'I met her once, yes. A very pretty and kind young woman.'

'She was a beauty queen,' Alice piped up.

'I know, and very well deserved.' Dolly took each of the girls by the hand. 'Now then, who would like to go to the funfair?'

The girls squealed with delight as Dolly led them across the road and onto the pier. Zoe and Dylan followed behind.

'She's not as scary as you made out,' Dylan said.

'I didn't say she was scary!' Zoe said. 'I said she was indomitable.'

'Same thing,' he said, biting into the last chip.

'Thanks for asking,' Zoe said, pointing at the empty carton.

Above the entrance to the pier was a new sign: *Delano's Pier and Funfair*, a colourful illustration of Eloise and her father in a collage of art. The women were reclaiming what had been taken away.

The two of them caught up with Dolly and the girls as Belle jumped up and down outside the Ghost House entrance.

'Mummy, *please?*'

Zoe remembered doing the same to Jane, pleading with her to let her go into the Freak Show. Jane always wanting to make her happy, to make her feel loved.

'You're too young, Belle. Why doesn't Dylan take you both on the carousel? I loved that as a kid.'

Belle stuck her bottom lip out, her arms crossed tightly over her chest. Dylan tickled her side, causing her to giggle and wriggle away.

'Come on, stinker, we can go in the arcade after.'

Zoe mouthed '*thank you*' to her son and watched as the three of them ran down the pier and disappeared into the crowds.

'Are you ready?' Dolly said.

Zoe looked up at the Ghost House, a shudder running down her spine. She had turned down Dolly's offer to see the progress on Eloise's new attraction over the winter, but now curiosity had gotten the better of her. The attraction had gotten rave reviews over social media, a *must see* on the *North-West Now!* website.

'As I'll ever be,' Zoe said, following Dolly past the long queue and into the house.

All of the 'scare' rooms had been revamped, the mannequins repainted and the props renewed where needed.

'Trevor has done a great job,' Zoe said, as a teen ran past them shrieking as he was chased by an actor wielding a chainsaw.

Screams echoed through the corridors and *mwuhahahas* boomed through amps as they reached the star attraction within the Ghost House.

The Last Supper

Eloise met them beneath the sign, kissing Zoe on the cheek. She put a temporary *Do Not Enter* sign on the wall and led them both through a dark corridor and into the room. Zoe stared down at the five lifeless figures around the table, frozen in gurning smiles and lascivious intent. Zoe walked, transfixed, towards the table. A shudder crawled up her spine as she studied the lifeless figures. Len, Bernard and Jeremy, Charlie's recognisable twisted grin and leering glassy eyes, and Dave, slouched back, a camera held in his wax hand.

'Ready?' Eloise said.

Zoe nodded tentatively. Eloise reached behind a curtain and flicked a switch, the room suddenly coming to life. Warped laughter and deep voices distorted, transforming the tableau into a macabre scene of greed and desire. Hatches around the room opened alternately, a Grim Reaper laughing loudly in one, in another a judge's head leaned out and called for 'order'. It was a manic, nightmarish scene, even to those that didn't share their secret. Five skeletons manipulated and formed into a funfair attraction. For years Dolly had kept Len, Bernard and Jeremy upstairs in the boarding house, waiting for the day when they could all be brought here. These men had wanted to rule Sunshine Sands, to use and abuse the women who surrounded them. Now they were finally at the mercy of the women they tried to silence.

Zoe noticed the guest book from the Forget-Me-Not, placed on a cabinet at the side of the room. She ran her fingers over the smooth cover.

'Why is this here? You're not closing down the boarding house, are you?'

A dark smile crept across Dolly's lips. 'Of course not. But that belongs here now. It's the last of my dad to leave the Forget-Me-Not.'

Zoe snapped her fingers away from the pale discoloured skin that stretched around the book.

EPILOGUE

Dolly licked her ice lolly, red food colouring bleeding down the wooden stick and onto her fingers. Zoe sipped from a paper coffee cup, and watched as Dylan hooked ducks, handing over cheap soft toys to his young sisters.

Dolly paused mid-lick and looked over to the waltzers. A tattooed fairground worker leaned over the car, his hand on a young girl's shoulder. The girl looked at the floor of the cart, her body rigid. He bent over further, whispering something in her ear as his hand slid under her T-shirt. The girl squirmed away, getting as far from his touch as the safety bar would allow.

'Did he just . . . ?' Zoe said, trying to follow the young girl's cart around the track.

The fairground worker sauntered to the next spinning car, moving up and down with the motion of the ride. He looked up and caught Dolly's eye, raising his hand as a nervous grin crept across his face. Dolly tilted her head as she watched his every move.

'You could just get him fired, Dolly. You don't have to . . .'

Dolly stepped closer, shaking her head and tossing the remains of the ice lolly in a bin. The man hopped off the ride, glancing back at Dolly as he tried to hide in the crowds.

'A woman's work really is *never* done,' Dolly said, following him up the pier.

THE END

ACKNOWLEDGEMENTS

This book is dedicated to my mum, Avril. I write a lot about dysfunctional mother-daughter relationships, and yet I have had one of the most loving and nurturing mums you could wish for. Thank you, Mum, for everything you did to make my childhood so happy, not least, making the best cheese-and-onion pie I have ever had. Thank you also to my lovely sister, Katrina. You have always been so supportive of my writing and have always been there when I needed you. To my friends — Mel, always a cheerleader, always an ear to bend and *always* the best one-liners! Thank you for everything, you are amazing. Nicola and Zoe, for the trips out and away and the laughter and support (but you can keep your weird jam-and-toast teabags to yourself!). Michelle, thank you for your ongoing encouragement and support: keep changing the world for the better, you are an inspiration.

To my 'Blackpool husband' and fellow writer, Daniel Sellers. Thank you for the encouragement to get me over the finish line. In what was a full-on year, it is great to have a fellow writer by my side.

Thank you to Sophia Spiers, my fellow writer and cheerleader (and lover of equally dark tales!).

To the readers and book bloggers, thank you for all the kind words and for the sharing and reviews that are so important to writers. I appreciate you more than you know.

Thank you to my agent Katie Fulford at Bell Lomax Moreton and to Joffe Books. I am forever grateful you believed in my stories. In particular to Jasmine, Hayley, Kate and Matthew, my editors at Joffe Books. Thank you so much for your attention to detail, and all the work you put in reining back this comma-loving writer! A huge thank you to Emma Grundy Haigh, not only for being the person who believed in my writing, but also for your ongoing support and being an A1 human being when I needed it most. Publishing is a tough world, but there are true lovely people out there, ones that will support you even when it's not about writing, and you are one of those.

To my son Gabriel, I am so proud of you and everything you are working towards. You are funny, smart and kind, and now a lifetime provider of free tattoos! I love you more than you will ever know. To Joe, my partner in crime and everything else. Thank you for being by my side, for making me laugh like no other and for all the love and adventures. Life wouldn't be half as much fun if you weren't in it. 'Love you, Joe!'

Finally, my love and eternal gratitude to the English seaside resorts I visited as a child. Ghost trains, fortune tellers, boarding houses, fish and chips and end-of-pier shows. Thanks to my dad's love of theatre and variety I saw most of the comedians of the time: Cannon and Ball, Les Dennis and Dustin Gee, Cilla Black, Freddie Starr and Tom O'Connor, to name but a few. These day trips to Blackpool were something to treasure and I always will. Most English seaside resorts today struggle to survive. As package holidays became more affordable, holidaymakers chose Benidorm over Blackpool, and Salou over Scarborough, and from then on most of our beloved resorts began to struggle. I love holidays to places where the sun is guaranteed and the sea is warm, but I'm not sure anything quite beats a walk down a British pier on a windy day, eating chips, before sitting down to win a cheap toy on the Donkey Derby.

THE JOFFE BOOKS STORY

We began in 2014 when Jasper agreed to publish his mum's much-rejected romance novel and it became a bestseller.

Since then we've grown into the largest independent publisher in the UK. We're extremely proud to publish some of the very best writers in the world, including Joy Ellis, Faith Martin, Caro Ramsay, Helen Forrester, Simon Brett and Robert Goddard. Everyone at Joffe Books loves reading and we never forget that it all begins with the magic of an author telling a story.

We are proud to publish talented first-time authors, as well as established writers whose books we love introducing to a new generation of readers.

We won Trade Publisher of the Year at the Independent Publishing Awards in 2023 and Best Publisher Award in 2024 at the People's Book Prize. We have been shortlisted for Independent Publisher of the Year at the British Book Awards for the last five years, and were shortlisted for the Diversity and Inclusivity Award at the 2022 Independent Publishing Awards. In 2023 we were shortlisted for Publisher of the Year at the RNA Industry Awards, and in 2024 we were shortlisted at the CWA Daggers for the Best Crime and Mystery Publisher.

We built this company with your help, and we love to hear from you, so please email us about absolutely anything bookish at feedback@joffebooks.com.

If you want to receive free books every Friday and hear about all our new releases, join our mailing list here: www.joffebooks.com/freebooks.

And when you tell your friends about us, just remember: it's pronounced Joffe as in coffee or toffee!

www.ingramcontent.com/pod-product-compliance
Ingram Content Group UK Ltd.
Pitfield, Milton Keynes, MK11 3LW, UK
UKHW020328171224
3696UKWH00049B/796

9 781835 269206